West Indian Stories

West Indian Stories

edited by

ANDREW SALKEY

FABER AND FABER
24 Russell Square
London

First published in mcmlx
by Faber and Faber Limited
24 Russell Square London WC1
First published in this edition mcmlxviii
Printed in Great Britain by
Latimer Trend & Co Ltd Whitstable
All rights reserved

© *this selection by Faber & Faber*
1960

Contents

7

Contents

Introduction

West Indian writing has been making a considerable impression not only in this country and in the United States of America, but also throughout Europe and Asia. In 1950, Edgar Mittelholzer's second novel, *A Morning at the Office*, attracted considerable critical attention and seemed to mark the beginning of a remarkable upsurge of new writing from the West Indies. Since then, fourteen other writers, including V. S. Reid, Samuel Selvon, George Lamming, John Hearne, V. S. Naipaul, Jan Carew, Ada Quayle and Neville Dawes, have joined Edgar Mittelholzer and have brought the total to fifty-two published books: forty-four novels, four autobiographies, one travel book, one book of literary criticism and two books of short stories. There have also been a number of books on Anthropology, West Indian History, Government and Economics. But even before 1941, when Mittelholzer's first novel, *Corentyne Thunder*, appeared, there had already been a number of books published by an older generation of West Indian writers—among them A. R. F. Webber, H. G. DeLisser, Alfred Mendes, Claude McKay, W. Adolphe Roberts, C. L. R. James, Eric Waldron, Neville Guiseppe and W. G. Ogilvie.

Both generations of writers have mainly written novels. In fact, of the present generation of writers only two, Samuel Selvon and V. S. Naipaul, have written books of short stories and have had them successfully published. In mentioning this, I am reminded of a statement I made eight years ago about the apparent dearth of West Indian short-story writers. At that time, along with a handful of writers who were all threatening to write their first novel, I believed that the West Indian short story had, somehow, been still-born. I also believed that its only

Introduction

hope of a second chance would be its possible emergence as a sort of by-product of the West Indian novel. Something like this had happened, after all, in South America, Central America, the United States of America, and Canada. On the evidence available, was there any reason to doubt that it would happen in the West Indies as well?

On reflection, though, I think that I was wrong. Established novelists like V. S. Reid, Roger Mais (now dead), George Lamming, Samuel Selvon, Jan Carew, and Neville Dawes were first of all noticed as short-story writers (and as poets, even before that) by successive producers and editors in the B.B.C.'s Caribbean and Colonial Service (Miss Una Marson, Henry Swanzy, E. R. Edmett, V. S. Naipaul, Edgar Mittelholzer, and now Miss Mary Treadgold) and by editors of West Indian literary reviews (Frank A. Collymore and W. Therold Barnes of *Bim*, A. J. Seymour of *Kyk-Over-Al*, and Mrs. Edna Manley of *Focus*).

It is nearer the truth to say that the West Indian short story and its logical development, the West Indian novel, have had dissimilar yet complementary midwives and guardians, at home and in exile; though, for many of the writers, especially those who seem to be on permanent loan from the West Indies to this country, the flexible term "exile" means "home away from home". It follows, as a consequence, that England and the West Indies must be held jointly responsible for the results of West Indian literary endeavour; and, at first look, this partnership seems both curious and possibly stultifying. But such is the inevitable fate of writers thrown up from a people without a literary tradition and without adequate facilities of their own for undertaking full-scale publishing. And there are other contradictions. To the West Indies, with its uncertain roots and highly original racial mixtures, with its scattered islands and its doubtful yet enthusiastic claims to nationhood, with its turgid colonial history, part rejected and part unconsciously absorbed, England has been a sort of necessary common denominator, a link holding all its constituent parts together. Out of seeming contradictions, a partnership has been established on more levels than one.

Introduction

Of course, the contradictions are there, and they are reflected in this anthology. Although I have avoided certain religious, social, and political stories, far weaker in their literary appeal than in their earnest documentary interest, I have tried to give the reader a mixture of comedy and tragedy, sometimes West Indian and sometimes not, but in each instance observed or interpreted by West Indian writers holding different points of view and cherishing widely differing ambitions. This attempt would seem both pretentious and unnecessary if it were not for the complex attitudes, intentions and sensibilities of the writers collected here: the Trinidadian's irreverent wit, wry humour, and, at the same time, his obtrusive sentimentality; the British Guianese and his penchant for mysticism, legend, and jungle lore; the Barbadian's regard for rhetoric and his overbearing seriousness; the Dominican's inventiveness and easy belief in superstition and myth; the St. Lucian's lyrical melancholy and brooding resentment of "Small Islandism"—a feeling of inferiority shared by most of the "small islands"; and the Jamaican's restlessness, class consciousness, and intolerable arrogance.

At best, these generalisations, diverting though they may be, are only mildly helpful as a guide to the uninitiated, because they become useless as differences and similarities, divergencies and parallels begin to emerge and overlap, as they must.

This is very much a personal selection and all the stories included are stories that I like myself. But they are by no means the *only* West Indian stories that I like. The space at my disposal was limited; and there are many writers not represented whose work I admire very much and for whom I would have found room if I possibly could: W. Therold Barnes, A. N. Forde, Joyce Gittens, Cecil Gray, Cicely Howland, Basil McFarlane, R. O. Robinson, Edward Scobie, Ulric D. Simmonds, Claude Thompson, F. D. Weller, John Wickham, Gordon Woolford and Sylvia Wynter. More than half the anthology is devoted to wit and humour because I think that West Indian short-story writers wear the comic mask with more assurance than the tragic. We are still without our prophets; but it is unlikely that the short story is the form in which to look for them, or to expect promise of their coming.

If I appear to be on the side of the "laughing boys", it is because they have made me laugh; and perhaps, too, because they have often made me pause for reflection afterwards. I very much regret V. S. Naipaul's absence from the anthology; for, with Samuel Selvon, he has probably contributed most to the comic genius which is the prime attraction of the West Indian short story. (I had intended to include two stories by V. S. Naipaul, but he felt unable to give me permission to do so. Such was the case also with Neville Dawes whose short stories have all, in one form or another, been incorporated in his first novel, *The Last Enchantment*.)

In selecting these twenty-five stories, I have tended to eschew the wilfully exotic or the bizarre though there is much of it— perhaps too much—in West Indian writing, both in the short story and the novel. I have selected as many as twenty-five stories in order to give as complete an overall picture as possible and to illustrate indirectly the direction in which West Indian writing seems to me to be heading: to self-conscious realisation of West Indian values through self-criticism. If self-criticism and, in certain instances, re-evaluation are going on, then the form of the short story lends itself admirably to just that sort of situation. Often the themes are passionately serious, themes of protest and revolt; and when not of them, inspired by them. But with Samuel Selvon, Stuart Hall, John Figueroa, Geoffrey Drayton, Barnabas J. Ramon Fortuné, and George Lamming's *A Wedding in Spring*, in particular, wit and humour are used as effective weapons for a serious purpose. Yet there are also those with different preoccupations and anxieties; those who have chosen the other path. Some of them are seen here with their axes raised for grinding; some are to be heard rumbling like ignored Vesuviuses.

I have tried to present both groups.

ANDREW SALKEY

A Morning at the Office

EDGAR MITTELHOLZER

(An excerpt from the novel, *A Morning at the Office*.
Excerpted and edited by permission of the author.)

"To hell with the bloody British Empire!"

"Shut up, Sidney! We're at the office!"

"What if we are! I don't care two ruddy ——!"

Sforzando! was how Miss Bisnauth, *the Manager's assistant
stenotypist, an East Indian*, dramatized the obscenity to herself.

Mr. Jagabir's face was expressive of disaster. Sudden and
irrational—but disaster. Jagabir, *the Assistant Accountant*, also
an East Indian, thought that the day had come, at last. They
were going to send him back to the estate to work in the fields.

Normally, Mr. Benson, *the Chief Clerk, coloured*, would have
scolded Miss Yen Tip, *the Chief Clerk's stenotypist, Chinese*, for
not attending to him (" . . . you don't attend to me, that's why
you're always making so many mistakes . . ."), but, instead, he,
too, had turned his head.

Mrs. Hinckson, *the Manager's secretary and chief stenographer,
coloured*, rigid with restraint, bit her lower lip, but Miss Henery's
mouth gaped slightly, her hand gripping the top of the type-
writer; Miss Henery being *the Accounts typist, coloured*.

Afterwards Miss Bisnauth described Miss Laballe, *the switch-
board operator, French creole and Portuguese*. "You looked like
Lot's wife. I was waiting for you to turn into a pillar of salt,"
she laughed.

Mr. Lopez, *Junior Accountant, Spanish creole*, was not at his desk; he had gone into the Men's Room only a moment before.

The widened stare of Mr. Lorry, *Customs Clerk, coloured,* was followed immediately by a slow smile. A smile of comprehension.

Horace, *office boy and negro,* was afraid to move, though he had risen. The instant he had heard the steps and voices on the stairs he had sensed trouble and had felt it his duty to intervene and remonstrate. But when he had seen that it was two white gentlemen, a subconscious fear had restrained him. He could not rebuke white people and good-class coloured people. This was something only a member of the main office staff could handle.

Mr. Murrain, *the Chief Accountant and Assistant Manager, an Englishman,* was already through the barrier-gate.

"Whitmer! I'm surprised at you!"

"You would be, Murrain. Exploiting snob!"

"You can't come in here . . ."

"Ignored your advice yesterday afternoon. Handed in my resignation thish morning to that old bashtard—Mr. Holmjh."

"Quiet, Sidney!"

The red-haired young man in a grey tropical suit was trying to wheel Sidney Whitmer back toward the stairs, but without success. Sidney staggered against the barrier, and the barrier vibrated. Mr. Murrain grasped his arm.

"Leggo, Murrain!"

"Quiet!"

"Stinking snobs! You Britishersh! Leggo my arm!"

"The Men's Room, Herrick. Get him in. Come."

"Take your hands off me!"

After a moment, he stopped resisting and let himself be led into the Men's Room.

"Mr. Lopez! Would you mind bringing in a chair, please!"

Mr. Lopez darted out—returned with a chair.

"Sit down, Sidney. Come on. Pull yourself together, man."

Mr. Lopez murmured to Mr. Murrain that Mr. Lorry had some Alka-Seltzer in his desk-drawer. Mr. Murrain nodded hastily, and Mr. Lopez was gone like lightning.

Sidney sat glowering at the floor. "Had to come and tell you, Murry. 'Pologies!" He put out a hand as red and perspiring as his face.

"That's all right, Sidney. That's all right," said Mr. Murrain, wincing.

"Resigning's all I could do. Couldn't stick it there any more. Wrote Mother telling her."

"I tried to stop him from coming here, sir," said Herrick in distress.

Mr. Murrain nodded.

Sidney began to laugh.

"Now, Sidney! Now! . . ."

"That's Mr. Lenfield's nephew," Mr. Jagabir was murmuring to Mrs. Hinckson. "One of de principals in London. What Mr. Lenfield going to say when he hear of dis?"

"Oh, is that Mr. Whitmer?"

"Yes, miss. Dat's Mr. Whitmer—Mr. Sidney Whitmer. Mr. Lenfield's nephew. It's Mr. Lenfield who get him de job and send him out here to Trinidad from England. But I hear 'e don't get on well wid de other overseers. He mix wid too much coloured people—and de overseers don't like him for dat."

"I see."

Without a glance at Horace, without a word of greeting to anyone, Mrs. Murrain walked into the office and headed for her husband's desk. She must have been half-way across when it seemed to occur to her that Mr. Murrain was missing. She paused and glanced around irresolutely. Her gaze rested, after a moment, on Miss Henery.

"Where's Mr. Murrain?"

Miss Henery went on typing as though deaf. Deaf and blind. Mrs. Murrain, tallish, thin, pretty in an English, narrow-faced way, not very well dressed, repeated the question—this time sharply.

Miss Henery typed on. Her mouth tightened, her eyes grew steely.

"You!" Mrs. Murrain pointed at Miss Henery. "I'm speaking to you. I'm asking where Mr. Murrain is."

Miss Henery stopped typing and looked up. "When you learn manners," she said, "I'll listen to what you're saying. Not before." She went on typing.

Mrs. Murrain's eyes and complexion reacted perhaps less expressibly than the stiffening of her body.

"Do you know who you're speaking to?"

"I'm perfectly aware *whom* I'm speaking to." (Cheap, thought Miss Henery, but I couldn't resist putting her right on her King's English.)

"You're impertinent!"

"You're disturbing me at my work!"

Mr. Jagabir's hands were clasped together tight. His eyes were the eyes of a man hypnotized.

Miss Yen Tip was silently convulsed—a convulsion of delight and approval.

Mr. Benson muttered, "Good. Good," with anguished approval. His eyes glittered. "The unmannerly white pig!"

"I shall report you for this!"

"You may do as you please!"

Mrs. Murrain turned. Her gaze moved in jerks about the office. It settled on Mr. Jagabir, still petrified beside Mrs. Hinckson, hands together.

"Mr. Jagabir!"

"Yes, miss! Yes, Mrs. Murrain!"

Mr. Jagabir moved toward her at a stumbling trot.

"Where is Mr. Murrain?"

"He—de boss—he in de Men's Room, miss. Somebody come." He trembled perceptibly. "He—he engaged at de minute, miss."

"Engaged? Engaged with whom?"

"Ah can't say—I mean, miss—Ah t'ink it's Mr. Whitmer from de estate."

Mrs. Murrain frowned at him, puzzled and uncertain, then turned and went toward her husband's desk. She seated herself in the chair near the safe, fumbling in her handbag for a cigarette. She lit it and flicked the match toward the window, tilted her face and exhaled, crossed her legs . . .

" . . . and look how she's dressed," Miss Laballe was murmuring to Miss Bisnauth. "Those down-at-heel shoes—and not even cleaned. And that dress looks as if she just took it from the clothes-basket." . . .

" . . . that's what I can't stand, Murrain! The blasted snobbery! The hypocrisy and the *nerve* of you English hounds. You come out to these colonies and squeeze the guts out of 'em—and then you *piss* on the natives! Insult to injury."

Sidney Whitmer's voice rang clearly through the office.

Mrs. Murrain's head tilted in alarm. She fidgeted. Her discomfiture was very apparent, but only Miss Bisnauth pitied her. Poor thing, thought Miss Bisnauth. She is overbearing, I admit, but such people should be pitied rather than despised or ridiculed.

"I can shake Miss Henery's hand."

"Yes, shake her hand," Mr. Benson muttered again half to himself, half to Miss Yen Tip. He hated negroes, but white people he hated twice as much.

Mrs. Murrain had risen. She began to look around again in that irresolute way. Suddenly she moved toward Mr. Benson.

"Mr. Benson, I think you're Chief Clerk here. Can you tell me what is happening in this office this morning?"

Mr. Benson stumbled to his feet. His breath hissed. His olive-sallow moon-face expressed pleasure, deep respect, concern in swift succession. "Well, the truth is, Mrs. Murrain, I'm afraid I'm just as . . ."

The telephone on his desk rang. He took it up.

"Excuse me a moment . . ."

He put down the instrument before it had reached his ear.

"Oh, Miss Yen Tip, please answer this for me! Come, come! Hurry!"

He was in such a dither of confusion that he took out his handkerchief and wiped his face hurriedly.

"The truth is, Mrs. Murrain, I've been so busy . . ."

"Is Mr. Murrain really in the Men's Room?"

"Yes, yes. I believe so. Is there—have you a message for him, Mrs. Murrain? Could I do anything for you?"

Mrs. Murrain clicked her tongue faintly. "But I can't understand what's going on here. Whose voice is that in there?"

"I think it's Mr. Whitmer. Could I go in—you wish me to call Mr. Murrain for you, Mrs. Murrain?"

"No, it's all right. Don't bother. I'll wait." She spoke curtly and turned off, returned to the chair near the safe. Her face was pale and tense.

Mr. Benson sat down, dabbing at his forehead with his handkerchief. He began to take up things and put them down. His face looked confused and ashamed. He called irritably to Miss Yen Tip, who had taken advantage of Mrs. Murrain's advent to cross over to Miss Henery with congratulations.

"What about that phone call? Didn't I tell you to answer . . .?"

"It was Barker's, Mr. Benson. They said they'd call back in a few minutes. I told them you couldn't speak to dem right away."

"Well, don't run off the moment I'm not looking. Take a letter!" . . .

" . . . I know! I know all about it! Everybody's ridiculing British imperialism nowadays! It's the vogue. But they're *right*!"

. . . and thudding noises . . .

" . . . Well, this is a *kommess*!" said Mr. Lorry to Mr. Lopez.

"We're making history this morning, boy!" grinned Mr. Lopez . . .

" . . . Y'haven't got to tell me that! I *know* I'm an Englishman, Murry! But I'm ashamed! Yesh! *Damned* ashamed!" . . . and urgent mumblings . . .

" . . . she may be arrogant, but for all we know, it might be a sort of shyness that makes her behave so. I've read of cases like that. These English people seem stiff and reserved, but it's really diffidence, that's all—and inhibitions. They only appear impolite and unfriendly. I think we should be sorry for them instead of despising or ridiculing them."

Mrs. Hinckson looked sceptical. "I'm afraid I can't quite see it that way, Edna," she murmured.

A Morning at the Office

Miss Bisnauth nodded. "I understand how you feel. I suppose it's foolish of me to defend them, but, somehow, I can never bring myself to condemn anyone outright. I always feel that if we looked beneath the surface we'd be able to discover that it's not their own fault, really. . . ."

They were bringing him out—supporting him between them. His head drooped on to his chest, and his knees kept bending abruptly. His eyes were open but unseeing.

" 'Pologies, Murry," he mumbled.

Mrs. Murrain rose, but her husband did not glance in her direction, his efforts too concentrated on the task in hand. His face was strained and red and twitched sensitively.

Sidney began to hiccup as they passed through the barrier.

Mrs. Murrain, a hand fumbling at her bosom, gazed after them. She sank on to the chair, then rose again at once and began to move with an air of uncertainty toward the barrier-gate.

We Know Not Whom to Mourn

EDGAR MITTELHOLZER

It was an afternoon of grey clouds like old rice bags, and the
wind strong and loud in its moaning, so loud that on the back
veranda where Harry, Hoolcharran's third son, sat in a bright-
blue wicker chair the voices in the house could not be heard.
The wind smelt of cow-dung and stagnant water and the iodine
of the sea, for the savannah surrounded the house on all sides,
and parts of the savannah were flooded from the rains of last
week, and on the dry parts small island-cakes of cow-dung lay
spotted: still, piteous islands amid the larger islands that moved,
for these were the cows and sheep and the goats. Now and then
the wind brought a lowing or a bleating, or the voice of a herds-
man, for this was the hour when the animals were coming home
to their pens, and it was the hour, too, when Hoolcharran, who
owned them all and the house, was dying.

Only Harry, the third son, sat on the back veranda, long-
headed, hands clasped in his lap, not smoking; just watching
the animals come home to pen, his eyes not sad but with a
haunted calm, as though he were a man to whom death was
not a thing for grief or fear but for thought. He seemed a lonely,
brooding man.

In the sitting-room and dining-room—only a large archway
separated the two rooms—were gathered Toolwa, an old aunt
of Hoolcharran's wife, Dookie. And Tommy, the eldest son, who,
at thirty-four, was one of the richest rice-millers on the Corentyne Coast, perhaps in the whole of British Guiana. And Gobin,
the dispenser from Kildonan, who was sixty-seven and an old

friend of Hoolcharran's. Hoolcharran and Gobin, as boys, had run in shirt-tails on the Public Road, and, naked, had caught *sherrigas* and *hassars* in the canals, had fought and quarrelled at school, and laughed and climbed mango trees. Gobin, in his little drug-store in Kildonan, had made up all the medicine Hoolcharran and his family had ever used. Also in the sitting-room and dining-room sat Doris and John and Edward, Tommy's children; Doris was fifteen (she was at High School in New Amsterdam), and John thirteen and Edward eleven. John and Edward were quiet boys, and today the awe of death made them quieter. But Doris, who could never keep back her giggles, was giggling now at a joke about two goats that Bella had just told her. Bella was present, too; she was the black cook, and had worked for the Hoolcharrans from the age of nineteen: she was forty-two now, and no other cook, it was said, on the whole Corentyne Coast, could make coconut curry like Bella. She was fond of telling jokes, especially smutty ones about *Burroo Goat* and *Burroo Tiger*.

Toolwa, the old aunt, gave Bella scolding glances, but did not try to scold her with words, because Bella was like a second mistress in the house. Bella's mother and Dookie (Mrs. Hoolcharran) had planted rice together as girls, and Dookie had always treated Bella as the daughter of her good friend rather than as a menial. Bella called Dookie Aunt Dookie, not ma'am. Hoolcharran's wealth had not turned Dookie's head, and Dookie, though she liked her big house and the car and all the things that money could buy, had never forgotten the old days of want. Bella had always been fat and plain—she had a cast in her right eye—and no man had ever asked her to marry him. Not that this made her any less cheerful.

In this hour of death, Dookie was upstairs in the room with the dying man. She sat on a large old trunk near a window, Phyllis Rambarry with her. Phyllis was the fourth child and only daughter; she was the wife of Jim Rambarry, a barrister-at-law who practised in New Amsterdam; she was educated and dressed well.

The doctor—his name was Ribeiro—and the nurse—a short black girl called Turpin—stood by the bedside doing what they could to save Hoolcharran. The doctor was a tall, slim Portuguese of thirty-five or so, and he was supposed to be the best doctor in Berbice. He had told Dookie that he would do all he could, but that, from what he could see, the chances were slim. He spoke with a sneer, for he was that kind of man. He did not like coloured people, especially East Indians. It was only because he was supposed to be the best doctor in Berbice that Dookie had sent for him when Hoolcharran got the stroke at around ten o'clock that morning. Only a few minutes before ten o'clock Hoolcharran had been laughing and talking in his jovial way, his fat paunch trembling, his silver hair glinting in a shaft of weak sunshine from the slightly overcast sky. Nobody in the big house, painted a bright yellow and blue, had guessed that death was so near Hoolcharran.

Doctor Ribeiro had ruled that no more than two members of the family could be allowed in the sick-room at a time. He wouldn't have a crowd, he had said—and had said it in a curt voice. Dookie had tried to persuade him to let her call in three more doctors, for she was so grieved and upset she felt that she must do everything she possibly could, with the aid of money, to save Hoolcharran. Doctor Ribeiro had given her a cold look, but, after an hour or so, he had agreed to have Doctor Bembridge from Skeldon, higher up the coast. Doctor Bembridge was an English doctor who had been practising for two or three years on the Corentyne Coast.

Maurice, the second son, was on his way from Georgetown, nearly a hundred miles off. Maurice had a big grocery shop in Georgetown. His wife was an invalid and could not travel. They had no children. Dookie was praying that Maurice would arrive before Hoolcharran died, because Maurice had been his father's pet son. Hoolcharran was not conscious, it was true, but, still, felt Dookie, his spirit might sense Maurice's presence if Maurice came in time. Dookie and Hoolcharran were Presbyterians. Hoolcharran never cared too much about the church, but Dookie

was a staunch believer in Jesus Christ and the Christian faith
as taught by the Presbyterians. She went to church every other
Sunday, and, whenever anyone in the house was sick, she
always prayed for their recovery. Hoolcharran had often laughed
at her and asked her if she forgot that her parents had been
Hindus, but he was always very generous in his gifts of money
to the church, and would sometimes even humour Dookie by
going to church with her.

Jim Rambarry, Phyllis's husband, had gone off in the car to
get Doctor Bembridge.

And now the wind moaned, and Harry, the third son, watched
the twilight deepen.

Toolwa got up and crossed over to where Gobin sat in a
rocking chair near the big cabinet radio set. She bent and whispered something. She asked him about the will. Did Gobin
know if Hoolcharran had made a will? Her manner was furtive
and scheming; she cast quick glances round at the others as
though feeling that she was doing something wrong. Her grey-
edged, dark-brown eyes were shiny with greed. The wrinkles of
her seventy-odd years looked like shadowed gutters of evil perhaps dug in the night by the jumbies strayed from the far-away
courida bush. Toolwa lived in a lonely wooden cottage three
miles away, and the wind and the rain, and perhaps the jumbies, were tearing it down shingle by shingle. Toolwa would
have liked some money to build a big house, though if she had
got the money she would not have built the house but would
have put the money in the bank. She had over three thousand
dollars in Barclay's Bank, for she was thrifty and saved as much
as she could out of the allowance Dookie made her. Her son,
Palwan, had died at the age of nineteen, and it was said that,
at that time, Toolwa had had a lot of money, for her husband
had owned two rice fields and had saved his money carefully in
the mattress of his bed. But Toolwa had been so stingy and had
denied Palwan good food for so long a time that he got tuber-
culosis.

Gobin shook his head and said he didn't know if Hoolcharran

had made a will, but he supposed so. He looked a little impatiently at her, and only because he was polite he checked himself from telling her to move away from him. Gobin was grieved. As soon as the news had reached him that his good friend had taken ill he had shut his drug-store and taken bus and come.

The telephone began to ring. It was in the dining-room: a wall-phone.

Doris sprang up and went and answered it. She said "yes" several times, then "no", then told the person at the other end that "yes", the doctor said there was little hope. "Yes", grandma was upstairs in the room with him and the doctor . . .

Toolwa asked Gobin if he thought Hoolcharran would leave anything for Harry. "Harry disappoint 'e bad," said Toolwa.

"Me can't tell you, Toolwa," said Gobin, shaking his head patiently. "Only 'e lawyer can tell you wha' 'e leff and wha' 'e ain' leff."

Toolwa glanced round again, and then asked: "Why 'e didn't tek Rambarry for 'e lawyer? Ent Rambarry 'e son-in-law?"

"Me can't tell you, Toolwa," said Gobin, fidgeting and frowning now.

"It funny," said Toolwa. "Ah believe 'e didn't too like Rambarry for Phyllis. Ah hear 'e did want Phyllis marry white overseer."

"Dat's a lie, Toolwa."

"So me hear. Me only tell you wha' me hear, Gobin."

Gobin made a puffing grunt of anger, and his lips moved soundlessly.

Toolwa tittered and moved off, went back to her chair by the upright piano.

And the wind moaned around the house, and Harry saw a weak light glowing in the distance where the gloom was dense. Harry smiled slightly, as though he could hear a voice in the wind that spoke only for him. Since he was a boy Harry had listened to the wind. No one knew what went on in his mind. He was not married. He was a schoolteacher and taught in the village school. He lived home here, and had many books, and when he came home went to his room. He sat some evenings alone on the back veranda, as he was sitting now. A strange, brooding man, Harry. As distant as the sea beyond the line of courida bush. Only the wind and the savannah knew him.

The drone of a car sounded. It was Rambarry, Phyllis's husband, coming back from Skeldon with Doctor Bembridge. John could see the headlights from the door. He had gone to the front door to catch a lizard which had streaked past his chair into the gallery and out under the door. John had a special piece of wire with a noose at the end for catching lizards. He liked to see a lizard squirm in the noose by its neck, and sometimes he would hold it over a fire if he was near a fire. Edward, who did not like to see any creature suffer, often scolded him for his cruelty, but John still went on catching lizards. Flies, too, and bees and pond-flies. One day, in New Amsterdam, John had gone hunting with a Daisy air-gun, and had shot four kiskadees and three blue sackies. He was a dead-shot with an air-gun. One of the blue sackies fell from a telegraph wire, only maimed in the wing, so John spread it out on the grass parapet and pinned it down with two stones. He brought out a box of matches and burnt every feather off it, and then stuck it with pins until it died.

The car bumped its way toward the house along the uneven grass and gravel track. And presently Rambarry came up the stairs with Doctor Bembridge, a thin, short, red-faced Englishman with a small brown moustache and a quick, nervous way of glancing this way and that way and smiling. He said "Evening! Evening!" to everybody in the sitting-room and dining-room as he passed on his way to the stairs that led to the upper storey. Tommy rose and said: "Good night, doctor!" his manner respectful and awed. For Tommy, in spite of the education Hoolcharran had given him, was still, at heart, a shy, salaaming coolie. Tommy, though he was one of the richest rice-millers on the Corentyne Coast, had never learnt how to be self-assured. He was timid in his relations with people. Only in business he knew how to be shrewd and bold. He never made a false move in business. But people, especially white people, frightened him. As a boy, he had often watched the white overseers on their mules aback of the nearby sugar-estate and trembled. Overseers, he had heard, kicked and shouted. They kicked the coolies who cut canes, and shouted curses at them, and threatened to shoot. One day he had seen an overseer kick a thin old coolie who was in charge of the oxen pulling the cane-laden punts along the canal.

Rambarry accompanied the doctor upstairs. And Tommy sat down.

Bella was telling Doris a story about *Bill, Burroo Rabbit* and *Burroo Monkey*. Doris giggled, and Edward asked her if she didn't know that Grandpa was ill upstairs.

Bella looked at him and said: "Boy, death can only come once to everybody. Wha' you hurting you' head for? Let de girl laugh!"

"You're too callous," said Edward.

Bella laughed softly and told him that it was what was inside your heart that mattered. "Not what you' face show. Dis is a life, boy, we never know who to mourn over. Sometimes it's de people who alive who we should cry for—not de dead ones, or de ones we t'ink dying. Run off and play wid you' marbles, boy." Her fat bulk shivered with fresh mirth, and Edward turned off and went sulkily toward the gallery.

And so the wind went on moaning round the house, and the clouds moved faster in the sky. They looked like inky cloaks now, for night had come, and Toolwa was calling to Bijoolie to bring in the gas-lamps. Bijoolie was the man-of-all-work. He was an illegitimate son of Hoolcharran's, for Hoolcharran had been a gay young man. He had drunk his rum and had had his women. The son of a cane-cutter, Hoolcharran had begun as a provision farmer, and lived in a mud house. All the land he possessed was an acre of swampy savannah. But he had mingled industry and thrift with his love for pleasure. The first cow he owned had strayed on to his land, and he could have had it impounded, but he saw a way of making it his own. It belonged to the widow of Poolram who lived a mile up the Public Road. Hoolcharran took the cow to Poolram's widow, and Beekwa— that was her name—was very grateful, and invited Hoolcharran to some curry and roti, as Hoolcharran knew she would have done. Beekwa was still young and pretty, and Hoolcharran was a handsome young man. Hoolcharran did not go home until the next morning. Six weeks later Beekwa made a present of the cow to Hoolcharran. The cow was with calf. Hoolcharran's career as a cattle-rancher had begun.

The moaning of the wind never stopped. It was still moaning past Harry's chair on the back veranda when (it was after nine o'clock) Phyllis brought the news from upstairs. Phyllis was breathless with excitement which she tried to suppress, for she moved with good-class coloured people in New Amsterdam and had to be careful not to show any vulgar feelings. Phyllis told them that Hoolcharran would live. Yes, the doctor said he had tided over the worst. It had been touch and go, she said, but he would recover. He might be laid up for several weeks, even months, but he would live. Oh, she was so glad—for Mother's sake. . . . A sigh of relief and joy went through the house, as though the wind had pushed a bright tributary out of its dark moaning in upon them.

But . . .

And then Edward's cry rose. Edward came in from the back veranda, pale and frightened-looking, and his cry rose. A cry of horror. Perhaps he was remembering, too, what Bella had told him an hour or two ago . . . "Dis is a life, boy, we never know who to mourn over. . . .' And they all went out on to the back veranda and looked at Harry who still sat in the bright-blue wicker chair. His head was slightly thrown back, and he was staring at the clouds in the wind. But his eyes were steady. And beside his chair, on the floor, lay the bottle, not bright-blue like the wicker chair, but a dark blue, and with a red label bearing a skull and cross-bones. A lonely, brooding man, Harry. About him was a smell of bitter almonds. About him the wind still moaned.

A Wedding in Spring

GEORGE LAMMING

London was their first lesson in cities. The solitude and huge-
ness of the place had joined their lives more closely than ever;
but it was the force of similar childhoods which now threatened
to separate them: three men and a woman, island people from
the Caribbean, who waited in separate rooms of the same basement, sharing the nervousness of the night.

The wedding was only a day away.

Snooker thought he could hear the sweat spilling out of his
pores. Talking to himself, old-woman-like in trouble, he started:
"Is downright, absolute stupid to make me harness myself in
dis mornin' costume. . . . I ain't no Prince Philip or ever want
to be. . . ."

A pause drew his attention to the morning suit he had rented.
The top hat sat on its crown, almost imitating itself. It provoked
Snooker. He watched it, swore at it, then stooped as though he
was going to sit on it.

"Now what you think you doin'?"

Snooker was alerted. He heard the closing creak of the door
and the blurred chuckle of Knickerbocker's voice redeeming the
status of the top hat.

Snooker was silent. He watched Knickerbocker hold the top
hat out like some extraordinary fruit in his hand.

"Is what Beresford think it is at all?" he said, turning his
back on the suit to face Knickerbocker. "My body, not to
mention my face, ain't shape for dis kind o' get-up."

"Even de beggar can be king," said Knickerbocker, "an' dis

28

A Wedding in Spring

is de kind o' headpiece kings does wear." He cuddled the top hat to his chest. "An' tomorrow," he added, lifting his head towards Snooker, "I goin' to play king."

"You goin' to play jackass," Snooker said sharply.

"So what?" Knickerbocker smiled. "Christ did ride on one."

"Is ride these clothes goin' ride you tomorrow," said Snooker, " 'cause you ain't got no practice in wearin' them."

"You goin' see who ride what," said Knickerbocker, "I sittin' in de back o' dat limousine jus' so, watch me, Snooker." He was determined to prove his passion for formal dress. He had lowered his body on to the chair, fitting the top hat on his head at precisely the angle his imagination had shaped. He crossed his legs, and plucked at the imaginary seams of his morning trousers. The chair leaned with him while he felt the air for the leather rest which would hold his hand.

Snooker refused to look. But Knickerbocker had already entered the fantasy which the wedding would make real. His head was loud with bells and his eyes turned wild round the crowd, hilarious with praise, as they acknowledged his white gloved welcome. Even the police had removed their helmets in homage to the splendour which he had brought to a drab and enfeebled London. He was teaching the English their own tune. So he didn't hear Snooker's warning until the leather rest refused his hand and the crowd vanished into the shadows which filled the room. The chair had collapsed like a pack of cards under Knickerbocker's body. He looked like a cripple on his back.

Now he was afraid, and he really frightened Snooker too, the way he probed his hands with fearful certainty under and across his thighs. His guess was right. There was a split the size of a sword running down the leg and through the crutch of the only pair of trousers he owned.

"You break up my bes' chair," Snooker said sadly, carrying the top hat like wet crockery across the room. It had fallen into the sink.

The crisis had begun. Knickerbocker crouched on all fours,

his buttocks cocked at the mirror, to measure the damage he
had done. The basement was still: Knickerbocker considering
his black exposure while Snooker collected the wreckage in both
hands, wondering how he could fit his chair together again.
They didn't speak, but they could hear, behind the door, a quiet
tumble of furniture, and after an interval of silence, the sullen
ticking of the clock in Flo's room.

She was alone, twisting her hair into knotty plaits that rose
like spikes out of her skull. She did not only disapprove of her
brother's wedding but she also thought it a conspiracy against
all they had learnt. Preoccupied and disdainful, she saw the
Vaseline melt and slip like frying lard over her hands. The last
plait done, she stuck the comb like a plough into the low shrub
of hair at the back of her neck. She scrubbed her ears with her
thumb; stretched the under lid of each eye to tell her health;
and finally gave her bottom a belligerent slap with both hands.
She was in a fighting mood.

"As if he ain't done born poor," she said, caught in that
whispering self-talk which filled the basement night. "Borrowin'
an' hockin' every piece o' possession to make a fool o' himself,
an' worse still dat he should go sell Snooker his bicycle to rent
mornin' suit an' limousine. Gran Gran. . . . Gawd res' her in de
grave, would go wild if she know what Beresford doin' . . . an'
for what . . . for who he bringin' his own downfall."

It was probably too late to make Beresford change his mind:
what with all those West Indians he had asked to drop in after
the ceremony for a drink: the Jamaican with the macaw face
who arrived by chance every Sunday at supper time, and
Caruso, the calypsonian, who made his living by turning every
rumour into a song that could scandalise your name for life.
She was afraid of Caruso, with his malicious tongue, and his
sly, secretive, slanderous manner. Moreover, Caruso never
travelled without his gang: Slip Disk, Toodles and Square Dick;
then there were Lice-Preserver, Gunner, Crim, Clarke Gable
Number Two, and the young Sir Winston. They were all from
"back home", idle, godless, and greedy. Then she reflected that

they were not really idle. They worked with Beresford in the same tyre factory.

"But idle or no idle," she frowned, "I ain't want Beresford marry no white woman. If there goin' be any disgrace, let me disgrace him first."

She was plotting against the wedding. She wanted to bribe Snooker and Knickerbocker into a sudden disagreement with her brother. Knickerbocker's disapproval would have been particularly damaging since it was he who had introduced the English girl to Beresford. And there was something else about Knickerbocker that Flo knew.

The door opened on Snooker who was waiting in the passage for Knickerbocker. Flo watched him in the dark and counted three before leaning her hand on his head. Her anger had given way to a superb display of weakness: a woman outraged, defenceless, and innocent of words which could tell her feeling.

"Snooker."

"What happen now?"

"I want all you two speak to Beresford," she said. Her voice was a whimper appropriate with grief.

"Let the man make his own bed," said Snooker, "is he got to lie down in it."

"But is this Englan' turn his head an' make him lose his senses." Flo crouched lower, tightening her hand against Snooker's neck.

"He keep his head all right," said Snooker, "but is the way he hearken what his mother say, like he walkin' in infancy all life long."

"Ma wasn't ever goin' encourage him in trouble like this," Flo said.

"Is too late to change anything," said Snooker, "except these kiss-me-tail mornin' clothes. Is like playin' ju-ju warrior with all that silk cravat an' fish-shape' frock they call a coat. I ain't wearin' it."

"Forget 'bout that," said Flo, "is the whole thing we got to stop complete."

George Lamming

Knickerbocker was slipping through the shadows, silent and massive as a wall which now rose behind Flo. The light made a white mask over his face. Flo seemed to feel her failure, sudden and complete. Knickerbocker had brought a different kind of trouble. He was fingering the safety-pins which closed the gap in his trousers. He trusted Flo's opinion in these details. He stooped forward and turned to let her judge whether he had done a good job.

"Move your tail out of my face," she shouted, "what the hell you take me for."

Knickerbocker looked hurt. He raised his body to full height, bringing his hands shamefully over the safety-pins. He couldn't understand Flo's fury: the angry and unwarranted rebuke, the petulant slam of the door in his face. And Snooker wouldn't talk. They stood in the dark like dogs shut out.

Beresford was waiting in the end room. He looked tipsy and a little vacant under the light; but he had heard Flo's voice echoing down the passage, and he knew the others were near. It was his wish that they should join him for a drink. He watched the bottle making splinters with the light, sugar brown and green, over the three glasses and a cup. The label had lost its lettering; so he turned to the broken envelope on his stomach and went on talking to himself.

All night that voice had made dialogue with itself about his bride. His mood was reflective, nostalgic. He needed comfort, and he turned to read his mother's letter again.

. . . concernin the lady in question you must choose like i would have you in respect to caracter an so forth. i excuse and forgive your long silence since courtship i know takes time. pay my wellmeanin and prayerful respects to the lady in question. give flo my love and my remembrance to snooker and knick. . . .

The light was swimming under his eyes; the words seemed to harden and slip off the page. He thought of Flo and wished she would try to share his mother's approval.

A Wedding in Spring

. . . if the weddin come to pass, see that you dress proper.
i mean real proper, like the folks in that land would have you.
hope you keepin the bike in good condition. . . .

The page had fallen from his hand in a moment of distraction.
He was beginning to regret that he had sold the bicycle to
Snooker. But his mood didn't last. He heard a knock on the
door and saw Knickerbocker's head emerge through the light.

"Help yuhself, Knick."

Beresford squeezed the letter into his pocket while he watched
Knickerbocker close in on the table.

"I go take one," Knickerbocker said, "just one."

"Get a next glass if the cup don't suit you."

"Any vessel will do," Knickerbocker said.

Knickerbocker poured rum like water as though his arm could
not understand the size of a drink. They touched cup and glass,
making twisted faces when the rum started its course down
their throats.

"Where Snooker?"

"Puttin' up the bike," Knickerbocker said. "But Flo in a
rage."

"She'll come round all right," said Beresford. "Is just that
she in two minds, one for me an' one 'gainst the wedding."

"You fix up for the limousine?"

"Flo self do it this mornin'," said Beresford, "they comin'
for half pas' four."

"Who goin' partner me if Flo don't come to the church?"

"Flo goin' go all right," said Beresford.

"But you never can know with Flo."

Beresford looked doubtful, but he had to postpone his mis-
givings.

Knickerbocker poured more rum to avoid further talk, and
Beresford held out his glass. They understood the pause. Now
they were quiet, rehearsing the day that was so near. The room
in half light and liquor was preparing them for melancholy: two
men of similar tastes temporarily spared the intrusion of female

company. They were a club whose rules were part of their
instinct.

"Snooker ask me to swap places wid him," Knickerbocker
said.

"He don't want to be my best man?" Beresford asked.

"He ain't feel friendly with the morning suit," Knickerbocker
said.

"But what is proper is proper."

"Is what I say too," Knickerbocker agreed. "If you doin' a
thing, you mus' do it as the done thing is doed."

Beresford considered this change. He was open to any
suggestion.

"Snooker or you, it ain't make no difference," he said.

"Then I goin' course wid you to de altar," Knickerbocker
said.

Was it the rum or the intimacy of their talk which had dulled
their senses? They hadn't heard the door open and they couldn't
guess how long Flo had been standing there, rigid as wire, with
hands akimbo, and her head, bull shaped, feeding on some
scheme that would undo their plans.

"Get yuhself a glass, Flo," Beresford offered.

"Not me, Berry, thanks all the same."

"What you put your face in mournin' like that for?" Knickerbocker said. He was trying to relieve the tension with his banter.
"Those whom God join together . . ."

"What you callin' God in this for?" Flo charged. "It ain't
God join my brother wid any hawk-nose English woman. Is his
stupid excitement."

"There ain't nothin' wrong wid the chick," Knickerbocker
parried.

"Chick, my eye!" Flo was advancing towards them. "He let
a little piece o' left-over white tail put him in heat."

"Flo!"

Beresford's glass had fallen to the floor. He was standing,
erect, wilful, his hands nervous and eager for action. Knickerbocker thought he would hit her.

A Wedding in Spring

"Don't you threaten me wid any look you lookin'," Flo challenged him. "Knickerbocker, here, know what I sayin' is true. Look him good in his face an' ask him why he ain't marry her."

"Take it easy, Flo, take it easy," Knickerbocker cautioned. "Beresford marryin' 'cause he don't want to roam wild like a bush beast in this London jungle."

"An' she, you know where she been roamin' all this time?" Flo answered. Knickerbocker fumbled for the cup.

"Is jus' what Seven Foot Walker tell you back in Port-o'-Spain," Beresford threw in.

Whatever the English girl's past, Beresford felt he had to defend his woman's honour. His hands were now steady as stone watching Flo wince as she waited to hear him through.

"That man take you for a long ride, Flo, an' then he drop you like a latch key that won't fit no more. You been in mournin' ever since that mornin' he turn tail an' lef' you waitin'. An' is why you set yuh scorpion tongue on my English woman."

"Me an' Seven Foot Walker . . ."

"Yes, you an' Seven Foot Walker!"

"Take it easy," Knickerbocker begged them. "Take it easy . . ."

"I goin' to tell you, Berry, I goin' to tell you . . ."

"Take it easy," Knickerbocker pleaded, "take it easy . . ."

Flo was equipped for this kind of war. Her eyes were points of flame and her tongue was tight and her memory like an ally demanding vengeance was ready with malice. She was going to murder them with her knowledge of what had happened between Knickerbocker and the English girl. Time, place, and circumstance: they were weapons which now loitered in her memory waiting for release. She was bursting with passion and spite. Knickerbocker felt his loyalty waver. He was worried. But Flo's words never came. The door opened and Snooker walked in casual as a bird, making music on his old guitar. He was humming: "Nobody knows the trouble I've seen". And his indifference was like a reprieve.

"The limousine man outside to see you," he said. "Somebody got to make some kind o' down payment."

The crisis had been postponed.

London had never seen anything like it before. The Spring was decisive, a hard, clear sky and the huge sun naked as a skull eating through the shadows of the afternoon. High up on the balcony of a fifth-floor flat an elderly man with a distressful paunch was feeding birdseed to a flock of pigeons. He hated foreigners and noise, but the day had done something to his temper. He was feeling fine. The pigeons soon flew away, cruising in circles above the enormous crowd which kept watch outside the church; then closed their ranks and settled one by one over the familiar steeple.

The weather was right; but the crowd, irreverent and forgetful in their fun, had misjudged the meaning of the day. The legend of English reticence was stone-cold dead. An old-age pensioner with no teeth at all couldn't stop laughing to the chorus, a thousand times chuckled: "Cor bli'me, look at my lads." He would say, " 'Ere comes a next in 'is tails, smashers the lot o' them," and then: "Cor bli'me, look at my lads." A contingent of Cypriots on their way to the Colonial Office had folded their banners to pause for a moment that turned to hours outside the church. The Irish were irrepressible with welcome. Someone burst a balloon, and two small boys, swift and effortless as a breeze, opened their fists and watched the firecrackers join in the gradual hysteria of the day.

Snooker wished the crowd away; yet he was beyond anger. Sullen and reluctant as he seemed he had remained loyal to Beresford's wish. His mind alternated between worrying and wondering why the order of events had changed. It was half an hour since he had arrived with the bride. Her parents had refused at the last moment to have anything to do with the wedding, and Snooker accepted to take her father's place. He saw himself transferred from one role to another; but the second seemed more urgent. It was the intimacy of their childhood, his and Beresford's, which had coaxed him into wearing the morning suit. He had to make sure that the bride would keep her promise. But Beresford had not arrived; nor Knickerbocker, nor Flo.

Snooker remembered fragments of the argument in the basement room the night before; and he tried to avoid any thought of Flo. He looked round the church and the boys from "back home" looked at him and he knew they, too, were puzzled. They were all there: Caruso, Slip Disk, Lice-Preserver, and an incredibly fat woman whom they called Tiny. Behind him, two rows away, he could hear Toodles and Square Dick rehearsing in whispers what they had witnessed outside. There had been some altercation at the door when the verger asked Caruso to surrender his guitar. Tiny and Slip Disk had gone ahead, and the verger was about to show his firmness when he noticed Lice-Preserver who was wearing full evening dress and a sword. The verger suddenly changed his mind and indicated a pew, staring in terror at the sword that hung like a frozen tail down Lice-Preserver's side. Snooker closed his eyes and tried to pray.

But trouble was brewing outside. The West Indians had refused to share in this impromptu picnic. They had journeyed from Brixton and Camden Town, the whole borough of Paddington and the Holloway Road, to keep faith with the boys from "back home". One of the Irishmen had a momentary lapse into prejudice and said something shocking about the missing bridegroom. The West Indians bristled and waited for an argument. But a dog intervened, an energetic, white poodle which kicked its hind legs up and shook its ears in frenzy at them. The poodle frisked and howled as though the air and the organ music had turned its head. Another firecracker went off, and the Irishman tried to sing his way out of a fight. But the West Indians were showing signs of a different agitation. They had become curious, attentive. They narrowed the circle to whisper their secret.

"Ain't it his sister standin' over yonder?"

They were slow to believe their own recognition.

"Is Flo, all right," a voice answered, "but she not dress for the wedding."

"Seems she not goin'," a man said as though he wanted to disbelieve his suspicion.

"An' they wus so close," the other added, "close, close, she an' that brother."

Flo was nervous. She stood away from the crowd, half hearing the rumour of her brother's delay. She tried to avoid the faces she knew, wondering what Beresford had decided to do. Half an hour before she left the house she had cancelled the limousine and hidden his morning suit. Now she regretted her action. She didn't want the wedding to take place, but she couldn't bear the thought of humiliating her brother before this crowd. The spectacle of the crowd was like a rebuke to her own stubbornness.

She was retreating further away. Would Beresford find the morning suit? And the limousine? He had set his heart on arriving with Knickerbocker in the limousine. She knew how fixed he was in his convictions, like his grandfather whose wedding could not proceed; had, indeed, to be postponed because he would not repeat the words: *All my worldly goods I thee endow*. He had sworn never to part with his cow. He had a thing about his cow, like Beresford and the morning suit. Puzzled, indecisive, Flo looked round at the faces, eager as they for some sign of an arrival; but it seemed she had lost her memory of the London streets.

The basement rooms were nearly half a mile from the nearest tube station; and the bus strike was on. Beresford looked defeated. He had found the morning suit, but there was no way of arranging for another limousine. Each second followed like a whole season of waiting. The two men stood in front of the house, hailing cabs, pleading for lifts.

"Is to get there," Beresford said, "is to get there 'fore my girl leave the church."

"I goin' deal wid Flo," Knickerbocker swore. "Tomorrow or a year from tomorrow I goin' deal wid Flo."

A Wedding in Spring

"How long you think they will wait?"

Beresford had dashed forward again, hailing an empty cab.
The driver saw them, slowed down, and suddenly changed his
mind. Knickerbocker swore again. Then: a moment of reve-
lation.

"Tell you what," Knickerbocker said. He looked as though
he had surprised himself.

"What, what!" Beresford insisted.

"Wait here," Knickerbocker said, rushing back to the basement room. "I don't give a goddam. We goin' make it."

The crowd waited outside the church, but they looked a
little bored. A clock struck the half-hour. The vicar came out
to the steps and looked up at the sky. The man in the fifth
floor flat was eating pork sausages and drinking tea. The
pigeons were dozing. The sun leaned away and the trees
sprang shadows through the early evening.

Someone said: "It's getting on."

It seemed that the entire crowd had agreed on an interval of
silence. It was then the woman with the frisky white poodle held
her breast and gasped. She had seen them: Beresford and
Knickerbocker. They were arriving. It was an odd and unpre-
dictable appearance. Head down, his shoulders arched and
harnessed in the morning coat, Knickerbocker was frantically
pedalling Snooker's bicycle towards the crowd. Beresford sat
on the bar, clutching both top hats to his stomach. The silk
cravats sailed like flags round their necks. The crowd tried to
find their reaction. At first: astonishment. Later: a state of
utter incomprehension.

They made a gap through which the bicycle free-wheeled
towards the church. And suddenly there was applause, loud and
spontaneous as thunder. The Irishman burst into song. The
whole rhythm of the day had changed. A firecracker dripped
flames over the church steeple and the pigeons dispersed. But
crisis was always near. Knickerbocker was trying to dismount
when one tail of the coat got stuck between the spokes. The

other tail dangled like a bone on a string, and the impatient white poodle charged upon them. She was barking and snapping at Knickerbocker's coat tails. Beresford fell from the bar on to his knees, and the poodle caught the end of his silk cravat. It turned to threads between her teeth.

The crowd could not determine their response. They were hysterical, sympathetic. One tail of Knickerbocker's coat had been taken. He was aiming a kick at the poodle; and immediately the crowd took sides. They didn't want harm to come to the animal. The poodle stiffened her tail and stood still. She was enjoying this exercise until she saw the woman moving in behind her. There was murder in the woman's eyes. The poodle lost heart. But the top hats were her last temptation. Stiff with fright, she leapt to one side seizing them between her teeth like loaves. And she was off. The small boys shouted: "Come back, Satire, come back!" But the poodle hadn't got very far. Her stub of tail had been safely caught between Flo's hand. The poodle was howling for release. Flo lifted the animal by the collar and shook its head like a box of bones.

Knickerbocker was clawing his rump for the missing tail of the morning coat. Beresford hung his head, swinging the silk cravat like a kitchen rag down his side. Neither could move. Flo's rage had paralysed their speech. She had captured the top hats, and it was clear that the wedding had now lost its importance for her. It was a trifle compared with her brother's disgrace.

The vicar had come out to the steps, and all the boys from "back home" stood round him: Toodles, Caruso, and Square Dick, Slip Disk, Clarke Gable Number Two, and the young Sir Winston. Lice-Preserver was carrying the sword in his right hand. But the poodle had disappeared.

Flo stood behind her brother, dripping with tears as she fixed the top hat on his head. Neither spoke. They were too weak to resist her. She was leading them up the steps into the church. The vicar went scarlet.

"Which is the man?" he shouted. But Flo was indifferent to his fury.

A Wedding in Spring

"It don't matter," she said. "You ju' go marry my brother."

And she walked between Knickerbocker and her brother with the vicar and the congregation of boys from "back home" following like a funeral procession to the altar.

Outside, the crowd were quiet. In a far corner of sunlight and leaves, the poodle sat under a tree licking her paws, while the fat man from the fifth-floor flat kept repeating like an idiot to himself: "But how, how, how extraordinary!"

Of Thorns and Thistles

GEORGE LAMMING

Mother Barton canted her head and removed her spectacles with an air of prophetic concern. With the spectacles removed and the crystal beads of rheum oozing from the half-closed eyes it was almost agonising to contemplate her features. Her nose and temples were deeply lined, and the skin lapped and sagged across the huge, round bones of her face.

The clock struck four and she clutched the banister, leaning her head cautiously against the upright. "Lenora, the witch-hazel, if you please," she demanded. She let her body fall level with the upright, and listened to the girl rummaging in the medicine cabinet. The sun struck full from the west, penetrating the green network of the cherry tree and throwing dark shapes on to the bleached clothes. Mother Barton looked round her critically, and thought that it was all the same the day before. She had shuffled out to the back gallery at the same hour, demanded the witch-hazel and the glass with which she washed her eyes, and with her instinct for particularising she had observed the sun like a big, outrageous bully lighting up everything about her. She wished to hear her daughter trotting through the house, yelling the hackneyed greetings, and the pattern would have been complete. The day would have repeated its predecessor with a shameless, unerring sense of triumph. For a while Mother Barton's emotional apparatus had become acutely receptive. That was the legacy of the maturing years, she thought, a pattern whose demands though unchanging seemed more irksome with each succeeding day.

Of Thorns and Thistles

Lenora returned with the witch-hazel and the glass and set them down on a small table. Mother Barton sidled up to the table and held them testingly. She sniffed the witch-hazel and passed her thumb with quiet, untiring thoroughness around the inside of the glass. "Twelve drops and a teaspoonful of water," she said, retreating to the banister. Her hands quavered and sweated as she watched the girl compounding the mixture. She could bear anything except the ignominy of dependence to which age and physical disability had reduced her. The indignity of acknowledging her weaknesses and having them laid bare like auction for other people's consideration was always a torture.

Lenora gave her the little globular glass and watched her fit it into the crease that ringed her eyes. She held her head back, letting the open eye wriggle sideways under the witch-hazel. It trickled past the prominent cheek bones into the hollow of her jaws like furtive, suppressed tears. When she tired, she brought the head up very slowly, letting the chin closet itself in the sink of her neck. The process was repeated with the other eye. When she had finished, her eyes were wet and bleared, and the lashes stuck together like drenched fur. The pain constricted the muscles of her throat and her lips curled away, revealing the solitary, black tooth that shot up from her naked gum. "Wash them and put them back," she gasped, fumbling through an adjoining room to her bed. She waited until she heard the clink and rattle of the phials in the medicine cabinet. Then she lay back, quiet and unthinking.

Angela came in late that afternoon. She wore soft, buff shoes which made no noise, and Mother Barton never suspected a third person in the house until the bed-spring creaked and sank beneath her. Angela wiped her eyes and kissed her on the mouth. Mother Barton turned on one side and gave her daughter's hand a tender squeeze. She had done that every afternoon for many years, and she had no other explanation for it but the affection which had grown out of a union that knew no third participant. Angela eased her shoes off and sprawled across the bed. The sun had gone down, and they lay holding hands in the early dark.

The night had crept unperceived over everything. Lenora washed the tea things and put out the fires. She touched up her hair, and gave her lips the customary smear before saying good-night.

"Stupid nigger," Mother Barton snapped, when the girl had left the premises. She stretched full length on the couch, her head thrown back, and her hands crossed across her waist. "It's a damn' shame," she went on. "A damn' shame to have to take about nasty pots an' pans all day. Nasty, that's what she is, damn' nasty."

Angela sat in the bent-wood chair opposite, stroking her brow and thinking. She didn't respond to her mother's protests; and although it was customary for Mother Barton to emphasise the servant's deficiencies and the petty fears which had afflicted her and the general run of the house, she felt increasingly aware of her own silence. She usually restrained Mother Barton, or consoled her. But to-night she sat quiet and preoccupied.

"I would have sent her away long ago," Mother Barton was saying, unaware of her audience, "sent her flyin' through the gate. But . . . you . . . you . . ."

"Mother," Angela interrupted. It was the first time she had spoken, and her tone was dry and resigned. Her skin was drawn and she seemed to tax her baffled, fatigued senses in an attempt to confess a blunder which she thought irrevocably stupid.

"What's it?" Mother Barton asked.

"I saw Rose to-day," she said.

She waited for the words to work their effect, and perceiving Mother Barton's failure to recognise the name, she continued: "And I asked her to come and see you."

"Who's Rose?" Mother Barton snapped in a manner that was neither friendly nor uncomforting.

"Rosie," Angela answered, placing the accent sharply on the last syllable. Mother Barton did not speak.

She couldn't wrestle against the surge of memories which that name recalled. The sound, the characters which combined to give it life and meaning seemed to merge into the vast, incalculable swamp of ill-will and deceit, leaving only the hollow, jeering skeleton of the word as a symbol of Mother Barton's hate. She had no adequate means of getting it off her chest. She could only resign herself to feeling and an acceptance of all she felt, and wait for time to bring her into harmony with the emotional conflict which she experienced. Angela had grasped the situation instinctively.

"There was nothing I could do," she said soothingly. "After all, it was such a long time."

Mother Barton's senses had retreated into disuse. She was aware of nothing but what she felt.

"She came to me," Angela continued. "How could I pretend not to know her or even to hate her? Fifteen years is a long time. It's fifteen years Rose was away."

The tears slipped down Mother Barton's face in large, solitary drops. Her skin, so thin and shrivelled, looked artificial under the light. Angela gave her a long, caressing look as she shuffled to her room.

It was all silence and darkness: the silence and darkness of the house at night, and the silence and darkness of Mother Barton's memory. She wrapped the sheets about her. She could feel the weight of her body as she wrenched from side to side, and the weight of that body had grown unbearable under the weight of her memories. She had ambled across the barren space of the years trying to piece out the events which had first united and then separated herself from Rose.

It was some thirty years ago, a time during which she had need of companionship. She had borne a child in very shameful circumstances, and the strain of disaster which followed that event had made life almost unbearable. She lost her job, the intimacy of those to whom she had always looked for friendship, and she had grown to distrust her own sense of values. To walk in the sunlight was an act of faith. It was then that Rose entered her life; and for both of them it was a sort of triumph.

Rose's devotion, coming at a time when no one else was eager
to offer their sympathy, had had a double significance. Rose
had helped her to regain her sense of proportion. Soon people
were referring to her in the ordinary way. She was simply
Barton with the little, "brown skin" child, Angela.

When Angela was three, Mother Barton left her to the care
of Rose. She wanted to start life afresh, and in order to do that
she thought she should tear herself away from her immediate
surroundings. She didn't believe that her wound would heal if
she remained among those who had helped to deepen it. She
worked her passage to Jamaica and there she lived and worked.
She had started life again.

Neither Rose nor Mother Barton was lettered, and the fragment of correspondence which soon petered out was sketchy
and vague. But during the twelve years that followed, Rose
had become a second mother to Angela. The latter had grown
into a charming little creature with long, curling hair and an
engaging smile. Her mother's sole physical legacy was a strong,
commanding brow. But she had her father's eyes, and the finely
chiselled nose and lips were thoroughly nordic in design.

She was fifteen when her mother returned from Jamaica. The
face bore evidence of a desperate, exhaustive struggle, and it
held no trace of recognition. Each had to re-establish an acquain-
tance. Moreover, Mother Barton was certainly in very bad
shape. Her body was thin and drawn, and Rose observed that
she never shifted her direction without some difficulty. Later
she explained how she had worked herself to the bone, and had
finally taken a cold which threatened her sight. In fact Rose
and Angela were hardly visible to her.

Angela had made no comment on her mother's arrival, but
it was clear to Rose that she herself had almost suddenly
developed a morbid sense of responsibility, and if she had sought
the real cause it was merely to dispel any feeling of guilt which
the situation might have warranted. She had never given Angela
a full account of her mother's career as she had known it, but
she had told her what she thought decent for a child to know.

She had made her aware of her mother's existence, and this knowledge had in a way given Angela an added confidence in their attachment.

But within two months of her mother's arrival there was a noticeable change in Angela's relation to Rose. Rose had remained devoted, affectionate and unselfish, but there was something which undermined every act of goodwill. Their relation had taken on a new shape and a new meaning. Illness, it seemed, had erected certain barriers between them. Neither Angela nor Rose could grasp the spiritual transformation which was taking place. Each tried in her way to cling to the other; but as her mother worsened, Angela sensed a gradual transference of allegiance from one to the other; from Rose to her mother.

For months they strove to relieve Mother Barton. The specialist had commended their efforts in order to steel them against his prediction that sooner or later she would lose her sight. It wasn't long before he witnessed the complete surrender of their will. Angela awoke one morning to discover that her mother was suffering temporary blindness. She could see for a minute or two, and then the vision failed completely before returning for another minute or two.

It was an unprecedented experience. The impact of the disaster had affected Rose no less, and once again, as if in revolt against a common misfortune, the barriers dissolved and they were thrown together. Angela stripped her fears naked and turned to Rose for a solution. It was an embarrassing situation. Rose was quite definite about her plans, but she couldn't imagine the reception they would get either from Angela or her mother. Angela, victimised by fear and enthusiasm, had clung to the likelihood of a temporary recovery. Rose, more dispassionate and objective, had emphasised the disagreeable fact that total blindness was a certainty. Her plans were quite simple. Two years before Mother Barton's arrival she had had an offer to settle in America, and she had intended taking Angela along. Mother Barton's arrival had disrupted her plans, but the nature of her illness now seemed to straighten them out again. Mother

Barton was forty-six, and quite helpless. Angela was sixteen, healthy, beautiful, with remarkable prospects. She could not reconcile the disparity. She suggested that they should send Mother Barton to an institute for the blind, and hope for the best. They would sail away together.

The suggestion had come upon Angela with a paralysing force. Whether it was due to the novelty of the idea or its apparent ruthlessness, she could not determine, but the effect was stunning. She could form no judgment on the matter and in the innocence of her years she consulted her mother and promised to accept her opinion.

The poor woman felt outraged. At first she had suspected Angela of playing a trick either on herself or Rose, but having been assured of the truth of the plans, she banished the past from her mind and surrendered herself to a consuming hate. She was convinced that Rose had expected some tangible remuneration for the time and labour she had spent in their behalf, and considering Angela a fair exchange she had tried to steal her. It was not only jealousy, Mother Barton thought, but treachery that had motivated those plans, and she swore by all the saints and the Mother of Jesus that she would never again speak to the woman who had regarded her illness as a good thing.

Rose was unusually calm. She refrained from argument. Angela and her mother had become fragments of an experience. She consigned the past to memory, and with her memory she departed.

Mother Barton had rehearsed the incidents in that order. She had placed out all the details of their attachment in order to reach a proper assessment of what had happened and discover some means of reconciling herself to Rose. But there was something about Rose that seemed to transcend all time. Rose could never be the same again.

It was six o'clock of a Friday evening, about fifteen years after Rose's departure, and exactly a fortnight since her return. Mother Barton lay supine on the bed. The counterpane was drawn up to her neck leaving her heels and toes exposed at the other end. Her eyelashes were damp and she squinted continually. The lingering stains of witch-hazel had given her cheeks a quiet, subdued warmth. Her sight had improved and now she seemed perfectly happy.

The door of her room opened and Angela entered on tiptoe. She kissed her on the eyes, squeezed her hand, and pressing her mouth to her ear whispered something. Mother Barton came to a sitting position, and peering from half-shut eyes spat her disapproval into Angela's face. Angela protested. Mother Barton was violent in her insistence. She refused to act against her will. The conflict proceeded in a crescendo of gasps and whispers. Angela persuaded. Mother Barton rebuked. Their patience was at an end, and Angela in a fever of indignation flung the door open and summoned Rose to the room. Mother Barton lay back quietly, her lids pressed to her eyes, her hands locked across her breast. Rose entered, and knelt beside the bed, remembering for a split second that it was their second reunion. Angela left the room, and for a while Mother Barton felt empty and dejected. It was seldom that Angela displeased her, but to-day she seemed unbearably callous. In spite of all that had happened she had insisted on seeing Rose again, and now she and Rose, whom she thought so hateful and wretched, were in the same room. If she were young and strong she would have avenged herself, but now she could only lie and think and hate. No word was spoken until Mother Barton craned her body up, and groped about the room.

"Barton, Barton," Rose cried through the stifling fog of sound that obstructed her words. Mother Barton, moving away from the direction whence the sound had come, held her hands out like searching antennae. When she spoke her tone was final and unsparing. "Your wish came true, Rose, I am blind."

The words had hardly awakened Rose's consciousness of the wound which they were intended to inflict, when Angela screaming her annoyance rushed into the room. "It's a lie," she cried, "it's a lie."

The mist of tears had formed into liquid beads of silver that winked and melted on Rose's cheek. Angela pressed her body to her, and for a moment the intimacy of their touch seemed to quicken a oneness which nothing could destroy. Mother Barton groped back to her bed. Her skin, thin and wrinkled, twitched continually. Her lids were relaxed, but she did not part them. Angela observed that passion had given her veins a mild inflation which rendered speech very difficult. She kept working the muscles of her face as if she had undertaken a labour which her strength could not accomplish. Angela clenched her firmly and sat her on the bed. Her full, round cheeks were highly coloured, and her body shivered with anger.

"It isn't true, you know it isn't," she shouted, strengthening her hold.

"But I can't . . . I can't . . ." Mother Barton was saying. The words were obstructed by her sudden gasps of breath. She kept working the muscles of her face as if she wanted to communicate to the other the terror which she felt. Angela released her hold, and leant over her. She brought the head against her breasts, and moved the lids away very gently. They closed back without effort, and for the first time it dawned on her that what she had always feared as a possibility had actually come to pass. The misfortune which Mother Barton was pretending had betrayed its purpose by confirming the truth of what she had told Rose. She was blind.

At the Stelling

JOHN HEARNE

"Dis one is no boss fe' we, Dunnie," Son-Son say. "I don' like how him stay. Dis one is boss fe' messenger an' women in Department office, but not fe' we."

"Shut your mout'," I tell him. "Since when a stupid, black nigger can like and don't like a boss in New Holland? What you goin' do? Retire an' live 'pon your estate?" But I know say that Son-Son is right.

The two of we talk so at the back of the line; Son-Son carrying the chain, me with the level on the tripod. The grass stay high, and the ground hard with sun. It is three mile to where the Catacuma run black past the *stelling*, and even the long light down the sky can't strike a shine from Catacuma water. You can smell Rooi Swamp, dark and sweet and wicked like a woman in a bad house back in Zuyder Town. Nothing live in Rooi Swamp except snake; like nothing live in a bad woman. In all South America there is no swamp like the Rooi; not even in Brazil; not even in Cayenne. The new boss, Mister Cockburn, walk far ahead with the little assistant man, Mister Bailey. Nobody count the assistant. Him only come down to the Catacuma to learn. John stay close behind them, near to the rifle. The other rest of the gang file out upon the trail between them three and me and Son-Son. Mister Cockburn is brand-new from head to foot. New hat, new bush-shirt, new denim pant, new boot. Him walk new.

"Mister Cockburn!" John call, quick and sharp. "Look!"

John Hearne

I follow the point of John's finger and see the deer. It fat and promise tender and it turn on the hoof-tip like deer always do, with the four tip standing in a nickel and leaving enough bare to make a cent change, before the spring into high grass. Mister Cockburn unship the rifle, and *pow*, if we was all cow then him shoot plenty grass for us to eat.

"Why him don't give John de rifle?" Son-Son say.

"Because de rifle is Government," I tell him, "and Mister Cockburn is Government. So it is him have a right to de rifle."

Mister Cockburn turn and walk back. He is a tall, high mulatto man, young and full in body, with eyes not blue and not green, but coloured like the glass of a beer bottle. The big hat make him look like a soldier in the moving pictures.

"Blast this sun," he say, loud, to John. "I can't see a damn' thing in the glare; it's right in my eyes."

The sun is falling down the sky behind us but maybe him think we can't see that too.

John don't answer but only nod once, and Mister Cockburn turn and walk on, and I know say that if I could see John's face it would be all Carib buck. Sometimes you can see where the Indian lap with it, but other times it is all Indian and closed like a prison gate; and I knew say, too, that it was this face Mister Cockburn did just see.

"Trouble dere, soon," Son-Son say, and him chin point to John and then to Mister Cockburn. "Why Mister Hamilton did have to get sick, eh, Dunnie? Dat was a boss to have."

"Whatever trouble to happen is John's trouble," I tell him. "John's trouble and Mister Cockburn's. Leave it. You is a poor naygur wid no schooling, five *pickney* and a sick woman. Dat is trouble enough for you."

But in my heart I find agreement for what stupid Son-Son have to say. If I have only known what trouble . . .

No. Life don't come so. It only come one day at a time. Like it had come every day since we lose Mister Hamilton and Mister Cockburn take we up to survey the Catacuma drainage area in Mister Hamilton's stead.

At the Stelling

The first day we go on the savannah beyond the *stelling*, I know say that Mister Cockburn is frighten. Frighten, and hiding his frighten from himself. The worst kind of frighten. You hear frighten in him voice when he shout at we to keep the chain straight and plant the markers where him tell us. You see frighten when him try to work us, and himself, one hour after midday, when even the alligators hide in the water. And you understand frighten when him try to run the camp at the *stelling* as if we was soldier and him was a general. But all that is because he is new and it would pass but for John. Because of John everything remain bad. From the first day when John try to treat him as he treat Mister Hamilton.

You see, John and Mister Hamilton was like one thing except that Mister Hamilton have schooling and come from a big family in Zuyder Town. But they each suck from a Carib woman and from the first both their spirit take. When we have Mister Hamilton as boss whatever John say we do as if it was Mister Hamilton say it, and at night when Mister Hamilton lie off in the big Berbice chair on the veranda and him and John talk it sound like one mind with two tongue. That's how it sound to the rest of we when we sit down the steps and listen to them talk. Only when Mister Cockburn come back up the river with we, after Mister Hamilton take sick, we know say all that is change. For Mister Cockburn is frighten and must reduce John's pride, and from that day John don't touch the rifle and don't come to the veranda except to take orders and for Mister Cockburn to show that gang foreman is only gang foreman and that boss is always boss.

Son-Son say true, I think. Trouble is to come between John and Mister Cockburn. Poor John. Here, in the bush, him is a king, but in New Zuyder him is just another poor half-buck without a job and Mister Cockburn is boss and some he cast down and some he raiseth up.

Ahead of we, I see Mister Cockburn trying to step easy and smooth, as if we didn't just spend seven hours on the savannah. Him is trying hard but very often the new boot kick black dirt

53

from the trail. That is all right I think. Him will learn. Him
don't know say that even John hold respect for the sun on the
Catacuma. The sun down here on the savannah is like the
centurion in the Bible who say to one man, Come, and he
cometh, and to another, Go, and he goeth. Like it say go, to
Mister Hamilton. For it was a man sick bad we take down to
the mouth of the river that day after he fall down on the wharf
at the *stelling*. And it was nearly a dead man we drive up the
coast road one hundred mile to Zuyder Town. We did want to
stop in Hendrikstadt with him that night, but he think him was
dying—we think so too—and him would not stop for fear he die
away from his wife. And afterwards the Government doctor tell
Survey that he must stay in the office forevermore and even
Mister Hamilton who think him love the bush and the swamp
and the forest more than life itself was grateful to the doctor for
those words.

So it was it did happen with Mister Hamilton, and so it was
Mister Cockburn come to we.

Three weeks we is on the Catacuma with Mister Cockburn,
and every new day things stay worse than the last.

In the morning, when him come out with the rifle, him shout:
"Dunnie! Take the *corial* across the river and put up these
bottles." And he fling the empty rum and beer bottle down the
slope to me and I get into the *corial* and paddle across the river,
and put the necks over seven sticks on the other bank. Then
him and the little assistant, Mister Bailey, stay on the veranda
and fire across the river, each spelling each, until the bottle is
all broken.

And John, down by the river, in the soft morning light, standing in the *corial* we have half-buried in the water, half-drawn
upon the bank, washing himself all over careful like an Indian
and not looking to the veranda.

"John!" Mister Cockburn shout, and laugh bad. "Careful, eh,
man. Mind a *perai* don't cut off your balls."

We have to stand in the *corial* because *perai* is bad on the
Catacuma and will take off your heel and your toe if you stand

in the river six inches from the bank. We always joke each other about it, but not the way Mister Cockburn joke John. That man know what him is doing and it is not nice to hear.

John say nothing. Him stand in the still water catch of the *corial* we half-sink and wash him whole body like an Indian and wash him mouth out and listen to Mister Cockburn fire at the bottle across the river. Only we know how John need to hold that rifle. When it come to rifle and gun him is all Indian, no African in it at all. Rifle to him is like woman to we. Him don't really hold a rifle, him make love with it. And I think how things go in Mister Hamilton's time when him and John stand on the veranda in the morning and take seven shots break seven bottle, and out in the bush they feel shame if four shot fire and only three piece of game come back. Although, I don't talk truth, if I don't say how sometimes Mister Hamilton miss a shot on the bottle. When that happen you know him is thinking. He is a man think hard all the time. And the question he ask! "Dunnie," he ask, "what do you see in your looking-glass?" or, "Do you know, Dunnie, that this country has had its images broken on the wheels of false assumptions? Arrogance and servility. Twin criminals pleading for the mercy of an early death." That is how Mister Hamilton talk late at night when him lie off in the big Berbice chair and share him mind with we.

After three weeks on the Catacuma, Mister Cockburn and most of we go down the river. Mister Cockburn to take him plans to the Department and the rest of we because nothing to do when him is gone. All the way down the river John don't say a word. Him sit in the boat bows and stare down the black water as if it is a book giving him secret to remember. Mister Cockburn is loud and happy, for him feel, we know say, now, who is boss and him begin to lose him frighten spirit. Him is better now the frighten gone and confidence begin to come.

"Remember, now," him say in the Department yard at Zuyder Town. "Eight o'clock sharp on Tuesday morning. If one of you is five minutes late, the truck leaves without you. Plenty of men between here and the Catacuma glad to get work." We laugh and say, "Sure, boss, sure," because we know say that already him is not so new as him was and that him is only joking. Only John don't laugh but walk out of the yard and down the street.

Monday night, John come to my house; I is living in a little place between the coolie cinema and the dockyard.

"Dunnie," he say, "Dunnie, you have fifteen dollar?"

"Jesus," I say, "what you need fifteen dollar for, man? Dat is plenty, you know?"

"All right," he say. "You don't have it. I only ask."

Him turn, as if it was the time him ask and I don't have no watch.

"Hold on, hold on," I tell him. "I never say I don't have fifteen dollar. I just say what you want it for?"

"Lend me. I don't have enough for what I want. As we pay off next month, you get it back. My word to God."

I go into the house.

"Where de money?" I ask the woman.

"What you want it for?" she ask. "You promise say we don't spend dat money until we marry and buy furnitures. What you want tek it now for?"

"Just tell me where it stay," I tell her. "Just tell me. Don't mek me have to find it, eh?"

"Thank you, Dunnie," John say when I bring him the fifteen dollar. "One day you will want something bad. Come to me then."

And him gone up the street so quick you scarcely see him pass under the light.

The next morning, in the truck going down to the boat at the Catacuma mouth, we see what John did want fifteen dollar for.

"You have a licence for that?" Mister Cockburn ask him, hard and quick, when he see it.

"Yes," John say and stow the new Ivor-Johnson repeater with his gear up in the boat bows.

"All right," Mister Cockburn say. "I hope you do. I don't want any unlicensed guns on my camp."

At the Stelling

Him and John was never born to get on.

We reach the *stelling* late afternoon. The bungalow stand on the bluff above the big tent where we sleep and Zacchy, who we did leave to look to the camp, wait on the wharf waving to us.

When we passing the gear from the boat, John grab his bundle by the string and swing it up. The string break and shirt, pant and handkerchief fly out to float on the water. Them float but the new carton of .32 ammunition fall out too and we see it for a second, green in the black water as it slide to the bottom and the mud and the *perai*.

Mister Bailey, the little assistant, look sorry, John look sick, and Mister Cockburn laugh a little up in the back of him nose.

"Is that all you had?" him ask.

"Yes," John say. "I don't need no more than that for three weeks."

"Too bad," Mister Cockburn reply. "Too bad. Rotten luck. I might be able to spare you a few from stores."

Funny how a man who can stay decent with everybody always find one other who turn him bad.

Is another three weeks we stay up on the survey. We triangulate all the stretch between the Rooi Swamp and the first forest. Things is better this time. Mister Cockburn don't feel so rampageous to show what a hard boss him is. Everything is better except him and John. Whenever him and John speak, one voice is sharp and empty and the other voice is dead, and empty too. Every few day him give John two-three cartridge, and John go out and come back with two-three piece of game. A deer and a *labba*, maybe. Or a bush pig and an *agouti*. Whatever ammunition John get him bring back meat to match. And, you know, I think that rowel Mister Cockburn's spirit worse than anything else John do. Mister Cockburn is shooting good, too, and we is eating plenty meat, but him don't walk with the gun like John. Who could ever. Not even Mister Hamilton.

The last Saturday before we leave, John come to Mister Cockburn. It is afternoon and work done till Monday. Son-Son and me is getting the gears ready for a little cricket on the flat piece under the *kookorit* palms. The cricket gears keep in the big room with the other rest of stores and we hear every word John and Mister Cockburn say.

"No, John," Mister Cockburn tell him. "We don't need any meat. We're leaving Tuesday morning. We have more than enough now."

Him voice sleepy and deep from the Berbice chair.

"Sell me a few rounds, Mister Cockburn," John say. "I will give you store price for a few rounds of .32."

"They're not mine to sell," Mister Cockburn say, and him is liking the whole business so damn' much his voice don't even hold malice as it always do for John. "You know every round of ammunition here belongs to Survey. I have to indent and account for every shot fired."

Him know, like we know, that Survey don't give a lime how much shot fire up in the bush so long as the men stay happy and get meat.

"You can't give three shot, Mister Cockburn?" John say. You know how bad John want to use the new repeater when you hear him beg.

"Sorry, John," Mister Cockburn say. "Have you checked the caulking on the boat? I don't want us shipping any water when we're going down on Tuesday."

A little later all of we except John go out to play cricket. Mister Cockburn and Mister Bailey come too and each take captain of a side. We play till the parrots come talking across the river to the *kookorits* and the sky turn to green and fire out on the savannah. When we come back to the camp John is gone. Him take the *corial* and gone.

"That damn' buck," Mister Cockburn say to Mister Bailey. "Gone up the river to his cousin, I suppose. We won't see him until Monday morning now. You can take an Indian out of the bush, but God Almighty himself can't take the bush out of the Indian."

Monday morning, we get up and John is there. Him is seated

on the *stelling* and all you can see of him face is the teeth as him grin and the cheeks swell up and shiny with pleasure. Lay out on the *stelling* before him is seven piece of game. Three deer, a *labba* and three bush pig. None of we ever see John look so. Him tired till him thin and grey, but happy and proud till him can't speak.

"Seven," him say at last and hold up him finger. "Seven shots, Dunnie. That's all I take. One day and seven shot."

Who can stay like an Indian with him game and no shot gone wide?

"What's this?" a voice call from up the veranda and we look and see Mister Cockburn in the soft, white-man pyjamas lean over to look at we on the *stelling*. "Is that you, John? Where the devil have you been?"

"I make a little trip, Mister Cockburn," John say. Him is so proud and feel so damn' sweet him like even Mister Cockburn. "I make a little trip. I bring back something for you to take back to town. Come and make your choice, sir."

Mister Cockburn is off the veranda before the eye can blink, and we hear the fine red slipper go slap-slap on the patch down the bluff. Him come to the wharf and stop short when him see the game. Then him look at John for a long time and turn away slow and make water over the *stelling* edge and come back, slow and steady.

"All right," him say, and him voice soft and feel bad in your ears, like you did stumble in the dark and put your hand into something you would walk round. "All right, John. Where did you get the ammunition? Who gave it you, eh?"

Him voice go up and break like a boy's voice when the first hairs begin to grow low down on him belly.

"Mister Cockburn," John say, so crazy proud that even now him want to like the man and share pride with him. "I did take the rounds, sir. From your room. Seven shot I take, Mister Cockburn, and look what I bring you back. Take that deer, sir, for yourself and your family. Town people never taste meat like that."

"You son of a bitch," Mister Cockburn reply. "You damned impertinent, thieving son of a bitch. Bailey!" and him voice scream until Mister Bailey come out to the veranda. "Bailey! Listen to this. We have a thief in the camp. This beauty here feels that the government owes him his ammunition. What else did you take?"

Him voice sound as if a rope tie round him throat.

"What else I take?" John look as if him try to kiss a woman and she slap him face. "How I could take anything, Mister Cockburn? As if I am a thief. Seven little shot I take from the carton. You don't even remember how many rounds you did have left. How many you did have leave, eh? Tell me that."

"Don't back chat me, you bloody thief!" Mister Cockburn yell. "This is your last job with Survey, you hear me? I'm going to fire your arse as soon as we get to the river mouth. And don't think this game is yours to give away. You shot it with government ammunition. With *stolen* government ammunition. Here! Dunnie! Son-Son! Zacchy! Get that stuff up to the house. Zacchy gut them and hang 'em. I'll decide what to do with them later."

John stay as still as if him was dead. Only when we gather up the game and a kid deer drop one splash of dark stomach blood onto the boards him draw one long breath and shiver.

"Now," Mister Cockburn say, "get to hell out of here! Up to the tent. You don't work for me anymore. I'll take you down river on Tuesday and that's all. And if I find one dollar missing from my wallet I'm going to see you behind bars."

It is that day I know say how nothing so bad before but corruption and rottenness come worse after. None of we could forget John's face when we pick up him game. For we Negro, and for the white man, and for the mulatto man, game is to eat sometimes, or it is play to shoot. But for the Indian, oh God, game that him kill true is life everlasting. It is manhood.

When we come back early in the afternoon, with work done, we don't see John. But the *corial* still there, and the engine boat, and we know that him not far. Little later, when Zacchy cook, I fill a billy pot and go out to the *kookorits*. I find him there, in the grass.

"John," I say. "Don't tek it so. Mister Cockburn young and foolish and don't mean harm. Eat, John. By the time we reach river mouth tomorrow everyt'ing will be well again. Do, John. Eat dis."

John look at me and it is one black Indian Carib face stare like statue into mine. All of him still, except the hands that hold the new rifle and polish, polish, polish with a rag until the barrel shine blue like a Chinee whore hair.

I come back to the *stelling*. Mister Cockburn and Mister Bailey lie into two deck chair under the tarpaulin, enjoying the afternoon breeze off the river. Work done and they hold celebration with a bottle. The rest of the gang sit on the boards and drink too. Nothing sweeter than rum and river water.

"Mister Cockburn," I tell him, "I don't like how John stay. Him is hit hard, sah."

"Oh, sit down, Dunnie," him say. "Have a drink. That damned buck needs a lesson. I'll take him back when we reach Zuyder Town. It won't do him any harm to miss two days' pay."

So I sit, although I know say I shouldn't. I sit and I have one drink, and then two, and then one more. And the Catacuma run soft music round the piles of the *stelling*. All anybody can feel is that work done and we have one week in Zuyder Town before money need call we to the bush again.

Then as I go to the *stelling* edge to dip water in the mug I look up and see John. He is coming down from the house, gliding on the path like Jesus across the Sea of Galilee, and I say, "Oh God, Mister Cockburn! Where you leave the ammunition, eh?"

But already it is too late to say that.

The first shot catch Mister Cockburn in the forehead and him drop back in the deck chair, peaceful and easy, like a man call gently from sleep who only half wake. And I shout, "Dive-oh, Mister Bailey!" and as I drop from the *stelling* into black Catacuma water, I feel something like a *marabunta* wasp sting between my legs and know say I must be the first thing John ever shoot to kill that him only wound.

I sink far down in that river and already, before it happen, I can feel *perai* chew at my fly button and tear off my cod, or alligator grab my leg to drag me to drowning. But God is good. When I come up the sun is still there and I strike out for the little island in the river opposite the *stelling*. The river is full of death that pass you by, but the *stelling* holds a walking death like the destruction of Apocalypse.

I make ground at the island and draw myself into the mud and the bush and blood draw after me from between my legs. And when I look back at the *stelling*, I see Mister Cockburn lie down in him deck chair, as if fast asleep, and Mister Bailey lying on him face upon the boards, with him hands under him stomach, and Zacchy on him back with him arms flung wide like a baby, and three more of the gang, Will, Benjie and Sim, all sprawl off on the boards, too, and a man more, the one we call "Venezuela", fallen into the grass, and a last one, Christopher, walking like a chicken without a head until him drop close to Mister Bailey and cry out once before death hold him. The other seven gone. Them vanish. All except Son-Son, poor foolish Son-Son, who make across the flat where we play cricket, under the *kookorits* and straight to Rooi Swamp.

"Oh Jesus, John!" him bawl as him run. "Don't kill me, John! Don't kill me, John!"

And John standing on the path, with the repeater still as the finger of God in him hands, aim once at Son-Son, and I know say how, even at that distance, him could break Son-Son's back clean in the middle. But him lower the gun, and shrug and watch Son-Son into the long grass of the savannah and into the swamp. Then him come down the path and look at the eight dead men.

"Dunnie!" him call. "I know you is over there. How you stay?"

I dig a grave for the living into the mud.

"Dunnie!" him call again. "You hurt bad? Answer me, man, I see you, you know? Look!"

At the Stelling

A bullet bury itself one inch from my face and mud smack into my eye.

"Don't shoot me, John," I beg. "I lend you fifteen dollar, remember?"

"I finish shooting, Dunnie," him say. "You hurt bad?"

"No," I tell him the lie. "I all right."

"Good," him say from the *stelling*. "I will bring the *corial* come fetch you."

"No, John!" I plead with him. "Stay where you is. Stay there! You don't want kill me now." But I know say how demon guide a Carib hand sometimes and make that hand cut throats. "Stay there, John!"

Him' shrug again and squat beside Mister Cockburn's chair, and lift the fallen head and look at it and let the head fall again. And I wait. I wait and bleed and suffer, and think how plenty women will cry and plenty children bawl for them daddy when John's work is known in Zuyder Town. I think these things and watch John the way I would watch a bushmaster snake and bleed in suffering until dark fall. All night I lie there until God take pity and close my eye and mind.

When my mind come back to me, it is full day. John gone from the *stelling* and I can see him sit on the steps up at the house, watching the river. The dead stay same place where he drop them. Fever burn in me, but the leg stop bleed and I dip water from the river and drink.

The day turn above my head until I hear a boat engine on the far side of the bend, and in a little bit a police launch come up mid-stream and make for the *stelling*. When they draw near, one man step to the bows with a boat-hook, and then the rifle talk from the steps and the man yell, hold him wrist and drop to the deck. Him twist and wriggle behind the cabin quicker than a lizard. I hear an Englishman's voice yell in the cabin and the man at the wheel find reverse before the yell come back from the savannah. The boat go down-stream a little then nose into the overhang of the bank where John's rifle can't find them. I call out once and they come across to the island and take me

63

off on the other side, away from the house. And is when I come on board that I see how police know so quick about what happen. For Son-Son, poor foolish old Son-Son, who I think still hide out in the swamp is there. Him have on clothes not him own, and him is scratched and torn as if him had try to wrestle a jaguar.

"Man," the police sergeant tell me. "You should have seen him when they did bring to us. Swamp tear off him clothes clean. Nearly tear off him skin."

As is so I learn that Son-Son did run straight as a *peccary* pig, all night, twenty mile across Rooi Swamp where never any man had even put him foot before. Him did run until him drop down in the camp of a coolie rancher bringing cattle down to the coast, and they did take him from there down to the nearest police post. When him tell police the story, they put him in the jeep and drive like hell for the river mouth and the main station.

"Lord witness, Son-Son," I say, "you was born to hang. How you didn't meet death in Rooi Swamp, eh?"

Him just look frighten and tremble, and the sergeant laugh.

"Him didn't want to come up river with we," he say. "Superintendent nearly have to tie him before him would step on the boat."

"Sergeant," the Superintendent say. Him was the Englishman I hear call out when John wound the policeman. "Sergeant, you take three men and move in on him from behind the house. Spread out well. I'll take the front approach with the rest. Keep low, you understand. Take your time."

"Don't do it, Super," I beg him. "Look how John stay in that house up there. River behind him and clear view before. Him will see you as you move one step. Don't do it."

Him look at me angry and the white eyebrow draw together in him red face.

"Do you think I'm going to leave him up there?" he say. "He's killed eight and already tried to kill one of my men."

Him is bad angry for the constable who sit on the bunk and holding him wrist in the red bandage.

At the Stelling

"No, Super," I tell him. "John don't *try* to kill you. If him did try then you would have take one dead man out of the river. Him only want to show you that him can sting."

But what use a poor black man talk to police. The sergeant and him three stand on the cabin roof, hold onto the bank and drag themself over. Then the Super with him five do the same. I can hear them through the grass like snakes on them stomach. John let them come a little way to the house, and then, with him first shot, him knock the Super's black cap off, and with him second, him plug the sergeant in the shoulder. The police rifles talk back for a while, and Son-Son look at me.

When the police come back, I take care to say no word. The sergeant curse when the Super pour Dettol on the wound and beg the Super to let him go back and bring John down.

"We'll get him," the Super say. "He knows it. He knows he doesn't stand a chance."

But him voice can't reach John to tell him that, and when them try again one man come back with him big toe flat and bloody in the police boot. When I go out, though, and walk along the bank to the *stelling* and lay out the bodies decent and cover them with canvas from the launch, it could have been an empty house up there on the bluff.

Another hour pass and the police begin to fret, and I know say that them is going to try once more. I want to tell them don't go, but them is police and police don't like hear other men talk.

And is then, as we wait, that we hear a next engine, an outboard, and round the bend come a Survey boat, and long before it draw up beside the overhang, my eye know Mister Hamilton as him sit straight and calm in the bows.

"Dunnie, you old fool," him say and hold me by the shoulders. "Why didn't you stop it? D'you mean to say you couldn't see it coming?"

Him smile to show me that the words is to hide sorrow. Him is the same Mister Hamilton. Dress off in the white shirt and white stocking him always wear, with the big linen handkerchief spread upon him head under the hat and hanging down the neck back to guard him from sun.

"I came as soon as I could," him say to the Super. "As soon as the police in Zuyder rang Survey and told us what you had 'phoned through."

You can see the Super is glad to have one of him own sort to talk with. More glad, though, because it is Mister Hamilton and Mister Hamilton's spirit make all trouble seem less.

"We might have to bomb him out," Super say. "I've never seen a man to shoot like that. He must be a devil. Do you think he's sane, Hamilton?"

Mister Hamilton give a little smile that is not a smile.

"He's sane now," he say. "If he wasn't he'd have blown your head off."

"What's he going to do?" Super ask.

Mister Hamilton lift him shoulder and shake him head. Then him go up to the cabin top and jump on the bank and walk to the *stelling*. Not a sign from the house.

I follow him and move the canvas from all the staring dead faces and him look and look and pass him hand, tired and slow, across him face.

"How did it go, Dunnie?" him ask.

I tell him.

"You couldn't have stopped him?"

"No," I say. "Him did have pride to restore. Who could have stop that? You, maybe, Mister Hamilton. But I doubt me if even you."

"All right," him say. "All right."

Him turn and start to walk to the house.

"Come back, man," Super shout from where him lie in the grass on the bank. Mister Hamilton just walk on regular and gentle.

John's first bullet open a white wound in the boards by Mister Hamilton's left foot. The next one do the same by the right. Him never look or pause; even him back, as I watch, don't stiffen. The third shot strike earth before him and kick dirt onto him shoe.

At the Stelling

"John!" him call, and Mister Hamilton have a voice like a howler monkey when him want. "John, if you make a ricochet and kill me, I'm going to come up there and break your ——ing neck."

Then I know say how this Mister Hamilton is the same Mister Hamilton that left we.

Him walk on, easy and slow, up the path, up the steps, and into the house.

I sit by the dead and wait.

Little bit pass and Mister Hamilton come back. Him is alone, with a basket in him hand. Him face still. Like the face of a mountain lake, back in the Interior, where you feel but can't see the current and the fullness of water below.

"Shirley," him call to the Super, "bring the launch up to the *stelling*. You'll be more comfortable here than where you are. It's quite safe. He won't shoot if you don't rush him."

I look into the basket him bring down from the house. It full of well-cooked *labba*. Enough there to feed five times the men that begin to gather on the *stelling*.

The Super look into the basket also, and I see a great bewilderment come into his face.

"Good God!" him say. "What's all this? What's he doing?"

"Dunnie," Mister Hamilton say to me. "There's a bottle of rum in my boat. And some bread and a packet of butter. Bring them over for me, will you? Go on," him tell Super. "Have some. John thought you might be getting hungry."

Him draw up the deck-chair in which Mister Cockburn did die. I go to the Survey boat and fetch out the rum and the bread and the butter. The butter wrap into grease paper and sink in a closed billy pot of water to keep it from the sun. I bring knife, also, and a plate and a mug for Mister Hamilton, and a billyful of river water for put into the rum. When everything come, him cut bread and butter it and pour rum for Super and himself, and take a leg of *labba*. When him chew the food, him eat like John. The jaws of him mouth move sideways and not a crumb drop to waste. The rest of we watch him and Super, and then we cut into the *labba* too, and pour liquor from the bottle. The tarpaulin stretch above we and the tall day is beginning to die over the western savannah.

"Why did he do it?" Super say and look at the eight dead lay out under the canvas. "I don't understand it, Hamilton. Christ! He *must* be mad."

Him lean over beside Mister Hamilton and cut another piece of *labba* from the basket.

"What does he think he can do?" him ask again. "If he doesn't come down I'm going to send down river for grenades. We'll have to get him out somehow."

Mister Hamilton sit and eat and say nothing. Him signal to me and I pass him the bottle. Not much left into it, for we all take a drink. Mister Hamilton tilt out the last drop and I take the billy and go to the *stelling* edge and draw a little water for Mister Hamilton and bring it back. Him draw the drink and put the mug beside him. Then him step from under the tarpaulin and fling the empty bottle high over Catacuma water. And as the bottle turn and flash against the dying sun, I see it fall apart in the middle and broken glass falling like raindrops as John's bullet strike.

We all watch and wait, for now the whole world stand still and wait with we. Only the water make soft music round the *stelling*.

Then from up the house there is the sound of one shot. It come to us sudden and short and distant, as if something close it round.

"All right," Mister Hamilton say to the Super. "You better go and bring him down now."

The Wind in this Corner

JOHN HEARNE

In the middle of the morning we drove out of the low, scrubby Queenshaven Hills and into the Braganza plain. It was very hot and dry outside, but in the car, going fast with the windows open, the heat was only pleasant: a warm, thick-textured rush of air, smelling of baked brick and a peppery, grass tang of the deep country. Charlie McIntosh was driving us in his car, the big, always dusty, hard-used Buick that had covered every road in Cayuna bigger than a bridle path; I was sitting behind with my forearms resting on the back rest of the driver's seat; and Roger Eliot sat beside Charlie.

"Well, it's a good day for it," Roger Eliot said.

"A good day for what?" Charlie McIntosh asked, before I could nudge him to keep quiet.

"A good day for murder," Roger told him. "I don't like committing murder in bad weather. That spoils everything. Don't you think so, Charlie?"

"Cho, God!" Charlie muttered. He was the older man but he sounded like a boy who has gone too far with adults and has been brutally snubbed. "You don't have to talk like that, Roger. It's not funny."

His florid, pleasant face was hurt and very Jewish, and as he squirmed in his seat, I felt the big car surge forward on a burst of new speed. Charlie always finds comfort and release, in any situation that seems to go beyond his grasp, by driving too fast, or by swimming furiously across harbour in which there are barracuda, or by getting drunk in a dozen widely separated bars, driving too fast to each of them.

"How are the other assassins?" Roger said and turned to look back past me and through the rear window. "Good. They're still keeping up. We won't have to do all the knife work alone."

"It might help if you shut up, Roger," I told him. "None of us is going to enjoy what we have to do. So why not stop whining as if you're the only one who hates it?"

His small green eyes were sombre and forbidding as they turned to me, and his long, pale, ugly face was too vivid and yet empty. It reminded me of the sad, dangerous face you see, sometimes, when a man has been smoking *ganja* and feels all his connections with other men are down and is getting ready to kill or maim simply to assure himself that the gap he senses can be bridged. I made a fist and punched Roger gently on the shoulder and smiled. Sometimes people like Charlie and me, in the party, tend to forget how young Roger Eliot is. He is so good that it is easy to forget.

"Go on," I said. "I know what the Old Man means to you. But what about us, eh? You think we don't feel it too?" He made a wry, tired grimace of disgust and turned away and looked before him again. We were travelling through the cane fields now but from the rear window I could still see the hills, close behind us and faded by the long dry season. They were a dusty grey-green, stark and inhospitable under the glowing sky. Where the road had been laid across the saddle there was a white gash of limestone looking strangely alive against the bleached out, dehydrated bush of the hill slope. The other cars were strung out along the straight road: Osbourne's Riley and Douglas's black Jaguar close together, and a good way behind, Dennis Broderick's old station waggon trailing a lot of dirty blue exhaust. The canes were all around us, close packed, tawny with the sun, stretching for ten miles down to the coast where the sky above the swamps was grey and hazy. The pink earth from the fields was dusted on the black road, and occasionally, as the tyres churned the soft surface, a tickling earth smell mingled with the sharpness of hot asphalt would swirl briefly about the car.

"Do we have time to stop for a drink at Sherwood Bridge?" Roger asked me.

"Sure," I said. "Do you need one?"

"Good God, yes, man. I don't want to go into him cold. Do you?"

"No," I agreed. "A drink would be a good idea. Get rid of this lead in my stomach. We don't want to get caught up in Sherwood Bridge, though. How long since you've been there?"

"About three months," Roger said. "When I was speaking at the Agricultural Show. But it's Charlie's territory. When were you over last, Charlie?"

"Ten days ago," Charlie told him. "There shouldn't be much to hold us up today. They won't have many new things that need listening to. Besides, it won't be a bad thing for Eugene to show his face. He's been so busy in the Eastmoreland divisions he hasn't had time for Braganza."

"How's he doing in Eastmoreland?" I asked. "Are we going to win down there?"

"You tell me," Charlie said. "Does anybody ever know how Eastmoreland is going to vote? Jesus, I'm glad I don't have to fight the election down there. Those Eastmoreland boys kiss you on Monday and hang you on Tuesday, and nobody ever knows why they do either."

"They're not the only ones," Roger said. His voice wasn't pleasant. It was flat and too precise and full of that angry sadness I had seen on his face. "When it comes to kissing and killing, we're doing all right, aren't we, Charlie?"

I saw Charlie's hands tighten on the wheel. He had big hands, firmly fleshed and virile like the rest of his body, covered with reddish freckles and a thick pelt of fine dark hairs. When he turned his face briefly to Roger, the full red lips were thinly compressed and the heavy bar of his moustache made a melancholy, decisive sweep across his profile.

"When we stop at Sherwood Bridge," he said, dead and even,

"you can take the car and drive back to town. Tony and I will go on with Eugene. If you don't want to do this, then you can back out now. Do anything you want but, for Christ's sake stop all the bull-shit. I've had enough. You hear me?"

"Me too," I said. "I know Charlie and me and the rest of us are pretty coarse, Roger, compared with you, but just stop reminding us how sensitive you are, eh."

The strange thing about it was that I think we all knew what we were trying to do. We were trying to get angry with each other so that when we reached the Old Man there would be enough anger left for us to do the job properly.

"Oh, shut up, both of you," Roger said. He passed his hand roughly over his pallid, heat-shiny face. "Let me think what I'm going to say to him. You have any cigarettes left, Tony?"

"Sure," I said, and smiled at him as he turned round and took one from the packet. "Take it easy, boy. We've given you a nasty job, but take it easy."

"You want me to do it?" Charlie asked. "I'll do it, Roger. It ought to have been me from the beginning. Not you. It was a son-of-a-bitch trick asking you to tell him."

Roger looked at him sideways and gave a warm, harsh snort of laughter.

"You know something, Charlie," he said. "You're a nice old bastard. Only your mother and I know it, but you're all right. No. I'll do it. I have to."

"Let me do it," Charlie said. "It ought to come from me."

"Don't be damn' silly," Roger said. "Of course I have to do it. If you or Tony or Eugene, or any of the others, initiated this it would finish him. When he thinks of the party and the movement now it's your faces he sees. All of you who were with him from the beginning, or who went to prison with him during the war. No, you couldn't do it. When I do it, I'll be speaking for the new guard, eh, for the hard young professionals who hope to govern this bloody island after the election. He'll understand that—just. I hope."

We drove on into the hot, sharp shadowed plain. Nobody

wanted to say anything more. We had said it all too often before this Sunday morning, and no amount of talking had made it any easier.

At Sherwood Bridge we stopped beside the yellow, plastered wall of the Chinese grocery; when we climbed from the car and stood on the gritty pavement, the heat rose from the concrete and enfolded us. The water in the gutter ran slimy and tepid around the tyres of the Buick, and a bright dense glare was flung into our faces from the whitelimed wall of the courthouse across the street. The little town had the dreamy, suspended feeling of Sunday morning and a church bell somewhere sounded thin and lost in the still air. In about a minute the first people began to gather round us, and by the time the other cars turned into the street there was a good crowd on the pavement outside the grocery. If only half of them meant to vote for us, it was still good to see that so many had collected so quickly.

There was a lot of excitement when Eugene Douglas's grey lion head emerged from his car, and further excitement, but lesser, when Osbourne and Broderick pulled up. Listening to the voices, I realised that unless the party did something very foolish we were in this time. Even allowing for the fact that this was the Old Man's parish, there was a note of recognition and pleasure in the voices that I had been hearing now for the last two months in other districts. It came from something more than the Old Man's personal influence, and we all had waited a long time for that sound from a crowd.

We went from the pulsing heat of the pavement into the green, bottle-glimmering coolness of the bar. Yap, the grocer, was standing behind the scarred wooden counter and smiling as he saw the crowd coming after us. Everyone was talking at once and somebody put a glass into my hand and Yap looked at me, pointing to a bottle of soda on the counter, and I nodded and he opened it, and handed it to me over the shifting heads. I splashed a little into the drink I had been given and watched the dark amber of the rum turn to pale gold and gave the bottle into a hand that reached out from the crowd.

John Hearne

This was the sort of gathering in which you realised how good Roger Eliot was. As I talked to the people around me, I could see him in the middle of his group, very tall, white-faced, with that distinctive, bony ugliness, turning from man to man unhurriedly. Each response was certain and intimate and you knew that he enjoyed this campaigning in the grass roots as most men enjoy being with a pretty woman. This was his gift. One of his many. Charlie McIntosh had it too, by background training and because being with the crowd made him feel happy, but he would never have, in addition, the cold, legalistic authority that Roger could turn on in the House like the controlled, merciless bursts from a machine-gun. In the House, apart from the Old Man, the only person who carried more sheer weight was Eugene Douglas, and then only because he had more experience and had been with the Old Man from the very beginning. And nowadays when you sat in the visitors' gallery, facing the opposition benches, and saw Roger Eliot and Eugene Douglas lounging side by side, each with that bleakly exultant histrionic barrister's keenness on his face, you realised that Roger was the greater man. He was greater because he was younger and we had given him a party and a machine to inherit. Sometimes, I wondered if we had asked too much of him too soon. It seemed to me that a lot of youth and a lot of gentleness had vanished from that intense, tautly preoccupied face while none of us was really looking.

He began to tell a clever and destructive story about the government and even the men talking with Eugene stopped to listen. I had heard it before, but listening to him tell it I found myself grinning. It was all very personal and rather obscene, as stories like that tend to be in Cayuna. We all pretend to be outraged when we hear them against ourselves, and then we start digging up one about our opponents. When he had finished the laughter crashed around us like surf.

"Den tell me, Mister Eliot," one of the men said; he looked like a cane worker or a small farmer, in for the day. "How we gwine do when election come? Who gwine win dis time?"

The Wind in this Corner

Roger grinned and pushed him roughly, like a father pushing a grown son with affection. Nobody else but Charlie or the Old Man could have done it in quite that way without patronage.

"Who gwine *win*?" he mocked the man, and appealed theatrically to the crowd. "Who gwine win? You hear him? We going to win, of course. How you can ask a dam' fool question like that, man? Lord, but we getting some milk an' water workers in the party nowadays. Who gwine win?"

He clapped the man on the shoulder, hard, and grinned down at him, enjoying what he was doing so genuinely that the man grinned too, with delight and confidence, as the rest had already begun to chuckle and repeat what Roger had said.

When it was time for us to go, the men in the bar came out to the pavement and watched us getting into the cars. They were very pleased that we were going on to see the Old Man, and they waved us down the street until we turned the corner by the Methodist Church.

Beyond the church there was an iron bridge spanning a shallow, dirty green river; sugar cane began on the far bank of the river and the great column of the sugar factory chimney towered red and harsh into the deep, soft sky. We could see the clean shimmers of heat rising from the road.

Two miles from Sherwood Bridge, Charlie turned the Buick into a pink, rocky side road, and as the big car lurched and jolted in the ruts, I could see, in the driving mirror, the others following. On the left there was a big, dried-out pasture with the Old Man's famous mules grazing on the dusty stubble, along with four lordly jacks and seven swollen mares. In the field on the left there was a stand of heavy maize and another of dense, cool-looking tobacco. Then the road began to rise a little and there, just under the crest of the hillock, was the Old Man's house, and the Old Man, who must have heard the cars, standing against a pillar at the head of his steps, lifting his hand as we drove into the yard and parked in the shade of a breadfruit tree.

"Well, gentlemen," he said, and came halfway down the steps to meet us. "What an unexpected pleasure. Charlie, you young scoundrel, I knew you were coming. But not everyone else."

The great, square, cropped head moved forward on the enormous neck as he squinted into the yard to where Eugene Douglas, Broderick and Osbourne were getting from their cars.

"Eugene!" he called as he took my hand and Roger's simultaneously. "I almost didn't recognise you. I thought you must have left the island. . . ."

"D.J.," said Eugene and came up and put his hands on the Old Man's shoulders. "How are you? I've been out of town every time you've come up. Things are tight in Eastmoreland and All Souls. We're going to need you in both places before the election. If we don't get at least one set of seats from those two we might lose again."

"We'll get 'em," the Old Man said crisply. "I promise you that. We have to, eh. We can't lose this time. Twice is as much as anyone can afford to lose in Cayuna. After that you're bad luck."

He stood, still holding Eugene by the arms, and smiling at us with the slight half-twist of his lips that, for as long as we could remember, had always accompanied his brief, almost aphoristic lectures on the strategy of practical politics. Each of us there, except Roger Eliot, could have written down about two hundred sentences, nearly proverbs, with which for over thirty years the Old Man had taught all he had learnt.

"No, gentlemen," the Old Man continued. "We cannot lose this time. Do not even entertain the idea. Now let's go in and spend a proper Cayuna Sunday morning. Good Heavens, but it's splendid to see you all like this."

He turned and led us up the broad steps: a short, bow-legged old man, with immense shoulders and a back as broad as a bank door, who yet managed to appear of a height in a crowd of tall men. Always, in the past, when you had bent your head to talk to him you had felt as if he were making the concession. And now, as I watched his stiff-collared, immaculately linen-suited figure between the bright-patterned, fluttering sports shirts and casual slacks of Roger and Eugene, there was still enough of the old demonic authority left to make those two towering men appear somehow slight.

"Mildred!" The marvellous gong of a voice carried through the darkened, cool rooms of the old house. "Mildred, we have guests. Tell the girl to bring ice and all the rest of it. Come, gentlemen. Draw up your chairs here. The wind in this corner is always cool for some reason. Some accident of architecture. On the hottest day it's always pleasant here. I know how you Queenshaven people complain about our Braganza heat. It makes men, though. You need a furnace for a good sword."

Watching us as we drew the wicker chairs into a semi-circle on the broad, wooden veranda, his old, wildly seamed face was firm and glowing with happiness. The huge, deer-like eyes sparkled. Once those enormous, liquid eyes and that compactly massive, squat body had been very nearly irresistible. All over Cayuna, now, you could see men and women, of all colours, with those same brown pools that beautified the plainest face, and with those same sloping, heavy shoulders.

"D.J.," Charlie said, "you have any of that whisky you gave me when I was over last week? Jesus, but that was a whisky, man. Don't give it to these crows. They wouldn't appreciate it. Save it for you and me."

The Old Man laughed: an emphatic, musical bark. He glared at Charlie with a furious love that became suddenly too naked to witness without embarrassment. From the beginning, he had respected Eugene and Osbourne as nearly his peers, or been fond of those like Broderick and myself, but it had been Charlie who filled his hunger for the legitimate son he had never been able to have. Now there was only his daughter: a grey, plump woman called Mildred; silent and distant like so many country spinsters.

"Any of that whisky?" the Old Man said. "Charlie McIntosh, you're a damned blackguard, as I've always maintained. Gentlemen, that person you see making himself at home on my veranda came here last week and under the pretence of talking party

business filled his gut with over a quart of the whisky I keep
for important guests. . . . Mildred, for God's sake, child, where
is the drink? You want these poor men to die of thirst?"

He raised his voice to an unconstrained shout, and rubbed his
hands hard together as if crushing his pleasure to get its essence.
Then as the maid came out with the drinks and Mildred followed
her, he sat down. We rose and Miss Mildred nodded to our greetings with a disdain that we knew was not directed at us personally but at whatever fate or chance had caused men to leave
her alone with only a genially tyrannical old father to care for.
She saw to the maid as the girl set the big mahoe tray with its
load of bottles, glasses and a bowl of ice on the low veranda
table. They both went inside again immediately. The maid was
a big, clumsy-looking girl, not wearing shoes, so I knew she
must be from far back in the country, probably from the St.
Joseph mountains. She seemed to be very apprehensive of Miss
Mildred.

"Now," said the Old Man. He was alight with anticipation.
Talking and drinking were two of the four or five things he had
always liked doing best. He took us all in with one quick, hot
glance. "Charlie, my boy, work for your living. Find out what
these gentlemen would like and give me a whisky and water.
You know how I like it."

"Yes," Charlie said, under his breath. "Five fingers of liquor
and the dew off a blade of grass."

"What's that? What did you say?"

"Nothing, D.J. Nothing. Just thinking aloud."

"I hope so. I hope that was all."

I felt the smile on my face become unbearably strained and
looked at Roger desperately, begging him in my mind to say
what he had come to say and stop this ritual exchange between
Charlie and the Old Man. Roger was carefully mixing himself
a rum and ginger-ale, not waiting for Charlie to help him, and
not looking at anybody. You could sense the crushing, Braganza
heat in the bright yard, but the wind in this corner of the
veranda was cool and gentle. As the Old Man had said it would

be. As I had known it would be. I had sat here often enough. After a long time Charlie gave me my drink.

"Here's to victory, D.J.," I said, and lifted my glass.

"I'll drink to that, Tony." He smiled, raising his glass first to me and then to the others, and then ran his square-tipped, coffee-brown fingers energetically through the cropped, silver lawn of his hair. "My God, I'll drink to that. It's been a long time, eh? Thirty years. You boys were in your twenties. And Roger . . . were you born yet, Roger?"

"Yes," Roger told him. "I was born. I wasn't taking much notice, you understand, but I was born."

"My God," the Old Man said again. "Sometimes it seems like thirty centuries and sometimes like thirty months. I used to think I was mad sometimes. Expecting this damned island to want independence. You remember what they called us then? 'The black man's party.' Well, if we never win an election we can be proud of that. There isn't a politician in the island now who wouldn't like to have that title for his party. That's our doing."

"You know what the government boys have started calling us these days?" Eugene asked him.

"No. What?"

"The white man's party. I heard Gomez saying that over in Eastmoreland the other day."

The Old Man threw his head against the back of his chair and laughed. The wickerwork gave that peculiar shushing creak of straw as the chair shook under him.

"Why?" he asked, and chuckled again. "Why?"

"Oh, because of Roger, I suppose. Charlie too, if you count Jews. Mostly because Fabricus is standing in Eastmoreland and is being very popular. It's his old parish, you know? Before he came to Queenshaven. He's beginning to frighten the government now, so Gomez decided to use his colour against him."

"Lack of colour, you mean," the Old Man said with delight. "Good. That's what I like to hear. Black man's party. White man's party. Jew man's party. Chinaman's party. They'll soon run out of labels. Each time they clap another one on us, it means we're hurting them somewhere."

"We've got them running, all right," Charlie said, "but it's going to be close. They could edge us out yet."

"Close!" the Old Man said. "Of course it's going to be close. But it's our election. I can smell it. If we get in this time, and the next, we're set for a long innings. Good God! After thirty years' fighting, to sit with men like you on a government front bench."

He leaned forward and gave his empty glass to Charlie. The stretched, deeply grooved skin of his face was burnished with the drink he had just taken. Charlie mixed him another quickly and he leaned back again. The long stomach was quite flat under the gleamingly starched linen waistcoat, and in the irreducible, worn bronze of his face, the eyes were much too young and adventurous.

Now, I said to myself, now, Roger. He's given you the cue. Say what you have to say. For all of us. If you don't say it now, when will you ever say it?

I heard the shallow heave of Eugene's breathing beside me. Broderick's fat yellow face was beaded with little unattractive drops of sweat. Charlie was a still, untidy heap in his chair, and Osbourne had begun to finish his drink in small, ridiculous sips.

"Look, D.J.," Roger said. "We haven't come out just to finish your liquor. We want to talk a few things over with you. Election business. And about afterwards."

His precise and resonant lawyer's voice was a little high. He looked into his drink, then swallowed half of it.

"Of course," the Old Man said. "I have a number of points I want to raise myself. I shall be putting them before the executive, officially, when we meet in Queenshaven next week, but so many of you are here this morning that I'd like to discuss them now."

"What we had in mind——" Roger said.

"I made a memorandum," the Old Man said. "Mildred was typing it for me last night. I'll go and get it. . . . Gentlemen, your glasses are empty. Charlie McIntosh, you dog, see to your duties or I'll cut you off with a shilling."

He stood up and his stiffness in getting from the chair was barely perceptible. And then we were looking at each other and listening to the slow, decisive footsteps going across the wooden floor of the old-fashioned drawing-room.

"He never even listened," Roger said. "Has he ever listened? He's run this damned party so long he thinks it's his personal property. There's no easy way out of it now, Eugene. I'm going to give it to him straight. He won't understand it otherwise."

"He *was* the party," Broderick said sullenly. "He was all the party this island had when you were still wetting your pants, Roger. When I was half your age, he was burning up Cayuna like a bush fire. He has a right to say his say. More right than any of us. My God!"

Roger turned on him with the speed of a biting dog, and I could almost touch the relief and eagerness with which he fastened on a cause for anger. On the excuse for any heat that might drive him through what he had to tell the Old Man.

"Right, Broderick," he said. "You do it. Or don't let's do it. Just as you all please. Say the word, gentlemen, and I'll stop where I started and we'll listen to what he has to say, as we always have. . . ."

He was shaking with desolate rage.

"We'll listen," Eugene said quietly. "We'll listen as we always have. And we'll learn something, as we always have. But not until you've told him he can't stand for election again, Roger. Not until you've told him that he has to leave the House. That's what we came out here for, and you are going to do it, aren't you?"

"Yes," Roger said, and the word was rough with the violence of his conflict. "Yes, I'm going to tell him what he should have realised for himself. But I don't want any of you old comrades-in-arms looking at me as if it's all my idea."

"Nobody is doing that," Charlie said heavily. "Just do what you have to and get it over. It's going to be kinder that way."

John Hearne

Then we heard the Old Man's emphatic footfall coming back across the drawing-room. He stood in the doorway studying two closely typed pages of foolscap, his rolled-gold spectacles pushed up on his forehead. God knows why the Old Man had ever worn spectacles. His vision hadn't altered much between seven and seventy-five. But he wouldn't read the posters on a wall without an elaborate performance of taking out the ancient, faded almost colourless, morocco case, removing the spectacles, putting them on carefully, and then, as carefully, pushing them up his forehead, almost to the hair line. This had become part of his legend. Cartoonists used it. Little, barefoot boys in the street acted it. Visitors to the House stayed to see it. It hadn't done us any harm at all.

"Gentlemen," the Old Man said, "I was considering our tactics the other night." Still studying his sheets he stepped onto the veranda and settled in his chair with a grunt. "I feel that we are going to need more emphasis in the north. Much more than we've given it up to now. It has always been our weak spot and we've always dodged it. Not any more though, gentlemen. We're going to take the fight to them——"

"D.J.," Roger said; his voice was calm now, and weary, but suddenly assured. As he sat there, leaning forward with his elbows on his knees and holding his glass in both hands, I could see two hectic smears of colour along the cheek-bones, beneath the very pale, normally waxen skin. "D.J., before you get on to the general plan of the campaign, there is something we'd like to discuss. It's very important."

The Old Man looked up, the frowning flicker of his impatience merely suggested within the lustrous vitality of his eyes, like the lightning you thought you saw behind the mountains at night. "Certainly," he said to Roger. "We have all day. You're all staying to lunch, by the way. I've told Mildred. What's come up, Roger? You sound worried." He sprawled easily, in that long familiar slouch of confident readiness, his face tightening into a still, sharply edged cast of experienced attention, the face of an old hunter to whom any problem is a repetition of

82

one known long ago and yet one needing care because some detail is always new. "Elections!" he said happily. "They always bring more trouble than any blasted thing I know. Even women. They're the price we pay for being politicians."

"D.J.," Roger asked him, "have you ever thought of giving up the House? Giving up parliamentary work, I mean, and using yourself on the trade union side?"

"Giving up the House?" We sat in a sort of hypnotised absorption as we watched bewilderment and then exasperated dismissal of an unworthy waste of time struggle for place in the Old Man. "Roger, boy, what the hell are you talking about? If that's what's on your mind, I'll settle it right away. No. I've never thought of leaving the House." He gave a short bark of laughter, half annoyed, half indulgent. "Not until the people of Braganza parish vote me out, at least. And they've been sending me up for thirty years now. What in God's name brought this on?"

"You," Roger said. "And the elections. And thinking about you after the elections."

"And what I'd be doing in trade union work at my age," the Old Man said, ignoring him still with the same wry anger that was no more than the quick reflex of a stallion at stud, "I don't know. What's the matter, has Brod been neglecting his duties there?" He winked at Broderick, who was the leader of the trade union congress that during the years had grown into affiliation with the party, and Broderick grimaced back at him stiffly as Roger got to his feet. He stood deliberately, and the three steps he made along the veranda and the three steps back were deliberate also, controlled and almost pensive, and when he stood above the Old Man, I thought, "Merciful Heavens, he looks just like the Old Man did that afternoon during the war when they came to arrest him for sedition as he left the House." And it was true. Roger as he stood there, elongated rather than merely tall, grotesquely thin, hunched in his bright shirt like a harlequin in the mime, all knobs, angles and elbows, with his tapered yet ugly hands jammed into his trouser pockets, was

83

invested with the same moment's quality that I had seen on the
Old Man when they arrested him, politely enough and on the
steps outside because members were immune while the House
sat: a quality at once angry and serene, dispassionately im-
placable with the sense of utter conviction.

"D.J.," Roger said. "Will you listen?" And the Old Man
looked up quickly, as the weight of that charged voice roused
in him his first serious apprehension. "Yes," the Old Man said.
"Go ahead, Roger."

"We're asking you to resign your seat," Roger said. "To
resign and not make it an official executive matter. We want you
to join Broderick in the trade unions and do the sort of field
work you still do better than anyone else. The executive want
you to present them with your resignation when you come up
next week."

"The executive," the Old Man said. "I didn't know the
executive . . ." His voice had become thick and uncertain and
when I saw the papers in his hand begin to shake I looked away.
I didn't want to look at the others. "The executive," the Old
Man said again, and then harshly, astonishment, not protest,
but stark incomprehension, lending strength to the uncertain
voice, "Why? I must have a reason for this." The great eyes as
they stared at Roger were dulled, opaque and absolutely still
and his face had a livid rigidity, as if he had gone beyond a
point of disbelief to where the personal shock was much less
than a sense of awed encounter with some fathomless and
abstract phenomenon. "Why?" he demanded.

"Because we are going to win this time," Roger said, "and
you could not stand five years as chief minister. No, listen, D.J.
Let me finish." He was pleading and almost anxious now, hurrying what he could into the destruction we had chosen him to
commit. "Do you have any idea what we're going to have to
do in the next five years, after we get in? What sort of mess we
have to clear up? There's five hours' paper work a night for any
minister. Let alone the business in the House during the day.
Half the year we'll be beating around Europe and America

raising capital investment. Off one damn' plane, into another, living out of suitcases, fighting it out at all-day conferences for an extra million dollars. Do you really think you could do that, D.J.?"

The Old Man's gesture was unthinkably distant and disinterested.

"I believe," he said conversationally, almost absently, "that I have proved my capacity for work in the past. Go on. I should like to hear this to the end."

His gaze travelled to each of us, with a flat, bleak absence of surprise that was far worse than recognition of treachery. It was then, I think, that the necessary, hungrily sought anger that had eluded Roger all morning finally seized him.

"Listen!" he shouted. "Listen, D.J." Not pleading and anxious now, but shivering in an ecstasy of inextricable rage and sadness. "You can't do it. You know you can't do it. However much you want to. It's a government you'll have to lead in October, not a radical opposition. You'd last a year, maybe two, and then you'd have to go. And even then you wouldn't have done your work properly. Well, we're not going to waste you like that, you hear. What you started in this island and what you built with us is too good to throw away. We want to use you where you'll do a job on the sugar estates or on the wharves, and among the fishermen. That's what you know. That's what you can do standing on your head. Tell me that isn't so. Tell me that isn't so, if you dare."

"I don't agree," the Old Man said.

"You don't agree." It was hard to tell whether the rasp in Roger's voice was savagery or tears or triumph. "Of course you don't agree. Not now. You want to be on the front bench with us. That's what you saw thirty years ago. A front bench with men like Eugene and Charlie and Tony and me. Well, you've got it for us. But it's not for you. And you'll know it tomorrow. You probably know it already because that's the sort of man you are. If you weren't, do you think I'd be standing on this blasted veranda saying what I've just had to say?"

John Hearne

He was bent over, folded from the waist in that slightly incredible fashion of the immensely tall whose skeletons seem to
struggle for release from the too scanty flesh, as if he were not
bent but suspended from the ceiling by a wire attached to the
base of his spine; his face, thrust close to the Old Man's, suffused
now with the uncontainable mixture of sadness and pure fury,
compelling from the Old Man, now, by some sheerly visible,
silent and terrific explosion of will, an acknowledgment not only
of those truths by which he had taught us to live in our work but
of how well he had taught those truths to us, both men locked
and isolated within that explosion of shared service, love and
integrity of purpose, neither man conceding one particle of his
anger or sorrow or stubborn righteousness until reluctantly,
tentatively, then with sudden and prodigal generosity, the will
of the older man recognised the faith behind the will of the
younger, recognised that and saluted, also, what it must have
cost a man as yet so young and vulnerable.

"Good God, boy," the Old Man said softly, "don't stand there
like that. I feel as if you're a tree about to fall on me. Sit down."

Roger sat, in the slow careful fashion of a man who has been
exhausted to a point where he dare not trust his muscles to
perform the simplest action. As slowly he took his right hand
and a handkerchief from his pocket and wiped the film of damp
and grease from his face. He grinned lopsidedly at the Old Man.
It was a hot day. Such as you get only in Braganza. In the
middle of the cane fields, on the south side of the mountains,
cut off from the northern trades and too far from the sea to
catch the breeze. Even in this corner of the Old Man's veranda
you could feel a declaration of heat, distinct and independent,
parasitically attached to the accidental current of cool air.

"I did not realise," the Old Man said, "that this was the
feeling of the executive. Of course I shall be proud to accept
whatever you may suggest. Gentlemen! Your glasses are empty
again. There is plenty of time for another before lunch. Charlie!"

His gaze, withdrawn but courteous, roved across our circle,
not so much repudiating contact as, for now, impervious to what

might mistakenly be offered as a substitute. Passed round us until it rested on Roger where he sat wrapped in his own exhaustion like a Mexican in his blanket.

Hot, I thought, dry hot. No rain. Much more of this and the Old Man will have to buy grass from the hills for his mules and his jacks and those mares in foal.

I don't know why this occurred to me then. Perhaps to protect me from an act of intimacy we had all witnessed but from which all but two of us had been excluded.

Knock On Wood

SAMUEL SELVON

The last time I see Jupsingh, he had a piece of a broomstick handle up in the lining of his coat. He say that he have that there because a Chinese fellar in Bayswater want to beat him, and he only waiting to crack this Chinese fellar head wide open with the handle.

But I feel Jup have that broomstick there because he like to knock wood for luck. In point of fact, Jarvis and myself see him lift the coat and take a little knock while we was talking to him, and at the same time he sort of make a half turn and kiss a cross that he have pin on his chest.

The first time I meet this test was one night Jarvis and me combing the Bayswater Road late to see if we could pick up a little thing to pass the time away. Same time, who should be coming down the road but Jupsingh, with a sharp thing holding on to his arm, a real chic chick.

"Oh God!" Jarvis say. "Boy, look Jupsingh. He is a real depressor, always bawling. He come from Trinidad. Listen to him when he come."

"What happening, what happening, man?" Jupsingh come up and hold Jarvis' shoulder. "Meet my new fiancée, Pat."

The thing shake hands with we. She had a babydoll face and it look like butter won't melt in she mouth. Jupsingh have on a colin-wilson and he keep pulling the long sleeves down to cover his fingers, like gloves. He have a bottle of South African sherry in his hand.

Jarvis haul him to one side and whisper, "Which part you get that piece of skin, Jupsingh?"

"Listen man, I in a jam," the old Jup say. "I bring this thing with me up from Woking and I ain't have no place to take she. What you think, boy? You think she all right? You think I could sleep with she tonight?"

"Well, you can't come by me," Jarvis say, "but I will ask my friend, he have a big room."

Jarvis ask me and I say all right, that at least we could polish off the bottle of sherry.

Up in my room Jupsingh anxious and restless as if he rusty and thirsty to hit one. Now and then, while Jarvis old-talking with Pat, he putting his hand to his face and saying Jesus Christ, and kissing a sign of the cross what he have pin on to the front of the colin-wilson. And he knocking wood. He knocking chair, table, floor—anything make out of wood in my room.

Meanwhile Jarvis talking with Pat and asking she which part she come from, and if she like London, and how she hurt her ankle, and Pat saying she come from Ireland, that she don't like London, and that she fall off a bicycle and hurt her foot.

I open the sherry and we finish off the bottle, with Jupsingh trying to force Pat to have more, but she won't. He ask she if she playing shy, and Pat smile and hang her head. You could see that the girl innocent and young, and only the good lord know how a evil test like Jupsingh manage to inveigle she to come up to London.

Well, whenever he get a chance Jupsingh asking either Jarvis or myself if we think the thing nice, and if we think she would spend the night with him, and the both of we telling him yes, yes, to keep him easy, because he restless like a racehorse at the starting line.

Pat begin to say it getting late and they have to catch the last train, but old Jup telling she to take it easy and relax, and he trying to cuddle her, but she pushing him off.

"If is anything, we could always sleep here," Jupsingh say, looking at me and winking.

"You can't sleep here," I say. "It have plenty hotels in the Water."

"You think I could get a room, boy?"

"Yes, man," Jarvis say.

Well, the four of we old-talk till it was late, then all of we went out to look and try and get a room for Jupsingh.

Outside in the road, Pat ask Jupsingh: "What are you going to do?"

"I will get a room, don't worry," he say.

You could see like he want to knock wood bad, and it chance to have some plane trees in the road where we was, and my boy went and knock the trunk of one and come back rubbing his face and saying Jesus Christ, and bending his head down and kissing the cross.

"I am not staying in a room together with you," Pat say.

"What happen to this girl at all?" Jupsingh say.

A big argument start up in the road. Pat have she hands folded and she cool as a cucumber, and you could see that she make up her mind that whatever happen she ain't going to bed down with my boy for the night. And the old Jup as if he in a kind of panic, he turning his back to kiss the cross and all the time he only asking Jarvis, "So what you think, what you think," like a recurring decimal.

"Well, let Pat go in the hotel and ask," Jarvis say. "You know how it is, they mightn't give you a room even if they have."

"How much hotel is around here?" My boy start to check up on how much money he have.

"This is a posh area, only aristocrats live here," Jarvis say, "but you might get one for one fifteen."

"Come on then, Pat, you coming?" Jupsingh holding the girl hand and pulling.

Eventually the two of them reach the entrance, but Pat stop and stand up and they argue a little, then Jupsingh breeze in alone.

Me and Jarvis stand up on the other side watching she.

"That man crazy," I say, "he can't see the girl don't want to sleep with him? What he believe? This is London, man."

"Look how she stand up there alone," Jarvis say.

"It look bad," I say. "Call she."

Jarvis call she with his hand and she cross the road.

"What is he trying to do?" Pat ask.

"Well you see," Jarvis say, trying to pacify the situation, "he gone to get a room for you."

"And where is he going to sleep?"

"With you."

"Oh no." The way Pat say that, any man but Jupsingh would throw in the sponge.

Jupsingh fly back out the hotel, rubbing his face and muttering Jesus Christ.

"No rooms, man, no rooms. Which part again we could try?"

"It have some other hotels in the next street," Jarvis say.

"Come on then." Jupsingh hold Pat and take off.

In the next street had a posh-looking hotel, and it had some people going in. Like they just come from theatre or something, with fur coat and bow tie and evening suit.

"It don't look like I would get a room there," Jup say uneasily. "You want to try, Pat?"

But the way Jupsingh thirst, he would of tried to get in the Savoy that night. He went in, but is either they dish him up quick or else he don't trust leaving Pat too long with we outside, because he come back in a hurry.

After that we start combing all over the Water for a hotel, but as if a hoodoo on the old Jup that night, he can't make a note. He only flying in and flying out, and sweating and smoking, and kissing the cross every chance he get, and now and then pulling Jarvis to one side and saying, "So what you think, boy? You think she will sleep with me? You think I stand a chance?"

By this time we reach down by Westbourne Grove and it had a taxi rank there, and Jarvis tell Jup to try the drivers, that they does know of places. But when Jup went, I don't know what the taxi fellar tell him, only thing he come back cursing and calling them bastards. And he vex too bad. He try to cuddle Pat and she turn away.

"I bet I slap you up here tonight!" Jup say. "I bet I start to get on ignorant!"

Poor Pat just stay quiet.

Jarvis say, "Man Jupsingh, you surprise me, man. You shouldn't tell the girl a thing like that. You letting me down. You from good family, man."

"I apologise," Jup say, coming quiet and turning and kissing the cross. "I apologise, Jarvis. Sorry, man."

We stand up there on the pavement, and I wondering at the arse I put myself in for this night.

"I know three fellars from Barbados living by Tottenham Court-road," Jup say. "We could go there and sleep. They have three bed."

"Where will I sleep?" Pat ask.

"With me, darling," Jup say.

"No," Pat say, and you could see she ain't weakening. As a matter of fact as the night wearing away so she getting stronger with the negatives.

"Jesus Christ," Jup say, looking around desperately for wood to knock, "I will sleep alone on the floor, and you have a bed to yourself. What happen, you don't trust me?"

"Listen, man," Jarvis say, "let we go up by Paddington, it have a lot of places there, we bound to get one."

So we start to walk up the road, and on the way we pass a wooden fence and Jup seize the opportunity to knock lightly as he pass.

We come up in a side street near to the station where it have some evil-looking joints where Londoners does go late in the night to make a stroke. Some frowsy-looking things going in, as if they just off a beat on the Bayswater Road, and some coming out, and one of them in a red dress scratching she thigh and chewing gum.

Another set of big argument start up as we stand up opposite a hotel with a neon sign. Pat won't go in with Jup, and we there arguing and flinging hands in the air and getting no place at all. To make things worse a police car making a rounds and coming up the road.

"Stop leaning on the wall like that, man!" Jup tell Pat. "You don't see the police coming? You want them to think we is criminals?"

Pat lean off the wall.

The police make a rounds, and they give we a look, but they drive on up the road.

Well, after about fifteen minutes of yes and no and kiss-the-cross Jup and Pat went inside the hotel, and me and Jarvis stand up outside waiting. We run out of cigarettes and I went up by the station to look for a machine. When I come back I see Pat there with Jarvis.

"What happen?" I say.

"I am not staying in that hotel with him," Pat say.

A minute after, the old Jup come out.

"I get the room," he say. "Is all right? The fellar waiting for we to make up we mind. What you say, Pat?"

"No," Pat say.

"Oh, Jesus Christ!" Jupsingh start up again. "You say you want to meet coloured people, and I take you around. Now you doing as if I is a criminal. I should of let you go with some of them damn' Jamaican and let them rough you up! What you think, eh? I sure if it was a white man you would of come!"

"It would not have made any difference," Pat say, and though she kind of uneasy about everything me and Jarvis had was to admire the consistency of the negatives she throwing at Jup.

"You shouldn't tell the girl such things, man," Jarvis say. "You shouldn't treat the girl like that."

Well, I don't know what would of happened there that night, the way things was going. The three of them argue and argue, and I draw to one side and every now and then I telling Jarvis, "I going home, eh," and Jarvis only waving his hand and telling me to wait for him, and Jup kissing the cross now without trying to hide, and rubbing his face and saying, "Jesus Christ!"

People come out of the hotel to watch the bacchanal, and Jup pointing to them and telling Pat look the man waiting on us.

At last, after about half an.hour, it look like my boy cool off and reconcile to the situation.

He turn to me. "Boy, I could sleep by you tonight?"

Now I frighten from what I see that this man run basic in my room, because I staying in a respectable house and I don't want no contention at this hour of the night, so I hesitating and hemming and hawing.

"Oh God, old man, we is Indian together, from the same island, man," he say.

It look as if the only way to settle the business is to say yes, so I say yes, and Jup throw his hand around my shoulder and repeating the song about how we is Indian together.

Well, it decided that Pat should stay in the hotel, Jup by me, and in the morning early please God he would come and meet she and the both of them would catch train go back to Woking.

We left Pat going in the hotel and start to walk back to the Water.

"What you think, boy? You think them fellars in the hotel would rape she? I tell she to shut the door and lock it. So what you think, boy? You think she good for me? She all right?"

The old Jup start up again, and only looking over his shoulder as if he mad to turn back and go to the hotel.

"Is all right, man, is all right," Jarvis pacifying him. "Take it easy. You have a place to sleep, and Pat have a place to sleep."

"Oh God!" Jup say suddenly, feeling in his pocket. "I forget to bring my sun-shades!"

"What the arse your sun-shades have to do with the position?" Jarvis want to know.

"Suppose sun shine bright tomorrow?" Jup want to know.

All the time we going, Jarvis telling Jup to look at the road good, so he won't get lost when he coming in the morning.

Knock On Wood

We break up when we reach the Water and Jup and me gone up in my room. I did tired and want to sleep, but Jup keep behind me all the time, asking me if I think Pat safe in the hotel, if he should go back and look after she.

When both of we in the bed he talking in a hoarse whisper, but every now and then as if his voice break and he talking naturally, and then as if he realise it sounding loud he fall back to whispering.

I was just falling asleep when I hear a knocking. I think perhaps the neighbour feel we making too much noise and I tell Jup to keep quiet and go to sleep. But the knocking still going on. When I look to see what it was, I see my boy leaning off the bed and lifting up the carpet to knock wood.

I start to get vex. "You best hads go and sleep in the chair if you can't sleep, man," I tell him.

"I can't sleep, man, this clock making too much noise. Put it under the bed. You set it to alarm at six in the morning?"

"Yes," I say, "and is nearly six already."

He keep quiet for five minutes then he start to cough. He start to cough some big cough that rattling the bed. Cough that coming from deep down as if the man dead and 'fraid to lay down. When at last he fall asleep he start to snore like a character in a animated cartoon.

Jupsingh wake up before the alarm went off. He knock wood and shake me at the same time.

"The alarm didn't go, man!" he saying.

"Is not time yet," I tell him.

"Well, I better get up anyway. You have any coffee?"

"It have some in the saucepan."

"Thank you, man, thank you."

He get up. I turn over and try to go back to sleep, but as if I hear a muttering. I look up and I see Jup kneeling by the side of the bed.

"Hail Mary . . . forgive us our sins . . . blessed is Mary child of God. . . ."

He finish prayers and kiss the cross. He knock wood and went

95

and drink the coffee cold from the saucepan. He get dress and come back by the bed.

"Thanks a lot, boy, God bless. Both of we is Indian together, boy. You is a real friend. Cheerio, boy."

Now this is a true ballad—if I lie I die—and it ain't have no fancy ending to end up with. In fact, it have some more to sing.

Who me and Jarvis should see breezing in the Water that weekend but my boy and Pat.

"I just went round by you, man!" Jup tell me after greetings.

"I don't live there any more," I say, because I want nothing more to do with this man. "I living in Camberwell now, I just come up here to see Jarvis."

Jup say that Pat hungry and he ask Jarvis if it have any good restaurants in the Water, and Jarvis send him down by one in Westbourne Grove.

"I didn't think she would ever go out with that test again," I tell Jarvis after they gone.

"It look as if she really like him," Jarvis say.

Well, about midnight that night my bell ring and I went downstairs, thinking that Jarvis was on a late lime and wanted some company. But when I open the door who I should see but my boy.

"I tell you I ain't living here any more, man," I say, pushing the door to close it.

"Listen man, Jarvis outside, he want to see you. Jesus Christ, boy, if you know what happen to me!"

I went outside and see Jarvis.

"My boy have a piece of wood in his coat lining," Jarvis tell me before Jup could come up. "He have a piece of broom handle and he knocking it all the time!"

"Yes, but why you-all ringing my bell at this hour, man?" Is what I want to find out.

"Boy," Jupsingh begin, "if you know what happen! You really can't trust these Nordic women. Today I take Pat round by my uncle. And all the time the man only sending me out to buy wine. Two-three times he send me. The last time I say,

Knock On Wood

'But a-a, why this man sending me out so all the time?' And I open the door quiet. Man, Pat laying down on the bed with my uncle! But my uncle right, you know. He tell me that she no good."

Jup haul up his coat and knock the broom handle.

"What the arse you doing with that broomstick?" I want to know.

"A Chinee fellar want to beat me, but I carrying this for protection."

"So you left Pat?" Jarvis ask him.

"I take she to the station and I give she three-four slap and left she." He turn to me. "Listen man, you could put me up tonight? I ain't have no place to sleep. You have anything to eat? Boy, all of we is Indian together, boy."

"Don't worry with that line, old man," I say. "I done tell you I don't live here any more. I only come to get my clothes and thing."

Jup hold on to me as I make to go. "At least give me two shillings to buy a train fare," he say. "I spend all my money on that girl and I ain't have a cent—if you stick me with a pin you wouldn't draw blood."

"You better ask Jarvis," I say. "I going. See you sometime."

When I turn to close the door I see Jup making a kiss of the cross that he have pin on under his tie. He and Jarvis start to walk up the road arguing.

My Girl and the City

SAMUEL SELVON

All these words that I hope to write, I have written them already many times in my mind. I have had many beginnings, each as good or as bad as the other. Hurtling in the underground from station to station, mind the doors, missed it!, there is no substitute for wool: waiting for a bus in Piccadilly Circus: walking across Waterloo Bridge: watching the bed of the Thames when the tide is out—choose one, choose a time, a place, any time or any place, and take off, as if this were interrupted conversation, as if you and I were earnest friends and there is no need for preliminary remark.

One day of any day it is like this. I wait for my girl on Waterloo Bridge, and when she comes there is a mighty wind blowing across the river, and we lean against it and laugh, her skirt skylarking, her hair whipping across her face.

I wooed my girl, mostly on her way home from work, and I talked a great deal. Often, it was as if I had never spoken; I heard my words echo in deep caverns of thought, as if they hung about like cigarette smoke in a still room, missionless; or else they were lost for ever in the sounds of the city.

We used to wait for a 196 under a railway bridge across the Waterloo Road. There were always long queues and it looked like we would never get a bus. Fidgeting in that line of impatient humanity I got in precious words edgeways, and a train would rumble and drown my words in thundering steel. Still, it was important to talk. In the crowded bus, as if I wooed three or four instead of one, I shot words over my shoulder, across seats;

My Girl and the City

once past a bespectacled man reading the *Evening News* who lowered his paper and eyed me as if I was mad. My words bumped against people's faces, on the glass window of the bus; they found passage between "fares please" and once I got to writing things on a piece of paper and pushing my hand over two seats.

The journey ended and there was urgent need to communicate before we parted.

All these things I say, I said, waving my hand in the air as if to catch the words floating about me and give them mission. I say them because I want you to know, I don't ever want to regret afterwards that I didn't say enough; I would rather say too much.

Take that Saturday evening; I am waiting for her in Victoria station. When she comes, we take the Northern Line to Belsize Park (I know a way to the heath from there, I said). When we get out of the lift and step outside, there is a sudden downpour and everyone scampers back into the station. We wait a while, then go out in it. We get lost. I say, "Let us ask that fellow the way." But she says, "No, fancy asking someone the way to the heath on this rainy night, just find out how to get back to the tube station."

We go back, I get my bearings afresh, and we set off. She is hungry. "Wait here," I say, under a tree at the side of the road, and I go to a pub for some sandwiches. Water slips off me and makes puddles on the counter as I place my order. The man is taking a long time and I go to the door and wave to her across the street signifying I shan't be too long.

When I go out she has crossed the road and is sheltering in a doorway, pouting. "You leave me standing in the rain and stay such a long time," she says. "I had to wait for the sandwiches," I say. "What do you think, I was having a quick one?" "Yes," she says.

We walk on through the rain and we get to the heath and the rain is falling slantways and carefree and miserable. For a minute we move around in an indecisive way as if we're looking

99

for some particular spot. Then we see a tree which might offer some shelter and we go there and sit on a bench wet and bedraggled.

"I am sorry for all this rain," I say, as if I were responsible. I take off her raincoat and make her put on my quilted jacket. She takes off her soaking shoes and tucks her feet under her skirt on the bench. She tries to dry her hair with a handkerchief. I offer her the sandwiches and light a cigarette for myself. "Go on, have one," she says. I take a half and munch it, and smoke.

It is cold there. The wind is raging in the leaves of the trees, and the rain is pelting. But abruptly it ceases, the clouds break up in the sky, and the moon shines. When the moon shines, it shines on her face, and I look at her, the beauty of her washed by rain, and I think many things.

Suddenly we are kissing and I wish I could die there and then, and there's an end to everything, to all the Jesus-Christ thoughts that make up every moment of my existence.

Writing all this now—and some weeks have gone by since I started—it is lifeless and insipid and useless. Only at the time, there was something, a thought that propelled me. Always, in looking back, there was something, and at the time I am aware of it; and the creation goes on and on in my mind while I look at all the faces around me in the tube, the restless rustle of newspapers, the hiss of air as the doors close, the enaction of life in a variety of forms.

Once I told her and she said, as she was a stenographer, that she would come with me and we would ride the Inner Circle and I would just voice my thoughts and she would write them down, and that way we could make something of it. Once the train was crowded and she sat opposite to me and after a while I looked at her and she smiled and turned away. What is all this, what is the meaning of all these things that happen to people, the movement from one place to another, lighting a cigarette, slipping a coin into a slot and pulling a drawer for chocolate, buying a return ticket, waiting for a bus, working the crossword puzzle in the *Evening Standard*?

My Girl and the City

Sometimes you are in the Underground and you have no idea what the weather is like, and the train shoots out of a tunnel and sunlight floods you, falls across your newspaper, makes the passengers squint and look up.

There is a face you have for sitting at home and talking; there is a face you have for working in the office; there is a face, a bearing, a demeanour for each time and place. There is, above all, a face for travelling, and when you have seen one you have seen all. In a rush hour, when we are breathing down each other's neck, we look at each other and glance quickly away. There is not a great deal to look at in the narrow confines of a carriage except people, and the faces of people, but no one deserves a glass of Hall's wine more than you do. We justle in the subway from train to lift; we wait, shifting our feet. When we are all herded inside, we hear the footsteps of a straggler for whom the operator waits, and we try to figure out what sort of a footstep it is, if he feels the lift will wait for him; we are glad if he is left waiting while we shoot upward. Out of the lift, down the street, up the road: in ten seconds flat it is over, and we have to begin again.

One morning, I am coming into the city by the night bus, 287, from Streatham. It is after one o'clock; I have been stranded again after seeing my girl home. When we get to Westminster Bridge the sky is marvellously clear with a few stray patches of beautiful cloud among which stars sparkle. The moon stands over Waterloo Bridge, above the Houses of Parliament sharply outlined, and it throws gold on the waters of the Thames. The Embankment is quiet, only a few people loiter around the public convenience near to the Charing Cross Underground which is open all night. A man sleeps on a bench. His head is resting under headlines: *Suez Deadlock*.

Going back to that same spot about five o'clock in the evening, there was absolutely nothing to recall the atmosphere of the early morning hours. Life had taken over completely, and there was nothing but people. People waiting for buses, people hustling for trains.

101

Samuel Selvon

I go to Waterloo Bridge and they come pouring out of the offices and they bob up and down as they walk across the bridge. From the station, green trains come and go relentlessly. Motion mesmerises me into immobility. There are lines of motion across the river, on the river.

Sometimes we sat on a bench near the river, and if the tide was out you could see the muddy bed of the river and the swans grubbing. Such spots, when found, are pleasant to loiter in. Sitting in one of those places—choose one, and choose a time—where it is possible to escape for a brief spell from Christ and the cup of tea, I have known a great frustration and weariness. All these things, said, have been said before, the river seen, the skirt pressed against the swelling thigh noted, the lunch hour eating apples in the sphinx's lap under Cleopatra's Needle observed and duly registered: even to talk of the frustration is a repetition. What am I to do, am I to take each circumstance, each thing seen, noted, and mill them in my mind and spit out something entirely different from the reality?

My girl is very real. She hated the city; I don't know why. It's like that sometimes; a person doesn't have to have a reason. A lot of people don't like London that way; you ask them why, and they shrug; and a shrug is sometimes a powerful reply to a question.

She shrugged when I asked her why; and when she asked me, why I loved London, I, too, shrugged. But after a minute I thought I would try to explain, because a shrug, too, is an easy way out of a lot of things.

Falteringly, I told her how one night it was late and I found a fish and chips shop open in the East End and I bought and ate in the dark street; walking; and of the cup of tea in an all-night café in Kensington, one grim winter morning; and of the first time I ever queued in this country, in '50, to see the Swan Lake ballet, and the friend who was with me gave a busker two-and-six because he was playing "Sentimental Journey" on a mouth-organ.

"But, why do you love London?" she said.

My Girl and the City

You can't talk about a thing like that, not really. Maybe I could have told her because one evening in the summer I was waiting for her, only it wasn't like summer at all. Rain had been falling all day, and a haze hung about the bridges across the river, and the water was muddy and brown, and there was a kind of wistfulness and sadness about the evening. The way St. Paul's was, half-hidden in the rain, the motionless trees along the Embankment. But you say a thing like that and people don't understand, at all. How sometimes a surge of greatness could sweep over you when you see something.

But even if I had said all that and much more, it would not have been what I meant. You could be lonely as hell in the city, then one day you look around you and you realise everybody else is lonely too, withdrawn, locked, rushing home out of the chaos: blank faces, unseeing eyes, millions and millions of them, up the Strand, down the Strand, jostling in Charing Cross for the five-twenty; in Victoria station, a pretty continental girl wearing a light, becoming shade of lipstick, stands away from the board on which the departure of trains appears and cocks her head sideways, hands thrust into pockets of a fawn raincoat.

I catch the eyes of this girl with my own: we each register sight, appreciation: we look away, our eyes pick up casual station activities: she turns to an automatic refreshment machine, hesitant, not sure if she would be able to operate it.

Things happen, and are finished with for ever: I did not talk to her, I did not look her way again, or even think of her.

I look on the wall of the station at the clock; it is after half-past eight, and my girl was to have met me since six o'clock. I feel in my pockets for pennies to telephone. I only have two. I ask change of a stander with the usual embarrassment: when I telephone, the line is engaged. I alternate between standing in the spot we have arranged to meet and telephoning, but each time the line is engaged. I call the exchange: they ascertain that something is wrong with the line.

At ten minutes to nine, I am eating a corned-beef sandwich when she comes. Suddenly now, nothing matters except that she is here. She never expected that I would still be waiting, but she came on the offchance. I never expected that she would come, but I waited on the offchance.

Now I have a different word for this thing that happened—an offchance, but that does not explain why it happens, and what it is that really happens. We go to St. James's Park; we sit under a tree; we kiss; the moon can be seen between leaves.

Wooing my way towards, sometimes in our casual conversation, we came near to great, fundamental truths, and it was a little frightening. It wasn't like wooing at all; it was more discussion of when will it end, and must it ever end, and how did it begin, and how go on from here? We scattered words on the green summer grass, under trees, on dry leaves in a wood of quivering aspens, and sometimes it was as if I was struck speechless with too much to say, and held my tongue between thoughts frightened of utterance.

Once again I am on a green train returning to the heart from the suburbs, and I look out of window into windows of private lives flashed on my brain. Bread being sliced, a man taking off a jacket, an old woman knitting. And all these things I see—the curve of a woman's arm, undressing, the blankets being tucked in, and once a solitary figure staring at trains as I stared at windows. All the way into London Bridge—is falling down, is falling down, the wheels say: one must have a thought—where buildings and their shadows encroach on the railway tracks. Now the train crawls across the bridges, dark steel in the darkness: the thoughtful gloom of Waterloo: Charing Cross Bridge, Thames reflecting lights, and the silhouettes of city buildings against the sky of the night.

When I was in New York, many times I went into that city late at night after a sally to the outskirts; it lighted up with a million lights, but never a feeling as on entering London. Each return to the city is loaded with thought, so that by the time I take the Inner Circle I am as light as air.

At last I think I know what it is all about. I move around in a world of words. Everything that happens is words. But pure expression is nothing. One must build on the things that happen: it is insufficient to say I sat in the Underground and the train hurtled through the darkness and someone isn't using Amplex. So what? So now I weave; I say there was an old man on whose face wrinkles rivered, whose hands were shapeful with arthritis but when he spoke, oddly enough, his voice was young and gay.

But there was no old man; there was nothing; and there is never ever anything.

My girl, she is beautiful to look at. I have seen her in sunlight and in moonlight, and her face carves an exquisite shape in darkness.

"These things we talk about," I burst out, "why mustn't I say them? If I love you, why shouldn't I tell you so?"

"I love London," she said.

Calypsonian

SAMUEL SELVON

It had a time when things was really brown in Trinidad, and Razor Blade couldn't make a note nohow, no matter what he do, everywhere he turn, people telling him they ain't have work. It look like if work scarce like gold, and is six months now he ain't working.

Besides that, Razor Blade owe Chin parlour about five dollars, and the last time he went in for a sandwich and a sweet drink, Chin tell him no more trusting until he pay all he owe. Chin have his name in a copybook under the counter.

"Wait until the calypso season start," he tell Chin, "and I go be reaping a harvest. You remember last year how much money I had?"

But though Chin remember last year, that still ain't make him soften up, and it reach a position where he hungry, clothes dirty, and he see nothing at all to come, and this time so, the calypso season about three four months off.

On top of all that, rain falling nearly every day, and the shoes he have on have big hole in them, like if they laughing.

Was the rain what cause him to t'ief a pair of shoes from by a shoemaker shop in Park Street. Is the first time he ever t'ief, and it take him a long time to make up his mind. He stand up there on the pavement by this shoemaker shop, and he thinking things like Oh God when I tell you I hungry, and all the shoes around the table, on the ground, some capsize, some old and some new, some getting halfsole and some getting new heel.

It have a pair just like the one he have on.

Calypsonian

The table cut up for so, as if the shoemaker blind and cutting
the wood instead of the leather, and it have a broken calabash
shell with some boil starch in it. The starch look like pap; he
so hungry he feel he could eat it.

Well, the shoemaker in the back of the shop, and it only have
few people sheltering rain on the pavement. It look so easy for
him to put down the old pair and take up another pair—this
time so, he done have his eye fix on a pair that look like Technic,
and just his size, too, besides.

Razor Blade remember how last year he was sitting pretty—
two-tone Technic, gaberdeen suit, hot tie. Now that he catching
his royal, everytime he only making comparison with last year,
thinking in his mind how them was the good old days, and
wondering if they go ever come back again.

And it look to him as if t'iefing could be easy, because plenty
time people does leave things alone and go away, like how now
the shoemaker in the back of the shop, and all he have to do is
take up a pair of shoes and walk off in cool blood.

Well, it don't take plenty to make a t'ief. All you have to do
is have a fellar catching his royal, and can't get a work noway,
and bam! By the time he make two three rounds he bounce
something somewhere, an orange from a tray, or he snatch a
bread in a parlour, or something.

Like how he bounce the shoes.

So though he frighten like hell and part of him going like a
pliers, Razor Blade playing victor brave boy and whistling as he
go down the road.

The only thing now is that he hungry.

Right there by Queen Street, in front a chinee restaurant, he
get an idea. Not an idea in truth; all he did think was: In for a
shilling in for a pound. But when he think that, is as if he begin
to realise that if he going to get stick for the shoes, he might
as well start t'iefing black is white.

So he open now to anything: all you need is a start, all you
need is a crank up, and it come easy after that.

What you think he planning to do? He planning to walk in

the chinee restaurant and sit down and eat a major meal, and then out off without paying. It look so easy, he wonder why he never think of it before.

The waitress come up while he looking at the menu. She stand up there, with a pencil stick up on she ears like a real test, and when he take a pin-t at she he realise that this restaurant work only part-time as far as she concern, because she look as if she sleepy, she body bend up like a piece of copper wire.

What you go do? She must be only getting a few dollars from the chinee man, and she can't live on that.

He realise suddenly that he bothering about the woman when he himself catching his tail, so he shake his head and watch down at the menu.

He mad to order a portion of everything—fry rice, chicken chop-suey, roast pork, chicken chow-min, birdnest soup, chicken broth, and one of them big salad with big slice of tomato and onion.

He begin to think again about the last calypso season, when he was holding big, and uses to go up by the high-class chinee restaurant in St. Vincent Street. He think how is a funny thing how sometimes you does have so much food that you eat till you sick, and another time you can't even see you way to hustle a rock and mauby.

It should have some way that when you have the chance you could eat enough to last you for a week or a month, and he make a plan right there, that the next time he have money (oh God) he go make a big deposit in a restaurant, so that all he have to do is walk in and eat like stupidness.

But the woman getting impatient. She say: "You taking a long time to make up you mind, like you never eat in restaurant before."

And he think about the time when he had money, how no frowsy woman could have talk to him so. He remember how them waitresses used to hustle to serve him, and one night the talk get around that Razor Blade, the Calypsonian, was in the place, and they insist that he give them a number. Which one it was again? The one about Home and the Bachelor.

108

Calypsonian

"Come, come, make up you mind, mister, I have work to do."

So he order plain boil rice and chicken stew, because the way how he feeling, all them fancy chinee dish is only joke, he feel as if he want something like roast breadfruit and saltfish, something solid so when it go down in you belly you could feel it there.

And he tell the woman to bring a drink of Barbados rum first thing, because he know how long they does take to bring food in them restaurant, and he could coast with the rum in the meantime.

By the time the food come he feeling so hungry he could hardly wait, he fall down on the plate of rice and chicken as if is the first time he see food, and in three minute everything finish.

And is just as if he seeing the world for the first time, he feel like a million, he feel like a lord; he give a loud belch and bring up some of the chicken and rice to his throat; when he swallow it back down it taste sour.

He thinking how it had a time a American fellar hear a calypso in Trinidad and he went back to the States and he get it set up to music and thing, and he get the Andrews Sisters to sing it, and the song make money like hell, it was on Hit Parade and all; wherever you turn, you could hear people singing that calypso. This time so, the poor calypsonian who really write the song catching hell in Trinidad; it was only when some smart lawyer friend tell him about copyright and that sort of business that he wake up. He went to America; and how you don't know he get a lot of money after the case did fix up in New York?

Razor Blade know the story good; whenever he write a calypso, he always praying that some big-shot from America would hear it and like it, and want to set it up good. The Blade uses to go in Frederick Street and Marine Square by the one-two music shops, and look at all the popular songs, set up in notes and words, with the name of the fellar who write it big on the front, and sometimes his photograph too. And Razor Blade uses to think: But why I can't write song like that too, and have my name all over the place?

109

And when things was good with him, he went inside now and then, and tell the clerks and them that he does write calypsos. But they only laugh at him, because they does think that calypso is no song at all, that what is song is numbers like "I've Got You Under my Skin" and "Sentimental Journey", what real American composers write.

And the Blade uses to argue that every dog has his day, and that a time would come when people singing calypso all over the world like stupidness.

He thinking about all that as he lean back there in the chinee man restaurant.

Is to peel off now without paying!

The best way is to play brassface, do as if you own the damn restaurant, and walk out cool.

So he get up and he notice the waitress not around (she must be serving somebody else) and he take time and walk out, passing by the cashier who writing something in a book.

But all this time, no matter how boldface you try to be, you can't stop part of you from going like a pliers, clip clip, and he feel as if he want to draw his legs together and walk with two foot as one.

When the waitress find out Razor Blade gone without paying, she start to make one set of noise, and a chinee man from the kitchen dash outside to see if he could see him, but this time so Razor Blade making races down Frederick Street.

The owner of the restaurant tell the woman she have to pay for the food that Razor Blade eat, that was she fault, and she begin to cry big water, because is a lot of food that Razor Blade put away, and she know that that mean two three dollars from she salary.

This time so, Razor Blade laughing like hell; he quite down by the Railway Station, and he know nobody could catch him now.

One set of rain start to fall suddenly; Razor Blade walking like a king in his new shoes, and no water getting up his foot this time, so he ain't even bothering to shelter.

Calypsonian

And he don't know why, but same time he get a sharp idea
for a calypso. About how a man does catch his royal when he
can't get a work noway. The calypso would say about how he
see some real hard days; he start to think up words right away
as he walking in the rain:

> *It had a time in this colony*
> *When everybody have money excepting me*
> *I can't get a work no matter how I try*
> *It look as if good times pass me by.*

He start to hum it to the tune of an old calypso (Man Centi-
pede Bad Too Bad) just to see how it shaping up.

And he think about One Foot Harper, the one man who could
help him out with a tune.

It had a big joke with One Foot one time. Somebody t'ief
One Foot crutch one day when he was catching a sleep under
a weeping willow tree in Woodford Square, and One Foot had
to stay in the square for a whole day and night. You could
imagine how he curse stink; everybody only standing up and
laughing like hell; nobody won't lend a hand, and if wasn't for
Razor Blade, now so One Foot might still be waiting under the
weeping willow tree for somebody to get a crutch for him.

But the old Blade help out the situation, and since that time,
the both of them good friends.

So Razor Blade start making a tack for the tailor shop which
part One Foot does always be hanging out, because One Foot
ain't working noway, and every day he there by the tailor shop,
sitting down on a soapbox and talking whole day.

But don't fret you head, One Foot ain't no fool; it had a time
in the old days when they uses to call him King of Calypso, and
he was really good. If he did have money, or education business,
is a sure thing he would have been up the ladder, because he was
the first man who ever had the idea that calypsonians should
go away and sing in America and England. But people only
laugh at One Foot when he say that.

Razor Blade meet One Foot in a big old talk about the time

when the Town Hall burn down (One Foot saying he know the fellar who start the fire). When One Foot see him, he stop arguing right away and he say:

"What happening paleets, long time no see."

Razor Blade say: "Look man, I have a sharp idea for a calypso. Let we go in the back of the shop and work it out."

But One Foot feeling comfortable on the soapbox. He say: "Take ease, don't rush me. What about the shilling you have for me, that you borrow last week?"

The Blade turn his pockets inside out, and a pair of dice roll out, and a penknife fall on the ground.

"Boy, I ain't have a cent. I broken. I bawling. If you stick me with a pin you won't draw blood."

"Don't worry with that kind of talk, is so with all-you fellars, you does borrow a man money and then forget his address."

"I telling you man," Razor Blade talk as if he in a hurry, but is only to get away from the topic, "you don't believe me?"

But the Foot cagey. He say, "All right, all right, but I telling you in front that if you want money borrow again, you come to the wrong man. I ain't lending you a nail till you pay me back that shilling that you have for me." The Foot move off the soapbox, and stand up balancing on the crutch.

"Come man, do quick," Razor Blade make as if to go behind the shop in the backroom. Same time he see Rahamut, the Indian tailor.

"What happening Indian, things looking good with you."

Rahamut stop stitching a khaki pants and look at the Blade.

"You and One Foot always writing calypso in this shop, all-you will have to give me a commission."

"Well, you know how it is, sometimes you up, sometimes you down. Right now I so down that bottom and I same thing."

"Well, old man is a funny thing but I never see you when you up."

"Ah, but wait till the calypso season start."

"Then you won't come round here at all. Then you is bigshot, you forget small-fry like Rahamut."

Calypsonian

Well, Razor Blade don't know what again to tell Rahamut, because is really true all what the Indian saying about he and One Foot hanging out behind the shop. And he think about these days when anybody tell him anything, all he could say is: "Wait till the calypso season start up," as if when the calypso season start up God go come to earth, and make everybody happy.

So what he do is he laugh kiff-kiff and give Rahamut a pat on the back, like they is good friends.

Same time One Foot come up, so they went and sit down by a break-up table.

Razor Blade say: "Listen to these words old man, you never hear calypso like this in you born days," and he start to give the Foot the words.

But from the time he start, One Foot chock his fingers in his ears and bawl out: "Oh God, old man, you can't think up something new, is the same old words every year."

"But how you mean, man," the Blade say, "this is calypso father. Wait until you hear the whole thing."

They begin to work on the song, and One Foot so good that in two twos he fix up a tune. So Razor Blade pick up a empty bottle and a piece of stick, and One Foot start beating the table, and is so they getting on, singing this new calypso that they invent.

Well, Rahamut and other Indian fellar who does help him out with the sewing come up and listen.

"What you think of this new number, papa?" the Blade ask Rahamut.

Rahamut scratch his head and say: "Let me get that tune again."

So they begin again, beating on the table and the bottle, and Razor Blade imagine that he singing to a big audience in the Calypso Tent, so he putting all he have in it.

When they finished the fellar who does help Rahamut say: "That is hearts."

113

But Rahamut say: "Why you don't shut you mouth? What all-you Indian know about calypso?"

And that cause a big laugh, everybody begin to laugh kya-kya, because Rahamut himself is a Indian.

One Foot turn to Razor Blade and say: "Listen to them two Indian how they arguing about we creole calypso. I never see that in my born days!"

Rahamut say: "Man, I is a creolise Trinidadian, *oui*."

Razor Blade say: "All right, joke is joke, but all-you think it good? It really good?"

Rahamut want to say yes, it good, but he beating about the bush, he hemming and hawing, he saying: "Well, it so-so," and "it not so bad," and "I hear a lot of worse ones."

But the fellar who does help Rahamut, he getting on as if he mad, he only hitting Razor Blade and One Foot on the shoulder and saying how he never hear a calypso like that, how it sure to be the Road March for next year Carnival. He swinging his hands all about in the air while he talking, and his hand hit Rahamut hand and Rahamut get a chook in his finger with a needle he was holding.

Well, Rahamut put the finger in his mouth and start to suck it, and he turn round and start to abuse the other tailor fellar, saying why you don't keep you tail quiet, look you make me chook my hand with the blasted needle?

"Well, what happen for that? You go dead because a needle chook you?" the fellar say.

Big argument start up; they forget all about Razor Blade calypso and start to talk about how people does get blood poison from pin and needle chook.

Well, it don't have anything to write down as far as the calypso concern. Razor Blade memorise the words and tune, and that is the case. Is so a calypso born, cool cool, without any fuss. Is so all them big numbers like "Yes, I Catch Him Last Night", and "That Is a Thing I Can Do Anytime Anywhere", and "Old Lady Your Bloomers Falling Down", born right there behind Rahamut tailor shop.

Calypsonian

After the big talk about pin and needle Rahamut and the fellar who does assist him went back to finish off a zootsuit that a fellar was going to call for in the evening.

Now Razor Blade want to ask One Foot to borrow him a shilling, but he don't know how to start, especially as he owe him already. So he begin to talk sweet, praising up the tune that One Foot invent for the calypso, saying he never hear a tune so sweet, that the melody smooth like sweetoil.

But as soon as he start to come like that, the old Foot begin to get cagey, and say, "Oh God, old man, don't mamaguile me."

The Blade not so very fussy, because a solid meal in his belly. But same time he trying to guile One Foot into lending him a little thing, he get an idea.

He begin to tell One Foot how he spend the morning, how he ups the shoes from the shoemaker shop in Park Street, and how he eat big for nothing.

One Foot say: "I bet you get in trouble, all-you fellars does take some brave risk, *oui*."

Razor say: "Man, it easy as kissing hand, is only because you have one foot and can't run fast, that's why you talking so."

Foot say: "No jokes about my one foot."

Razor say: "But listen, man, you too stupid again! You and me could work up a good scheme to get some money. If you t'iefing, you might as well t'ief big."

"Is you is the t'ief, not me."

"But listen, man, Foot," the Blade gone down low in voice, "I go do everything, all I want you to do is to keep watchman for me, to see if anybody coming."

"What is the scheme you have?"

To tell truth, the old Blade ain't have nothing cut and dry in the old brain; all he thinking is that he go make a big t'ief somewhere where have money. He scratch his head and pull his ears like he did see Spencer Tracy do in a picture, and he say: "What about the Roxy Theatre down St. James?"

Same time he talking, he feeling excitement in his body, like if waves going up and coming down and he hold on to One Foot hand.

The Foot say: "Well yes, the day reach when you really catching you royal. I never thought I would see the time when my good friend Razor Blade turn t'ief. Man, you sure to get catch. Why you don't try for a work somewhere until the calypso season start up?"

"I tired try to get work. It ain't have work noway."

"Well, you ain't no t'ief. You sure to get catch, I tell you."

"But, man, look how I get away with the shoes and the meal! I tell you all you have to do is play boldface and you could commit murder and get away free."

The Foot start to hum a old calypso:

> "*If a man have money today* . . .
> *He could commit murder and get away free*
> *And live in the Governor's company.* . . ."

The Blade begin to get vex. "So you don't like the idea? You think I can't get away with it?"

"You ain't have no practice. You is a novice. Crime does not pay."

"You is a damn coward!"

"Us calypsonians have to keep we dignity."

"You go to hell! If you won't help me I go do it by myself, you go see! And I not t'iefing small, I t'iefing big! If I going down the river, I making sure is for plenty money, and not for no small time job."

"Well, papa, don't say I ain't tell you you looking for trouble."

"Man Foot, the trouble with you is you only have one foot so you can't think like me."

The Foot get hot. He say: "Listen, I tell you already no jokes about my one foot, you hear? I ain't taking no jokes about that. Curse my mother, curse my father, but don't tell me nothing about my foot."

The Blade relent. "I sorry, Foot, I know you don't like nobody to give you jokes."

116

Calypsonian

Same time Rahamut call out and ask why they keeping so much noise, if they think they in the fishmarket.

So they finish the talk. Razor Blade tell One Foot he would see him later, and One Foot say: "Righto, boy, don't forget the words for the song. And I warning you for the last time to keep out of trouble."

But the minute he leave the tailor shop Razor Blade only thinking how easy it go be to pull off this big deal. He alone would do it, without any gun, too, besides.

Imagine the Foot saying he is a novice! All you need is brass-face; play brazen; do as if you is a saint, as if you still have you mother innocent features, and if anybody ask you anything, lift up you eyebrows and throw you hands up in the air and say: "Oh Lord, who, *me*?"

He find himself quite round by the Queen's Park Savannah, walking and thinking. And he see a old woman selling orange. The woman as if she sleeping in the heat, she propping up she chin with one hand, and she head bend down. Few people passing; Razor Blade size up the situation in one glance.

He mad to bounce a orange from the tray, just to show that he could do it and get away. Just pass up near—don't even look down at the tray—and just lift one up easy as you walking, and put it in you pocket.

He wish One Foot was there to see how easy it was to do.

But he hardly put the orange in his pocket when the old woman jump up and start to make one set of noise, bawling out: "T'ief, t'ief! Look a man t'ief a orange from me! Help! Hold him! Don't let 'im get away!"

And is as if that bawling start the pliers working on him right away; he forget every thing he was thinking, and he start to make races across the savannah.

He look back and he see three fellars chasing him. And is just as if he can't feel nothing at all, as if he not running, as if he standing up in one spot. The only thing is the pliers going clip clip, and he gasping: Oh God! Oh God!

Waiting for Aunty to Cough

SAMUEL SELVON

It had a late lime what few of the boys acquainted with. That don't mean to say it was anything exclusive, but as far as I know Brackley was the only fellar who get in with a thing that living far from London, and had was to see the piece home every night, going out of the city and coming back late, missing bus and train and having to hustle or else stay stranded in one of them places behind God back.

I mean, some people might say a place like where Brackley used to go ain't far, and argue even that it still included in London, but to the city boys, as soon as you start to hit Clapham Common or Chiswick or Mile End or Highgate, that mean you living in the country, and they out to give you tone, like: "Mind you miss the last bus home, old man," and, "When next you coming to town?" or, "You could get some fresh eggs for me where you living?"

Well, Brackley in fact settle down nicely in Central, a two-and-ten room in Ladbroke Grove, with easy communications for liming out in the evenings after work, and the old Portobello Road near by to buy rations like saltfish and red beans and pig foot and pig tail. And almost every evening he would meet the boys and they would lime by the Arch, or the Gate, and have a cup of coffee (it have place like stupidness now all over London selling coffee, you notice?) and coast a talk and keep a weather eye open for whatever might appear on the horizon.

But a time come, when the boys begin to miss Brackley.

"Anybody see Brackley?"

"I ain't see Brackley a long time, man. He must be move."

"He uses to be in this coffee shop regular, but these days I can't see him at all."

All this time, Brackley on one of them green trains you does catch in Charing Cross or Waterloo, taking a ride and seeing the girl home.

Though Brackley living in London for eight years, is as if he start to discover a new world. Brackley never hear name like what he reading as they pass them stations—Gypsy Hill, Penge West, Forest Hill.

"You sure we on the right train?" Brackley frighten like hell the first time, feeling as if they going to Scotland or something. "How far from London you say this place is?"

"It is in London, I keep telling you," the girl say patiently.

"All of this is London?" Brackley look out and see a station named Honor Oak Park. Houses fading away and down there real grim as if is a place far out in the country.

"Yes," Beatrice say.

"And every day, you have to come all this way to work in London?"

"Yes."

"Oh, you must be one of those commuter people I read about in the papers."

Brackley look at his wristwatch. "I don't like this lime," he say.

"Oh, you'll get accustomed to it," Beatrice say. "It is like nothing to me now."

"I wonder what the boys doing in the coffee shop in town," Brackley mutter.

"That is all you ever worry about—wasting your time," Beatrice start to sulk.

"It ain't have no high spots this side of the world?" Brackley ask. "If it have, we could go out down here instead of staying in London and coming home late every night."

"You know I like to go out in the city," Beatrice pout. "The only place we could go to down here is near to Croydon."

"Croydon!" Brackley repeat. "Where the aeroplanes come from all over the world? You mean to say we so far from London?"

"There are frequent trains," Beatrice say anxiously.

"Frequent trains!" Brackley repeat. "Frequent planes, you mean! I don't like the lime at all."

But all the same, Brackley like the thing and he was seeing she home every night.

Well, he start to extend his geographical knowledge from the time he going out with Beatrice, and when he was explaining his absence from the city to the boys, he making it sound as if is a grand lime.

"Man," he boasting, "you-all don't know London! You think London is the Gate and the Arch and Trafalgar Square, but them places is nothing. You ever hear about Honor Oak Rise?"

"Which part that is, behind God back?"

"That is a place in London, man! I mean, look at it this way. You live in London so long, and up to now you don't know where that is. You see what I mean?"

"Man Brackley, you only full of guile. This time so that woman have you stupid and travelling all over the country, when you could be liming here. You staying tonight? It have two sharp things does come for coffee here—I think they from Sweden, and you know over there ain't have no inhibition."

"I can't stay tonight."

"Today is Saturday, no night bus."

But Brackley in hot with Beatrice at this stage and that ain't worrying him. What happen that night was he find himself walking to Kent afterwards, thinking that he was on the way to London, and he would have found himself picking hops or something if a fellar didn't put him right.

One night Brackley was taking a cuppa and a roll in a little place it have near Charing Cross, what does stay open all night for stragglers like him. The set-up is this: three-four frowsy women, and some tests who look as if they only come out at night. I mean, if you really want to meet some characters, is to lime out there by the Embankment after midnight, and you sure to meet some individuals.

That night, two fellars playing dominoes. A group stand up round a fire that they light with wood to keep warm. Suddenly a big commotion start, because the police take Olive and a test say it serve her right.

A woman start to 'buse the fellar who say it serve Olive right.

"What do you know about it?" the woman snarl. "Keep your ——ing mouth shut."

She start to scratch her thigh. Same time another woman come hustling up with the stale news that the police take Olive.

"Yes," the first woman say, "and this bastard here say that it served her right." She turn to the fellar again. "Keep your ——ing mouth shut," she say, though the fellar ain't saying anything.

Suddenly she turn on Brackley and start to 'buse him, saying that he was responsible. Poor Brackley ain't have a clue what the woman talking about, but three-four frowsy-looking sports gather around him and want to beat him up.

Brackley ease away and start to go up by Whitehall, and the starlings kicking up hell on the sides of the tall buildings, and is almost three o'clock in the morning and he thinking what a hell of a thing life is, how he never ever hear about any Olive and look how them women wanted to beat him up.

Well, to get back to the heart of the ballad, one rainy night Brackley and Beatrice went theatre, and theatre over late, and they catch the last train out of town. While they on the train —and Brackley like a regular commuter these days, reading the *Standard* while Beatrice catching up on some knitting—Beatrice suddenly open her handbag and say: "Gosh, I think I've lost my key!"

"You could always get another one," Brackley say, reading How The Other Half Laughs.

"You don't understand," Beatrice moan. "Aunty is always complaining about my coming in late, and by the time we get home it will be long after midnight, and the door will be shut."

"Ring the bell," Brackley say, laughing at a joke in the paper.

"I daren't wake Aunty at that hour," Beatrice say, putting aside the knitting to worry better.

"Don't worry, I will open a window for you," Brackley say.

But when they get to where Beatrice living she was still worrying what to do. She tell Brackley to wait by the gate. She went inside and pick up a tiny pebble and throw at the window, which was on the first floor. It make a sound ping! but nothing happen. After a little while she throw another one ping! but still nothing happen.

Brackley stand up there watching her.

She turn to Brackley helplessly. "I can't wake Aunty," she say.

Brackley open the gate and come inside and pick up a big brick from the garden to pelt at the people glass window. Beatrice barely had time to hold his hand.

"Are you mad?" she say in a fierce whisper.

"Well," Brackley say, "you don't want to get inside?"

"You are making too much noise already," Beatrice whisper. "I will have to stay on the steps until Aunty gets up."

"What time is that?" Brackley ask.

"About six o'clock," Beatrice say. "She is an early riser."

"You mean to say," Brackley say, "you spending the night here in the damp? Why you don't make a big noise and wake she up?"

"No, no," Beatrice say quickly, "we mustn't make any noise. The neighbours are very troublesome. Let us wait here until Aunty gets up. She is restless at night. When I hear her coughing I will throw another stone."

So Brackley and Beatrice sit down on the wet steps, waiting for Aunty to cough.

One o'clock come and gone, two o'clock come and gone. Three o'clock rain start to pelt slantways and fall on the steps wetting Brackley. This time so, as Brackley look around, the world grim. Rain and fog around him, and Beatrice sleeping on his shoulder.

He shake her.

Waiting for Aunty to Cough

Beatrice open her eyes and say, "What is it, did you hear Aunty cough?"

"No. It look as if her cold get better, I don't think she going to cough tonight at all."

"She always coughs in the night. As soon as she does I will throw some stones again."

"Why you don't make a big noise and finish with it? Back home in Trinidad, you think this could happen? Why——"

"Hush, you are speaking too loudly. I told you it would cause trouble with the neighbours."

"Why you don't wake up the people on the ground floor?"

"Nobody is there—they work nights."

"I ain't even have a cigarette," Brackley grumble, wondering what the boys doing, if they get in with the two girls from Sweden and gone to sleep in a nice warm room.

Beatrice went back to sleep, using poor Brackley as pillow.

Four o'clock come, five o'clock come, and still Brackley waiting for Aunty to cough and she wouldn't cough. This time so he have a sizeable stone in his hand and he make up his mind that the moment Aunty cough he going to fling the stone at the window even if he wake up everybody in the street. Sleep killing Brackley but the doorway small and he bend up there like a piece of wire, catching cramp and unable to shift position. In fact, between five and halfpast Brackley think he hear Aunty cough and he make to get up and couldn't move, all the joints frozen in the damp and cold.

He shake Beatrice roughly. "Aunty cough," he say.

"I didn't hear," Beatrice say.

"I hear," Brackley say, and he stretch out slowly and get up.

Brackley augment the stone he had with three others and he fling his hand back and he pelt the stones on the people glass window before Beatrice know what he doing.

Well, glass cracks and break and splinters fly all about and the noise sound as if the glasshouse in Kew Gardens falling down. Same time Aunty start one set of coughing.

"You see?" Brackley say, "I tell you Aunty was coughing!"

"You fool!" Beatrice say. "Look what you have done! You had better go quickly before you cause further trouble."

And before Brackley knew what happening Beatrice hustle him out to the pavement and shut the gate.

Well, a kind of fore-day light was falling at that hour of the morning and when Aunty fling open the window to see what happening, she see Brackley stand up out there. Only, she not so sure, because Brackley blend in nicely with the kind of half-light half-dark. But all the same, Aunty begin to scream murder and thief.

Brackley take off as if he on the Ascot racecourse.

Some nights later he tell the boys the episode, making it sound like a good joke though at the time he was frighten like hell. But that was a mistake he make, because since that time whenever the boys see him they hailing out:

"Brackley! You still waiting for Aunty to cough?"

The Coming of Amalivaca

JAN CAREW
A Guianese legend

In long-time-past days Wind was a lonely man. And for a long time he keep loneliness tie up in he belly 'til the day come when he couldn't bear it no more and it burst out and drive poor Wind mad. He start howling through the valleys, roaring over the savannah, crying like a baboon-mother who loss she one-child, and he couldn't bear to see he own face in he madness so every time he see quiet water he used to ruffle it up and make it fretful.

One night Wind hear drum beating and people singing in a Accewayo village near the big waterfall called Kaietuk and he creep up and spy on what was going on, pretending to be a shadow.

That night the music from the gorge which the river sprites was making sound like a million humming birds whirling they wings, and a big-belly drummer-man sit under the mora tree near to the shadow that was Wind, and he start to fondle the goatskin like if it was a woman flesh.

There was music that the river sprites make like humming bird wing, and music from the thunder bird echo, and music from the big-belly drummer-man, and Wind couldn't dance, Wind who foot can turn light like silk-cotton blossom. But the people dance and make mirth and drink kasheri and a drunken dancer spill a calabash full of kasheri in Wind mouth while he was lying under the mora tree playing shadow. Wind drink, and he blood warm-up and he belly begin to swell. The drink make he madder and madder and he bellow out, "Is why the music stop? Play on, drummer-man!"

"Yes, Lord Wind," drummer-man say and he beat up a scatter-brain tune and he right hand didn't know what he left hand was doing and suddenly Wind start to dance. The first swirl he make root up the big mora tree and it kill half the people at the fête. Thunder Bird come out of he cave and he try to tie Wind up with bush rope until he sober up, but Wind dodge and hide and break heself up in pieces and join the pieces together again, and all the time he was howling like a forest full of red baboons.

Wind frolic about 'til sleep catch he and then he curl up and lie down on the flat top of Roraima, the red mountain, and that is where Thunder Bird find he next morning. Was no trouble to catch Wind once he was sober and Thunder Bird tie he up and carry he back to the cave behind Kaietuk. Now while the big gods was talking 'bout Wind and what they was going to do to punish him, he turn over on he side and watch through the cave-mouth. Sun was shining on the mist before the fall and for the first time Wind see Rainbow combing she hair. The vision of Rainbow in the mist put the gift of music in Wind throat and he start to sing a song sweeter than a piper owl song. When Wind begin to sing the big gods stop growling and fretting and they listen to the song and one god say,

"I never heard a song so sweet!"

And another god grumble and say,

"Is only the devil can sing so!"

But the other gods standing all 'bout the place start to hush them up and the singing echo up and down the cave and when Sun hear it, he begin to dance up and down Rainbow hair. Now, long-time-past the gods did weave Rainbow hair out of water tumbling down the fall and all along the cliff face by the side of the fall they plant orchid so that Rainbow could pick them and stick them in she hair. The old people in the bush say that Rainbow had the river sprites in a spell, she work obeia on them so that they can play bamboo flute night and day and when

The Coming of Amalivaca

Sun or Moon or Star come to listen she does steal they light to comb she hair. That's why, the old people say, she hair always so shiny. Wind sing to Rainbow 'til she stop brushing she hair and she let the orchid she pick tumble down in the gorge and get crush up against the sleeping-rocks.

The power-gods make Wind promise that whatever he do or however mad he get he will sing every now and then. Wind promise to sing but he say the gods must put harp-strings on all the forest trees and they must make some of the savannah grass stems hollow so that when he lie down he can whistle and flute through the grass. The gods say they would do what Wind ask and they set Wind loose and he rush out the cave and press heself against the length and breadth of Rainbow body 'til Sun get jealous and hide behind a cloud. Wind press against Rainbow so hard that he scatter she hair all over the place. It get tangle-up with the rocks and knot-up on the trees nearby and the river Watchman, Kai, who does guard Rainbow, turn heself into a flight of swallows and fling a shadow cloak round Rainbow—one minute Wind was holding Rainbow and the next minute she vanish. From then on everywhere that there was mist Wind chase behind it looking for Rainbow, over the snow mountains, over rivers, and trees, at day-clean, over the savannah when rain fall and the earth start to steam—but Wind couldn't find Rainbow nowhere because the river people lock she up in a deep well by the sky-rim where the savannah does melt away.

One day a fire-plume woodpecker tell Wind that Rainbow had a child by him, a boy child, and Rainbow say that if he want to see the child he must scoop a cradle out on top the red mountain before the horned moon turn up in the night sky again.

Next day Wind scoop out the cradle and he fill it up with young tamarind leaves and he sit down to wait for the horned moon. While he was waiting he didn't even stir a leaf on a cassava stem or press he finger-tip 'gainst a blade of grass. And without Wind-music the forest people start fighting 'mongst theyself but Wind wouldn't budge to help them. At last the day come when the horned moon rise. Rainbow appear through a mist over the mountain top with a baby in she arms and she put the baby in the cradle Wind make but when Wind try to reach her he scatter the mist and Rainbow vanish again.

Wind name the boy-child Amalivaca, the child of searching. Amalivaca was a bright-eyed child with a voice full of singing and the music of Father Wind in he bones. He playground was the table-top of the red mountain, Roraima, and he playmate was macushi ants and an old condor bird named Gé. Gé was a bird who the old people say when ugliness was sharing, he take all. He had brown lack-lustre feather, mournful, smoky eyes and a crinkle-up naked neck and he voice was so raucous, was a pain to listen to it, every word used to grate 'gainst you ears like a rough tree bark. But Gé was wise and he had a kind heart and Father Wind lef' he one-boy, Amalivaca, in Gé charge.

Amalivaca used to sit down on a rock whole day and listen to Gé, the old condor bird, and watch the macushi ants building towers and storing up food. When rain fall on top of the red mountain clear water used to cascade down to the valley below, and the waters running tongues carry the news that there was a dreaming, bright-eye boy living on top the mountain and the boy was the son of Father Wind.

One fore-day-morning the big chibat, Akarai, send Trumpeter Bird to call Amalivaca down from the red mountain. Trumpeter Bird come and knock 'gainst the rock that does guard condor nest.

"Who is there?" condor ask.

"Is me, Trumpeter; the big chibat, Akarai, send me to talk to the boy who is the son of searching Wind."

"Then I will bring the boy, Trumpeter, and you can talk to he yourself. A-m-a-l-i-v-a-c-a! Amalivaca, the time come for you to go, the big chibat, Akarai, send Trumpeter to call you."

And the boy with the brightness of jewel stone in he eyes come to Trumpeter and listen.

"Akarai say you must go to the valley people, in the valley

of Uitshi where the Accewayos does live. He say you father wrong these people and you must make recompense."

And Amalivaca hug old condor round he wrinkle-up neck and the water from he eye fall on a lack-lustre wing and left two bright jewels.

"You got to go, boy, you got to go," old condor keep saying and he smoky eyes was sad. And when Father Wind hear that he one-boy had to go down to the valley people he knock he fist 'gainst the cliff-side and cry out loud:

"Akarai, let me boy-child live free on the red mountain, the boy got the brightness of Rainbow, and he heart is soft like a humming bird wing, he don't even know what hate is." And when Akarai hear Wind crying out, he shout from he mountain peak near the weeping wood. He say:

"Is only Amalivaca, the boy with Rainbow brightness, can save the valley people. Let him go Father Wind and give him the gift of music, and magic to play the harp strings on the trees, and the grass flutes on the wide plain."

And Father Wind do what Akarai beg him to do and he float the boy on condor back down to the valley and they lef' Amalivaca in a grove of weeping trees. Amalivaca sit down on the dead leaf under the tree and take out the silver bally flute that Father Wind give he and begin to play. The creek nearby pick up the tune and carry it through the forest and greedy toucan lef' a mango tree and fly to the grove of weeping trees and marudi, maam, humming bird, piper owl and even vampire, blind as night, gather round, and all the wild brute-beast and the snake, the alligator, and even the fish, arapaima and hassar, come to listen. The rainbow boy bring brightness to the forest for the first time since the black snake push the land up out of the sea and the news spread like fire that Father Wind chase down the savannah grass, that a Prophet come to end strife in the whole world from the green sea at Kamakusa to the rock of Patagonia.

Amalivaca come and make the Accewayo woman belly fertile and he bring macushi ants with he and lef' them to teach the village people how to work and the village turn a bright place. And mad Father Wind used to watch over he, and if Amalivaca call for rain, Wind would call out Thunder Bird from he cave and make he empty the water from the lake on his back, and if Amalivaca the child of Wind searching, ask for dry weather, Wind used to gather the clouds together in flocks and drive them over the rim of the sky.

Amalivaca was the first prophet of light, the child of Wind searching, the son of Rainbow, and he end strife amongst the forest people from the river of the weeping wood to the mountain of the moon-shadow.

Mr. Dombey, the Zombie

GEOFFREY DRAYTON

Mr. Dombey, the zombie, took the 8.10 train every morning of the working week. On the way to London he read a newspaper, carefully digesting the spate of words so that its essence might be spewed up again in a form acceptable to his *hounsi*.* His *hounsi* was always interested in the latest murders and rapes, but her interest was never sufficient to let her read through whole columns for the sake of the few sharp thrills they might provide. Anyhow, it was to save herself such bother that she had gone to the trouble of acquiring a zombie. Mr. Dombey not only read the newspapers and books—Crime Club for the most part—but he kept her garden tidy, mowed the lawn, washed the dishes. He could not, of course, earn very much money because, being a zombie and capable only of habitual action, he was forced to work at mechanical tasks, under orders from a superior.

At times this annoyed her and she berated him for it; but since it was not really his fault—and, in any case, he could not argue back—she was restricted in her displeasure. Usually she vented it by imposing on him some especially disagreeable task —like cleaning out the chicken-coops or scrubbing the kitchen floor. The chickens were an unfriendly lot, perhaps because they knew that they were only kept to serve as sacrifices at the right times of year; they never appeared to lay eggs—or so Mr. Dombey would have been led to presume if he had been capable of presuming anything. They pecked him when he came near; but by his nature he was oblivious to the pecking of hens. No doubt

* A voodoo priestess, according to Haitian Houngan rites.

if he had been human he would have been less oblivious, perhaps even fearful.

As it was, his only fear was of the woman who had charmed his spirit out and obtained control of his body. His spirit was now imprisoned in a large, curiously carved and decorated gourd which reposed on the mantelpiece in the sitting-room. Until the gourd was broken, and the spirit rejoined the body, Mr. Dombey would be incapable of dying, would have to continue in serfdom indefinitely.

This state of affairs had gone on for more than thirty years, when suddenly one day the *hounsi* fell ill. She tried various herbs and remedies of her own concoction, even certain spells that she had inherited from the *mamaloi* of her faith; but all to no avail. Eventually she was forced to take to her bed; and since she could not trust anyone else in the house, Mr. Dombey no longer caught the 8.10 train to his daily task in the city. He remained by her bedside, fetching and carrying. She grew worse. At last she decided to summon a doctor. Obviously the god *Damballa* was angry with her. She had gone through the rites necessary for his placation, but all had failed; she could now do herself no further harm by resorting to the sorceries of Science.

But the *hounsi* had waited too late. The doctor discovered her in the final grimaces of life. In the post-mortem he diagnosed death by arsenical poisoning.

It was all a ghastly mistake. The *hounsi* had been in the habit of taking a stomach-powder—for some strange disease of her kind known as flatulence. The last time he had been sent to purchase this commodity, Mr. Dombey had been ordered to buy arsenic as well—for killing rats. A malignant hand of Providence —*Damballa's* no doubt—had substituted the arsenic for the stomach-powder, with the result that the *hounsi* had been attempting to cure her flatulence with arsenic.

The newspapers blamed Mr. Dombey, the zombie. They were, of course, quite mistaken; but neither the journalists concerned nor, later, the police knew anything about voodoo and zombies; and Mr. Dombey was incapable of informing them. The result

Mr. Dombey, the Zombie

was a gross miscarriage of justice. Mr. Dombey was found guilty of murder and sentenced to death by hanging.

Had matters proceeded in an ordinary fashion there would be no merit in recounting this old tale. But at that point what had seemed straightforward suddenly became bizarre. The newspapers screamed with delight and Mr. Dombey was transformed, overnight, into a sort of hero. Some even found proof of his innocence—as with the mediæval Ordeals—in the fact that he could not be hanged. On the first occasion the trap-door failed to open. The rope broke on a second attempt. But—great climax of all—when the apparatus finally worked and Mr. Dombey had been seen to swing in orthodox fashion, the corpse showed a most unexpected co-operation in helping his executioners to lift itself down.

Mr. Dombey's sentence was commuted to life imprisonment. He was said to be nearly sixty at the time, and, judging by his gauntness, the death-like pallor of his face, and the fact that he had recently undergone unnerving experiences, everyone who thought about it decided that the State would not have to support him for long. At that point the newspapers turned their attentions elsewhere, though keeping the matter in mind, anticipating an obituary in which the sensational hanging might again be used to edify the public.

But newspapermen die, and their dreams die with them. Mr. Dombey, on the other hand, persisted in living. He was still alive seventy years later—growing parched and withered to be sure, but by no means an invalid. He had seen many prison wardens, many convicts come and go. But as he did nothing to bring himself to their attention, he was successfully forgotten and his age attracted no comment.

Mr. Dombey was, in fact, a hundred and thirty years old when his great-great nephews decided to springclean their attic.

After the death of Mrs. Dombey and the imprisonment of her supposed murderer, Mr. Dombey, the zombie, relatives had taken over the ill-omened house, the chickens and the gourd. They had slaughtered the chickens; but not knowing what to do with the strange sitting-room ornament, they had put it in the attic along with several other inherited monstrosities. There the gourd had remained, for two generations, growing wizened and dusty, but with Mr. Dombey's spirit safe in its bowels. Now, on the day of springcleaning, it was again brought forth. Quite unceremoniously—since who was to know it had a value above that of a cremation-urn?—it was thrown on the bonfire. Without a murmur it dissolved into ashes.

And so Mr. Dombey, the zombie, again cheated the newspapers and the seekers after truth—and, to be exact, the police records. If a little pile of ashes in a prison courtyard had been able to speak it might have related that Mr. Dombey had felt a sudden raging fever. The next moment he was dust. Then the wind blew and Mr. Dombey was dispersed among the other particles.

The Covenant

WILSON HARRIS

(An excerpt from the novel, *Far Journey of Oudin*.
Excerpted by permission of the author.)

The stars shone faint in the stream on the windy night and
they penetrated a flying cloud. The lights shining far across the
river were uncertain and distant, close to the ground, and one
with glimmering heaven. The shape of a cow loomed on the
opposite bank, so enormous it blotted out the lights and invisible windows of the far scattered settlements: it loomed like
a cloud, shapeless and massive in the dreaming faint light,
slithering down the bank suddenly into the water, washing the
stars away as it swam across the night.

He awoke with a drowning sensation in his mouth as unlike
the memory of creek-water as rum tastes like *padi*. The tasteless
dawn shone through the window; a dim radiance of ancient pearl
and milky rice washed the ground and settled in his eyes, moving
stealthily, circulating within the room until he saw in the image
of his limbs the dry brown stalks of harvest. He had been reaped
and he lay staring and dead as a naked cliff or as a window that
had fallen from its house to rot on the earthen floor until there
sprouted forth the solitary relics of grass.

Oudin knew it was still a dream, the dream of the heavenly
cycle of the planting and reaping year he now stood within—
as within a circle—for the first time. He felt his heart stop where
it had danced. It was the end of his labour of death. The night
and the day were finished as the starlight and the lantern-light
of every dying human settlement and flame.

It was a new freedom he now possessed. He roused himself to
stand on his dry dreaming feet, and to swallow his saliva over

135

and over again. There was a shot of rum on the shelf in the room and he poured it out into a cup as a miser counts the change he hoards—stealthily as a ghost swallowing the last drop. The vague harvested bundles lying on the floor of the room began to stir.

Oudin's hut stood against the river looking dressed and drenched in dew on a high round mound in the savannahs. The early light circled it with a spray of vapour in the same way as the sea encounters an ancient foreshore and clothes the first sentinel and tree. The tide beneath the mound and house was dark: yet it seemed white on the surface, still and lifeless, and only the mist of the dawn appeared to drift.

The hut emerged suddenly, ordinary and dead as day. The vague eternity and outline vanished. There was no mystery in the poverty of its naked appearance—a few planks nailed together and roofed by bald aluminium.

Oudin saw it in the corner of his eye as if for the first time: so clearly he might never have seen it before. The stark light in which he beheld it was a mystery to him, the first real mystery and power of apprehension he possessed.

The dark surface of the river cleaned suddenly, showing in the running tide a deeper spirit and across the track of spiritual reflection stood the hanging heads of horses and cows. The day cleared in the new light of his eye and the land was a wilderness on which had fallen the curious naked spoil of his conquest and death. He possessed it all now as one would a match-box world surrounded by its models and furniture, their head still outstretched to crop the ground beneath every windless and breathless tree. Oudin held it all in the corner of his eye. And it seemed to him that the first outcry from within the hut—the wailing voice of his wife and child—had happened in the depth of time long before the vain echo of the announcement could be heard in the still air he had ceased to breathe.

"Oudin dead. Oudin dead. Oudin dead."

It was a senseless outcry and it ran over him as water from a duck's back and became part of the flimsy scaffolding of the world.

Beti ran and stood half-wailing, half-breathless, outside the door. She had the refined, emaciated face of an East Indian and Guianese woman that looked older than it was, bearing the stamp of a well-known ornament.

Destiny had fulfilled itself in dividing Oudin and herself after thirteen years together in the blind eye of the world. They had never known each other in reality as far back as they knew. Oudin saw this now—as it had always been—in a new way of self-possession that overcame the folly of grief and lent him an image of transparency and compassion.

She wore her long unbelted dress; her elbows were pressed hard against her stomach and her hands outstretched beseechingly, intent on making an awkward catch. Her black hair escaped on all sides from the cloth over her head and her wrists and ankles were adorned with bracelets which reflected the light. The cry she raised was as involuntary as a bird's or animal's. She always relished standing in this light, advertising a mournful need and curiosity, waiting for something to happen and fall into her hands. Her cry and wail were the oldest expression and tradition of inviting and deceiving everyone, and herself in the bargain, so that there stood upon her now the stamp of timeless slavery, rather than selection and freedom, and of belonging to someone and something living and dead, like a commodity everybody instantly recognised. She was Oudin's wife and she cried both hopelessly and hopefully—"Oudin dead."

Oudin understood how she was the representation of a slave despite her secret longing and notion to be free.

"Beti, Beti, is what happen? Oudin can't be dead. You talking foolish. Me and he had a lil' drop yesterday. He did send he boy-picnie to the road for a bottle. Remember? Oudin been strong-strong then I tell you. Beti is what happen? Oudin and me got pressing business and contract on hand. . . ."

Beti shrank from the man who had approached and questioned her as from a sudden unwelcome visitor. His house was near to Oudin's and he had been cleaning his teeth and had come running in his singlet and old pyjamas still chewing the stem of sage bush he used as a brush. He turned to implore the child—standing beside his mother—whom Oudin had sent yesterday for a bottle of rum to seal the contract—"Is where you daddy, picnie? Where you daddy?" The child bowed his head to the ground without a word. He saw the hard grey toe-nails staring up at him from the man's feet where they protruded from the pyjamas. He was fascinated and repelled: they reminded him of his father's nails and feet, grey and hard as stone. Ram looked down at the boy's bent head and neck and he feared the unwelcome silence.

He regretted everything, now running across to Oudin so quickly and standing chained to the ground where Oudin had overpowered him, holding him firmly in the corner of a dreaming eye. His shadow crossed the door entering the hut with the rising sun, fearful of this involuntary bondage and servility.

"Oudin really dead?" he asked himself under his breath. He was frightened, frightened of the gliding shadow of the sun and a prospect of calculation circulating around him, his cattle and ricefields. The news of Oudin's death had come to him as such a sudden and unexpected reversal of fortune that it struck him as a trick possessing and activating everyone and everything.

The empty rum bottle stood on the shelf and he looked reproachfully and accusingly at the body lying on the floor. Oudin had been able to buy this with Ram's money and not a drop now remained though Ram was sure last night they had not drunk all of it.

Oudin was smiling at the superstitious conceit like an observant host who knew every desire in the craftiest reflection.

"Oudin dead?" Ram's mind was once more assaulted by an incredible image of possession and dispossession. A crowd of voices had started outside the house. He felt he must bar them until he had cornered the impossible smiling thing. He scanned the room frantically and blindly, knowing it was full to bursting with a rich secret: his miserly instincts were frustrated and aroused. "Oudin dead?" The gliding thought that Oudin was *alive* and in process of catching him—rather than being caught —filled him with panic. He trembled, unable to discern the wall and the shadow of the sun he wished to corner and possess with every grain of rice he harvested in the present and the future and every acre of land he acquired from his tenants, who had mortgaged their labour and their world to him.

Ram returned to Oudin after the funeral—a man making many steps and still not moving one from the blazing eye of the rising sun bright and tropical. "Oudin dead and buried?" Ram blinked, wondering whether the blinding shock he had felt when he first heard the wailing impossible cry (a million dreaming years ago it was) had burst his inner tube to flatten him and rob him of air, and fill him with a drowning sensation he had never had before. He seized the empty rum bottle to plunge it into the river outside but stealthily replaced it.

Beti forced herself to address him—"Is who you want, Mr. Ram?" She thrust out her hands to him, helplessly inviting and warding him off—"Oudin gone, Mr. Ram."

Ram stared at her. He knew she was in league against him as she shrank from him. "In league with whom?" Everyone in the savannahs dreaded him, and it made him cold and uncomfortable all of a sudden to see her watching him intently. There was a time when he would not have known the slightest misgiving and discomfiture. What was it that made him see himself as a foul obnoxious shadow against the world? His heart plunged with the force of a cricket ball falling in a stream of air and emptying him of concentration. Emptying him like a fieldsman who stared into the sun at a blind catch. Oudin was encircling all and dispossessing him.

"I looking for a piece of paper," Ram blurted out softly and unseeingly. "Oudin tek it from me the same-same night before he dead. . . ." His voice was a pleading whisper.

Beti glared at him in terrible astonishment. She was stunned by the plea and the subservience. And she felt that such awful confidence called for a whisper in return so that she would not be overheard. Overheard by whom? Oudin had vanished from the hut. Her outstretched hands writhed and struggled to seize a spirit that had always eluded her and the heart of Ram stared, hanging on her breath.

"You see it?" he cried hopefully. "You see it? You know where it is?"

Beti was startled and the spell of the moment slipped from her mind. "I dunno is what you mean," she said, falling back.

Ram was disappointed and enraged. "Suppose is me life Ah sign away and you drop and lose it?" he cried accusingly. "You *stupid*." He turned to the shelf in the room where the empty rum bottle stood, picking up a pen and rusty nib still smeared with ink. "Is this Ah use to sign. *Stupid!* Where the ink gone?" he demanded. "It been next to the rum."

"Mr. Ram, Ah don't know nothing," Beti wailed and shouted. All of a sudden she was conscious of the dreadful menace she addressed; she recalled his notorious power and his avarice that had faded a little from the field of her recollection a moment ago in the light of intuition.

"Mr. Ram, Ah don't know nothing."

"Hush, woman!" Ram said, rebuking her for her outcry.

They both stood and listened.

The wind blew upon the hut and shook the roof just over their heads. Every window had been closed to conform with the rule in a dead man's house. Half-light and vision circulated through the space of the door and long lines in the walls where the rough-sawn boards had been nailed blind together.

Ram crinkled his eye looking along the sights of an imaginary gun and peering through a slit outside. He saw Oudin's boy chasing a cow. It was a fleeting glimpse that looked distant and still as a rolling game and a dream.

"The picnie deh far," he said, turning to Beti. "He can't hear we."

The Covenant

A curious frightened intimacy enveloped them once again, the intimacy of perhaps belonging to no one and nothing and yet of being overheard and caught by someone and something. They were growing conscious of a presence whose apparent nothingness was more real and penetrating and commanding than anything they had ever known.

Ram suddenly remembered and looked on another shelf on the opposite wall. "Ink," he said. "Ah sign me name with this ink."

"Look, paper," Beti said. She tore him a scrap of old newspaper, sensing his need and desire. It had been lying crumpled on the floor. Ram smoothed it carefully. "Ah sign like this," he said. He scratched his name with precision. The paper had acquired a thin film of dung as it lay on the ground and the nib disturbed its flaky surface as Ram wrote upon it until the smell rose into his nostrils. "Is dog dung," he cried in disgust, flinging the pen from him.

He opened his mouth wordlessly and his tongue curved into a dreaming wave turning up towards the ragged burnt edge of one of his teeth that appeared like floating planks in their sockets.

"I only know to mek me mark on paper," Beti cried half-fearfully, half-craftily observing him. "I never learn to read and write clever like you, Mr. Ram." She felt herself drawn closer to him than ever in fresh surprise at his insecure humanity. "No paper with *you* writing been in here when Oudin dead." She spoke in artless wonder, bringing an intonation of vehement secrecy into her voice. "I swear I don't know and I never see it. Look!" She started undressing before him as if to prove she was as naked as the walls around her.

Ram stared at her with a sense of dreadful hallucination and assault and intimacy. He wanted to feel that she was still part of—and belonged to—Oudin's boarded walls. The listening catching spirit in the room drew him to her—in his evil curiosity to plumb the depths of appearance—as to a worthless abandoned place and shelf, or to a priceless mystery in which had been hidden the contract he had made a couple of days ago with

141

Oudin. He felt he dared not speak aloud to her or the husband
of silence might reply and crush him. It was impossible to plead
with a presence he could neither seize nor possess. He saw her
cruel nakedness and the injustice of her position like a man who
had made a blinding covenant with a ghostly phenomenon and
life.

"The only place lef' to look, Mr. Ram," Beti said at last, "is
under the floor in the bowels of the earth." Ram felt that she
had begun to despise him—in the intimacy of self-knowledge
—now that his assault on her had served to yield nothing.

"Oudin put you up to this," he raved, "you bitch!"

Beti's smile trembled, scorning his self-evident powerlessness
and defeat.

Ram had no alternative but to follow the enormous blind
vigil he had started. He must watch Oudin's hut in the impossible hours of sleeping and waking to see who entered and
who departed. He had spies and obsessions to warn him if anyone visiting or leaving contemplated a trip downriver to the
public road on Beti's behalf. He felt he must confront every
appearance she made until he had willed her to gain no help to
spell and read the lines he had signed and written. It was a
gesture of control he made over himself, and the world he used
to govern, speaking inwardly and indefatigably to himself. The
truth was—and this he never uttered aloud even in the silence
of his heart—it was her contempt for him that conceived an
indifference to his power and possessions. This, he sensed—
remembering the time he had searched her, squirming under her
scorn—was his salvation. His contract was pointless in her eye
and what was the use of learning the contents now? It was
Oudin's dead business and desire, not hers. Ram was drawn to
this conclusion and it helped to comfort him in the misery of
impotency and understanding.

Still, it was a secret he must wrest from Oudin's property, he
told himself, or he would never sleep for fear of Beti taking it
into her head to do something after all.

The Covenant

Oudin was no longer available and responsible Ram knew in essential chagrin. Every process would have been normal and regular then. He had disappeared like a thief, leaving behind him a naked wall and legacy. It was unprincipled and grotesque in the extreme that Ram should be excluded from finding what belonged to him in a way he had never bargained for or realised in the nature of the contract.

Ram learnt to approach the door of the hut in the dark. From afar off he could see the flickering light through the invisible curtain and wall, blowing it seemed to him in the wind, as if it were nowhere at all and the whole thing was the reflection of a star. He followed it: his eye was drawn by the thin silver radiance across the dark earth to the hidden treasure of his life.

The door was never securely barred, only tied he knew by a filthy piece of twine that had been wound through a hole and around a post.

Ram learnt to retire at last with the coiled twine in his eye, and he knew in his dreams, when he snatched a couple hours of sleep before dawn, the slightest interference with the coil of twine on the door would start him cruelly awake in his bed. The twine, he was aware, would uncoil before him, so that stretched taut at last it would draw him forward as Oudin walked backward into the distance like a sleepwalker, until their vision would meet in a way that shattered him to the core. He tried to shout across the distance his gratitude and his horror all at once that his vigil was fixed and established. It was because of his stupefaction and sense that Oudin had not really deserted him. Oudin knew not only what he wanted but was intent as well on overthrowing every misconception and inferior relationship in their contract, the fulfilment of which had become a matter of spiritual conscience to him. Ram was filled with fear as he was drawn from his waking sleep to Oudin's unsleeping watch, until it seemed he no longer understood whether the covenant lay with a reality beyond him or an appearance of life and death within and around him.

Jamaican Fragment

A. L. HENDRICKS

Every day I walk a half-mile from my home to the tram-car lines in the morning, and from the lines to my home in the evening. The walk is pleasant. The road on either side is flanked by red- and green-roofed bungalows, green lawns and gardens. The exercise is good for me and now and then I learn something from a little incident.

One morning, about half-way between my front gate and the tram track, I noticed two little boys playing in the garden of one of the more modest cottages. They were both very little boys, one was four years old perhaps, the other five. The bigger of the two was a sturdy youngster, very dark, with a mat of coarse hair on his head and coal-black eyes. He was definitely a little Jamaican—a strong little Jamaican. The other little fellow was smaller, but also sturdy—he was white, with hazel eyes and light-brown hair. Both were dressed in blue shirts and khaki pants: they wore no shoes and their feet were muddy. They were not conscious of my standing there watching them; they played on. The game, if it could be called a game, was not elaborate. The little white boy strode imperiously up and down and every now and then shouted imperiously at his bigger playmate. The little brown boy shuffled along quietly behind him and did what he was told.

"Pick up that stick!" The dark boy picked it up.

"Jump into the flowers!" The dark boy jumped.

Jamaican Fragment

"Get me some water!" The dark boy ran inside. The white boy sat down on the lawn.

I was amazed. Here before my eyes, a white baby, for they were little more than babies, was imposing his will upon a little black boy. And the little black boy submitted. I puzzled within myself as I went down the road. Could it be that the little dark boy was the son of a servant in the home and therefore had to do the white boy's bidding? No. They were obviously dressed alike, the little dark boy was of equal class with his playmate. No. They were playmates, the little dark boy was a neighbour's child. I was sure of that. Then how was it that he obeyed so faithfully the white boy's orders? Was it that even at his early age he sensed that in his own country he would be at the white man's beck and call? Could he in such youth divine a difference between himself and the white boy? And did the little white youngster so young, such a baby, realize that he would grow to dominate the black man? Was there an indefinable quality in the white man that enabled his baby, smaller and younger than his playmate, to make him his slave? Was there really some difference between a white man and a black man? Something that made the white superior? I could find no answer. I could not bring myself to believe such a thing, and yet, with my own eyes I had seen a little dark boy take orders from a little white boy—a little white boy obviously his social equal, and younger and smaller. Were we as a race really inferior? So inferior that even in our infancy we realized our deficiencies, and accepted a position as the white man's servant?

For a whole day I puzzled over this problem. For a whole day my faith in my people was shaken. When I passed that afternoon the little boys were not there. That evening I thought deeply on the subject.

The next morning the boys were there again, and a man was standing at the gate watching them. I stopped and looked, just to see what the white boy was making his little servant do. To my utter astonishment the little dark boy was striding

145

imperiously up and down the lawn, while the white youngster walked abjectly behind him.

"Get me a banana!" The little white boy ran into the house and reappeared shortly with a banana. "Peel it for me!" The little white boy skinned the banana and handed it to his dark master.

I saw it now. This was indeed a game, a game I had played as a child. Each boy took it in turn every alternate day to be the boss, the other the slave. It had been great fun to me as a youngster. I smiled as I remembered. I looked at the man standing by the gate. He was a white man. I remembered what I had thought yesterday. He, no doubt, I thought to myself, was wondering if the black race is superior to the white. I laughed gently to myself. How silly grown-ups are, how clever we are, how wonderfully able we are to impute deep motives to childish actions! How suspicious we are when we have been warped by prejudice! This man, I said to myself, will puzzle all day on whether the blacks will eventually arise and rule the world because he thinks he sees a little black boy realizing at a tender age his superiority over the white. I will save him his puzzle. I will explain it to him. I went across to him.

"I know what you're thinking," I said. "You're thinking that maybe the black race is superior to the white, because you just saw the little dark youngster on the lawn ordering the little white boy around. Don't think that, it's a game they play. Alternate days one is boss, the other the servant. It's a grand game. I used to play it and maybe so did you. Yesterday I saw the little white boy bossing the dark one and I worried all day over the dark boy's realization of his inferiority so young in life! We are silly, we grown-ups, aren't we?"

The man was surprised at my outburst. He looked at me smiling.

"I know all about the game," he said. "The boys are brothers —my sons." He pointed to a handsome brown woman on the veranda who had just come out to call in the children. "That's my wife," he said.

Jamaican Fragment

I smiled. My spirit laughed within me. This is Jamaica, I said in my heart, this is my country—my people. I looked at the white man. He smiled at me. "We'll miss the tram if we don't hurry," he said.

Arise, My Love

JAN WILLIAMS

Ever since Frank could remember, he had lived on the island. There was the high blue smudge of St. Vincent to the north on clear days and nearer and clearly marked, if you turned your head, the sharp, saw-toothed hills of Union Island, with Carriacou as a blue backdrop beyond. He knew all the islands by name—all rocky, dry and reluctantly giving up during the short rainy season a pathetic little crop of cotton, corn and peas.

"Ain' nothin' ever happen," Frank had been saying since he was small, although big enough to lend a hand in the boat and pull on an oar as he went out with Grandmere into the clear green waters within the reef to tend the fishpots and dive for lobsters and conches.

"Ain' nothin' ever happen nowheres 'cept birth an' death an' livin' in between," Grandmere would say, pursing her thick lips and resting on her oar as she wiped the sweat off her face. And then she would go on rowing in short, swift jerks from the wrist, stopping every so often to peer into the clear green depths or to slip over the side to dive towards some rocky cavern in which her sharp eyes could see a lurking lobster or a bed of rock where the conches clung thickly.

Sometimes at low tide they would row within the waters of the reef out to Shell Island, a sandy shell-strewn split on which in the old days a few coconut-palms had fought their losing battles against the sea. Nothing was left of them now but a few stumps, soggy and shell-covered, in a desert of whitened shells and coral, brightened at times by a yellow sea fan, a pink

148

conch, a large, dappled brown cowrie hurled up by the rising tide and left to fade under the merciless sun and to whiten like old bones.

Frank loved Shell Island. So did Fibi, his little cousin. Fibi's mother, Frank's Tante Mallie, had died when she was born; of a broken heart, some folk said, when the young Bajan from St. Vincent had stopped coming to the island in his sloop, leaving Mallie to fend for herself, as men so often did. Frank remembered when she had died; remembered the muffled crying of Grandmere as she followed the coffin down through the valley and along the narrow hillside path to the little cemetery. He remembered, too, the shock of realisation that Mallie's voice was forever muted, leaving in its turn the weak wailing of Fibi, that was so easily silenced by a rag dipped in sweet water or by gentle rocking.

When she was a baby he used to sit for hours on the step of their thatched hut, holding her in his arms, marvelling at her pale-gold skin, the soft fair hair like the down of a baby chick, and her blue eyes flecked with brown like little freckles. His small black hands looked so dark and out of place as they held her and in his mind he early set her apart.

When she was big enough to go out in the boat with Grandmere and himself, he plaited her a hat from wild cane to protect her hair and face from the sun. But in time the sun had its way and Fibi at fifteen was a warm golden brown, her hair bleached yellow by salt water and sun.

Frank's heart would twist within him at the sight of her thin body in the sea-stained and tattered dress which was practically the only garment she possessed, her golden legs powdered grey by the dry dust or glistening a deeper gold when she scrambled back into the boat with a lobster or a conch.

"Fibi hadn't oughta look like dat," he told himself, seeing in his mind's eye a picture of Fibi dressed like the girls in the magazines the padre sometimes gave him. He saw her in a clean white dress, her hair combed smooth, with perhaps a ribbon in it, instead of tangled and flying in the wind, or plaited pickny

fashion by Grandmere on a Sunday, until the smooth strands
escaped and grew tousled again in the wind. She would look
good, too, he told himself, with lipstick and a dab of powder on
her straight little nose with the gold freckles sprinkled across its
bridge.

"One a dese days," he told himself, "I gettin' 'way from dis
island. I going to Aruba or Trinidad or some place an' earnin'
plenty plenty money for Fibi." But he knew that as long as
Grandmere lived he would have to stay, since there was no one
to work their little plot of land or to catch fish to eke out their
crop of dried peas and cornmeal.

His dark eyes would grow broody as he remembered the time
when going out in the boat with Grandmere had been an
adventure.

But that had quickly dulled with the passing years and had
become, as Fibi and he had grown older, a grim, everyday search
for food, as it was for Grandmere and most of the other people
on the island. But the dream of earning money persisted, tinged
though it was with hopelessness when he thought of Fibi and all
he wanted to do for her. Her casual acceptance of things as they
were crushed him at times into despair. His love she accepted
too, without being aware of his growing fear of the day when the
quiet backwater of her childhood would burst the dam and fling
her into the stormy waters for which her comeliness had des-
tined her. To Frank, Fibi was the one lovely thing in a life which
held out no hope for the future; but behind the loveliness was
fear.

Then one night it came upon him with full force like a blow
between the eyes: he had to do something positive to prove his
love for Fibi. He was returning to the village after hours spent
on the rocks, catching crabs for bait by the light of a flambeau.
He was going to catch fish from the rocks the next day, for they
needed more mullet and chub than they could catch to make a
meal, now their corn was all gone, and there was no money to
buy any from the shop. He was going to try for something bigger
—a red snapper or two, perhaps, or a cavalli. Then he might

manage to sell one or two, to the agricultural officer who had just arrived at the government rest house. There were so few visitors to the island, this was an opportunity he dare not miss.

Picking his way carefully along the stony track that wound round the hill towards the village, he saw the slender mast of a sloop at anchor in the bay, silhouetted against a sky studded with stars and in which hung the silver thread of the new moon. Then he heard voices—the deep rumbling of a man's and the shrill laughter of a girl. It was Fibi. On an island where everybody knows everybody else, Frank knew that the man was a stranger. He stood still and listened. All he could hear was a faint rustling among the sea grape bushes bordering the beach.

"Dat yo, Fibi?" he called.

He waited and thought he caught a faint "ah" followed by a suppressed giggle.

"It latem, Fibi," he persisted. "It time yo' in bed long long time."

The only answer was the sound of the sea lapping the white sand with deep sighs. He walked to the village slowly.

He lay in his corner in an agony of misery. Grandmere was snoring. A rooster crowed and another answered it. And somewhere a dog howled. The sound was mournful and eerie in the night. Until now he had seen Fibi as a child—a gay, uncomplaining companion of days in the boat or out hoeing in the hot sun—a golden creature whom he, dark and uncouth though he was, would one day rescue from a way of life into which an unkind fate had flung her. His mind stumbled numbly over the fact that Fibi, for all her golden skin and blue eyes, was as coarse as her environment had moulded her; that she was no different from the other girls on the island. Fibi in a temper could curse like the rest, pull out hair and throw stones. Fibi noisily sucking up fish tea from a tin pot, sucking and gnawing a fish-head and spitting out the bones, belching loudly and wiping her mouth clean with the back of her hand, might look different from the darker girls, but she was no different really.

The realisation of this was like the stubbing of a toe against a sharp stone. It hurt.

Frank carried the hurt around for weeks, helplessly casting about for the right to speak to her, to make her understand; but finding that he had no right. Who was he, he asked, to tell Fibi that he loved her?

After a few days, the sloop sailed, and Fibi's nocturnal disappearances ended, though Frank, watchful, saw a subtle change in her as the weeks merged into months. Always thin, she grew thinner, and the fine modelling of her face grew even finer, giving her a look of transparency which the blue veins at her temples accentuated.

She no longer sang as they rowed the boat. And once or twice he heard her crying in the night. He longed to take her in his arms, as he had done so often when she had been small; but he knew that his desire for the feel of her thin body against his own was for his own comfort as much as for hers. But she would only say, as she had been accustomed to saying, recently, whenever he touched her tousled head, "Tak yo' han's offen me," in a sharp, bitter voice so unlike her own. He retreated with his misery, just as Fibi did with her own.

One morning Grandmere did not get up. She lay on the torn canvas cot against the wall of the hut, her legs drawn up to her lean belly, shivering and mumbling to herself. Without the white cloth she usually wore twisted around her head, she looked very old, Frank thought, binding the leads along the edge of his cast-net while Fibi bent over the coal-pot by the door. His belly growled as he watched Fibi stirring sugar in the milk-can of hot water and then pouring it into the three tin pots.

"Ain' got no bakes this mornin'. Ain' got no more flour," Fibi told him as she handed him the pot of sweet water.

"Dat a'right, Fibi. I ain't pertickler hungry dis mornin'," he replied.

He wanted to make an early start because the agricultural officer had said he would like some lobster and a big string of mullet to take back to St. Vincent with him on the launch that afternoon. With luck they might catch enough to buy a little cornmeal and flour. Fibi could go into the shop. The sight of the tins of sardines, corned beef and salmon, the barrel of biscuits, the rum on the shelves, was torment to Frank. And the shopkeeper liked Fibi. Sometimes she managed to wheedle a penny loaf or a handful of broken biscuits from him.

Grandmere turned her head to the wall when Fibi took her the "tea". She left it on the floor beside her as they went out, Fibi carrying the net and gaff and Frank the oars and rowlocks.

Rowing in silence, Frank kept his eyes on the church and the huddle of thatched huts that had once been a prosperous village in Grandmere's youth, when most of the island had been one estate. Frank wanted to look at the little gold tendrils of Fibi's hair and to imagine the lay of muscles under the bedraggled loose dress with the patch across the back—a patch that in its turn was soon going to need yet another patch. He wanted, too, to grip her arms until he hurt her, to shake her and say: "Listen, Fibi, you gotta listen. Yo' gotta be different to de other girls, see, yo' just gotta."

Then as they left the bay and were out round the point in the shallow green water within the reef, he became grimly intent on the day's work; years of habit, years of grappling with the sea to give up its life for food, translating from thought to instinct. And, as if by unspoken agreement, they both began to pull more slowly, their eyes searching the green depths for what they sought.

Twice he shipped his oar, slipped silently over the side, dived, came up for air, dived again, his grimy sea-and-work-stained shorts and shirt which were a miracle of patching, clinging to his lean body. Then he pulled himself into the boat, throwing Fibi a smile as he threw a lobster, tail thrashing, into the bilge. Time and again he and Fibi slipped over the side into the clear depths, until they reached Shell Island, for it was on the ledge of rock that ran like a spar out into the deeper water towards the reef that he would stand waiting to cast his net, while Fibi cruised around in the shallower water on the look out for lobsters and conches.

Just before they reached the ledge, Fibi suddenly shipped her oar and leaned over the gunwale, retching miserably. Frank, appalled that what he had feared was now a fact, was filled with a blinding rage, not only against Fibi and himself, but against the island itself that had bred her. It crashed over him like a gigantic wave and the blood pounded in his head.

The instinct to destroy blotted out all else. Fibi was suddenly no longer to be rescued but to be destroyed to banish his own anger and shame. Hardly knowing what he did, he suddenly brought his fist down on her golden head, bent miserably over the boat's side, with a violence that jarred his whole body.

Then, because the crumpled figure, with head lolling in the bilge where she had fallen, urged in him the stirring of fear and pity he could no longer bear to feel, and with a wild, searching glance at the shimmering white sand of the beach and the impertinent blue of the sea beyond, he lifted her and dropped her over the side of the boat. He leaned over and watched her, a wavy-edged, distorted figure in the clear water, as he had watched her many times before.

Then before he knew it, he had dived towards her and she was no longer distorted like a figure in a fantasy but close and near to him. He tried to take hold of her but time after time she eluded him, carried this way and that by shifting currents. Again and again he rose to the surface, filled his lungs with great gulps of air and dived. When at last he managed to hold her and felt her body limp in his arms as he brought her to the surface, he suddenly became panic-stricken at what he had done. Thought, and with it terror, seeped into him again slowly.

Taking a deep breath, he dived again, down into the familiar depths they both had known so intimately in the past. Fighting the pressure of the water until little explosions went off inside his head, he pushed her body with all his remaining strength into a cleft in the rocks; went up for air and dived again to seize a huge chunk of coral to wedge her body more securely in the cleft.

Exhausted, he dragged himself to the hot white sand and coral of the Island, staring dully at the sky and the white scudding clouds racing across it, not sure if the thunder he heard was his own blood pounding in his head or the thunder of the surf on the reef. Love for Fibi burst like a great white light over him, wave after wave of timeless white light until, blinded by it, he slid into the water to escape its searing brightness. He had to see her once more. He could never go back now, back to Grandmere and life, any more than Fibi could. He saw one golden-brown arm waving in the water like a reed, and touched it, dislodging the rock that had held her down. Opening his mouth, he tried to speak, and that was the last he saw of her as her slim brown body rose gracefully to the surface.

There's Always the Angels

F. A. COLLYMORE

"Have you ever been a god?"

It was with difficulty that I murmured a perfunctory "I beg your pardon" to the old gentleman who was occupying the seat on the park bench beside me. I'd certainly never been asked that question before.

He repeated it, a faintly humorous smile playing round his lips as he did so; but his large brown eyes were very sad.

"Why, no," I replied after another moment of hesitation.

He eyed me thoughtfully, critically, as though he was making up his mind about something. Then he spoke again with a little sigh, wistfully, as though making a confession of something he wasn't too proud of, "I have, you know."

"Oh!" I said. It didn't mean anything, but then what else could I have said?

"Yes," he repeated slowly, "I have."

He sat there lost in meditation looking over across the trim lawn to where against a background of dim mahogany trees a couple, a young man and a girl, were pacing slowly, arm in arm, up and down.

I looked at him closely for the first time. I hadn't paid him much attention when I'd taken my seat. Indeed, I'd thought at first he was a clergyman, one of those elderly retired clergymen you see taking an evening stroll, sitting in the park for a few moments before, refreshed by the sight of the trees and flowers, they move on slowly homewards, before it grows dark. But on closer inspection I decided he wasn't a clergyman. He wasn't dressed like a clergyman. His clothes, a bit shabby, had nothing suggestive of the clerical about them. And he wore a very bright blue tie that was in some way . . . an artist, that's what he was. The tie, those long tapering fingers. Musician, painter? I stole a glance at his face now in profile. It must have been a very handsome face once, I thought. Even now, despite the many wrinkles and a slight grey stubble, it was worth while looking at. There was a peculiar air of aloofness about its expression, a sort of brooding absorption. The sort of face . . . Ah, I was sure now: a scientist.

"Pardon me," I began, but at that moment he turned and said:

"Life. Life on this planet of ours. It's not what it ought to be, you know. Don't you find it very confusing?"

I was about to reply but he continued:

"Yes, you must have given the matter some consideration. It's inevitable. It all could be so pleasant. So very pleasant."

He broke off again. He spoke in jerks, but smooth little jerks, if you know what I mean.

"Over there. That boy and girl. In love and planning for happiness. And what? A background of pain and evil and disease and death. And war. Always war. Always evil. Why?"

I replied to the effect that I supposed it was in the nature of things.

"But surely it oughtn't to be in the nature of things. It wasn't intended. I know it wasn't. I . . . ." He ran a hand through his thinning greyish hair.

"Yes?"

"You see, knowing this, I thought: Why not make another universe I could control? A universe from which pain and violence and evil would be excluded? Where there'd be only life and joy and happiness? You understand?"

"Quite. Only it's . . . well, it's not so easy, creating a universe, is it?"

He took me up rather sharply. "That depends, my dear fellow, that depends."

F. A. Collymore

"Upon what?"

"This universe as you know it, what is it really? I will tell you. It is a thought in the mind of the one who created it, of God. Now I ask you, can't you draw the inference?"

"Well, I suppose anybody could *think* out a universe, if that's what you mean," I replied cautiously. "But I shouldn't imagine it would be a very real sort of universe."

"That's where you're utterly mistaken." He was rather heated now. "I admit it isn't very easy, but it can be done. I tell you I know what I'm talking about. Because I've done it."

Again I ventured a noncommittal "Oh!"

He was looking out now, over the tops of the darkened mahogany trees, into the late afternoon glow of the sunset and there was a sort of nobility about the face that touched me.

"At first, you know, there was chaos. Confusion. Nothing and everything. It's difficult to think of everything. But it's more difficult to think of nothing. Have you ever tried thinking of nothing?"

But he didn't seem to be expecting any answer and he went on:

"Yes, it was all terribly difficult in the beginning. But at last I felt I could begin. It was all here." He tapped his forehead. "All here in the same way . . ."

He broke off again. He seemed to be thinking of something else.

"In the same way?" I prompted.

"Let's not talk of that now," he said. "As I was saying, I began again."

"Again?"

"One must experiment, you know. I wanted this universe of mine, this new universe, if I may put it that way, to be perfect. Well, I began in the orthodox manner. Light first. It's funny, but it's got to be so. I suppose you've often wondered about that part of the Bible story. Light first, sun and so on afterwards. But it's really so. You try it, if you don't believe me. Yes, the first thing has got to be light. So I began. I worked on the approved model. I shan't tire you with a detailed description, of course. Only I did want to have a moon all the year round."

"And why didn't you?"

"No, I couldn't forgo the starlight. And then, you can't improve upon the stars, could you?"

I made no comment.

"And so I went on and on. I thought of introducing a few new varieties of plant life, but somehow . . . And it was delightful creating the birds."

"Did they prey upon one another?" I ventured.

But he didn't reply. He went on. "And so, at last, I came to the final creation, man."

"With or without appendix?" You see, I was just convalescing from an operation.

But he ignored that question, too.

"My masterpiece."

"What did he look like?"

This time he replied. "Well, he was rather like . . . like me. Me, but much younger, of course. I wasn't a bad-looking young man. But that was long ago. However. Still I wasn't satisfied; so I created a partner for him. A woman."

"Rib?"

His answer led me to think he was a little hard of hearing.

"Never mind about the name. But she was very beautiful. And they were happy in the garden. Very happy. And I thought: Now this is where things went wrong in the other garden. So I didn't put any restrictions upon them. No tree. No inhibitions. I felt I was wiser. I'd read Freud in the meantime. And then . . . and then . . ."

He broke off and buried his face in his hands. I had a suspicion he was sobbing, sobbing very quietly.

After a suitable pause, I coughed. It was getting late.

He looked up. His eyes *were* wet.

"And then?" I reminded him.

"I don't know."

"You don't know?"

He shook his head sadly. "No. I don't think I shall ever know."

There was something so hopeless in the tone of these words that suddenly I was filled with an overwhelming wave of pity for the old man. I looked away. I couldn't bear to think of this fantasy of his. How could it have had such an effect upon him? A tall man was walking slowly in our direction. A man in a tweed suit and a felt hat. I could barely see that it was a tweed suit in the gathering darkness.

"I don't *want* to know! I don't *want* to know!" He was clutching me by the arm.

I gave his hand a reassuring clasp.

"I don't *want* to know, I tell you." He was sobbing now unashamedly.

I squeezed his hand again. "Oh, it's sure to be all right," I said. "After all, you made your little universe; you can make things go how you want them to."

"But that's the awful part," he moaned. "Look at what's happening to the one you're living in."

"But . . ." I began smilingly.

The man in the tweed suit had come alongside us and touched his shabby felt hat to us.

"Good evening," I returned.

The old gentleman didn't notice him. He withdrew his hand and looked at me intently. There was something extremely disconcerting in his regard. "You see, I made the one you're living in also."

The man in the tweed suit smiled at me not unsympathetically, and touched the old gentleman on the shoulder.

"Come along, sir. Nearly seven o'clock, you know."

"Yes, I know, Michael."

He rose, wiped his eyes in a faded silk handkerchief and blew his nose softly.

"Good evening," he said to me. "Must be off." He patted the man affectionately on the shoulder. "After all, there's always the angels." And he gave me a knowing wink.

There's Always the Angels

They moved away. The lovers had long since departed. The park bell rang for closing time.

Good Lord, I thought, what a sad case! And such a nice old fellow, too! And I hadn't even discovered who he was. At least I could have asked the keeper his name.

I got up and tried to overtake them. But it was no good; I couldn't walk very quickly. When I reached the gate, they had disappeared. I've made enquiries about them, but strangely enough, I've never been able to trace them.

The Fig-Tree and the Villager

ROY HENRY

The village begins where the road from the plain ends its winding ascent into the hills. Down over the hills and across the plains about twenty miles away the sea merges into the coastline of Jamaica. Here, the road descends into a fertile valley. It continues winding for a mile. Here and there the open fields are decorated with gaily coloured shacks and small Spanish-walled houses and well-fed animals. At this end of the valley, where the road meets another road and begins to climb once more, you come upon the village centre, with its four shops and a huge fig-tree with its branches about and beyond them all. The district is called "Castle", but is better known as "Uncle Eddy's Castle".

The fig-tree is as old as the village. But only the size of its trunk and the rugged dried-up roots, chipped, chopped, blood-spattered and barky come to the surface to suggest its antiquity.

Like the tree, Castle (Uncle Eddy had taken the name of the village) had seen more flourishing years. In those years he had wandered afar in search of sustenance and a better life. In Cuba he had worked as a cane-cutter, learnt to strum the guitar and led a small dance orchestra. He had been a policeman in Costa Rica and an engineer and magistrate in Panama. But he had ended up in America as a waiter during the depression with nothing but his experiences to comfort him. Now an old man, retired from his minor foreign expeditions, he looked as weather-beaten as the tree and as tattered as his shack, both of which stood on the only material possession he had worth having—

one quarter of an acre of land. Even this property, a legacy, was shared with his sister and her son, Sam—a shopkeeper.

On his return to the village, a little over ten years ago, he had found himself privileged and respected. There was so little informed conversation to be had that he was painfully aware of the advantage of the wider horizon of his experiences. True, he had little money. But as the situation of the land he partly owned was attractive to the many who hoped to do business in the village, the fear of being destitute was not inevitable. Moreover, the fig-tree was strategically placed for his battles against the ignorance he saw around him. He was convinced for the first time that his life had a noble purpose.

At first he led the respectable life. He went to church every Sunday. He owned and rode a horse. He showed great fondness for children. When dressed, he always wore a bunch of violets in his buttonhole. He had an order at the Post Office to supply him with a copy of the island's only daily newspaper. And as if that were not sufficient, he bought a couple of the weekly ones as well. Often with his guitar hanging from his shoulder, he would sit under the fig-tree strumming and singing to his soul's delight and the pleasure too of the many villagers who would gather to listen and join in the choruses. He had even been known as a man of parts when he had led the local cricket team successfully.

But that was ten years ago. Now, he no longer went to church. He no longer owned a horse. Instead of buying the daily and weekly papers, he borrowed them from one of the shops. He would comfort himself that his new habits were not due to his lack of means or a mark of niggardliness, but a privilege he had earned; for the shop in which he read the newspapers on any particular day would surely be the one to make the best sales. The shopkeepers considered it a privilege to accommodate him and even vied to fête him with alcohol.

But he was a proud man and never risked the indignity of consuming more than he could hold. He was proud as only one who could read and write and tell tales of a foreign land to those who know little of these privileges could be proud. Accordingly he rationed his services. Most days he would read in no shop at all but have the papers sent to him. Then sitting at the roots of his fig-tree, he would read it aloud. The village lads, the loiterers, the passers-by, would surround him.

It was here, too, that he presided at all sorts of meetings, for all political parties, all denominations, all visiting magicians and conjurers.

And for fear of what might befall him, had often taken the chair and eulogised would-be herbalists whom everyone suspected of being more obeah-men than herbalists.

But he drew the line at peddling. His dignity would only allow him to give redress to those whom he considered "done" by a salesman or vice versa. And there were many of both types. Then in the position of arbiter, he would administer justice with all the finality of the law courts. Soon with his gift of eloquent persuasion, his opinions came to have the authority of the law. He was contemplating running for a seat in the island's House of Representatives when he and the fig-tree were confronted with a struggle for their lives.

"A man like you with the ton of education you have, should keep yourself quiet and not be a humbug to a man business." This was Sam, Castle's nephew, noted more for passionate outbursts than business acumen. Proprietor of the smallest shop in the village, he had become sore with the old man when the merchants had started to press him. Sam, in fact, as the old man's nephew, had expected some show of favour in the development of his little business venture. He felt his uncle could at least have frequented his shop more often. Failing to get this privilege, he had found a way to unsettle the old man. To get rid of his uncle and the menace of his association with the tree, Sam was prepared to buy his uncle's share of the property.

Castle was sitting on the fig-tree strumming his guitar that evening and, as some of the village lads throwing dice behind the tree had overheard Sam's contention, he did not reply. His pride was hurt. But discretion as always restrained him from having an open brawl. He made as if to walk away without answering Sam. But Sam became more abusive.

"All day long you giving high-brow talk around here and wouldn't even build yourself a decent house to live in. All you full up of is talk, talk, talk, from morning till night. But a goin' to cramp you style. A goin' to get rid of you and dat tree. After all, people come out here to shop and all you do is play guitar and get them into argument bout things that can't give nobody bread."

Castle seemed to have had a thousand voices to answer for him. "Quiet yourself, boy, quiet yourself. What wrong wid you?" "Who you tink you is? Dat old man worth ten like you." "If he ever answer you, you will wish you wasn't born."

The words came from so many lips that for a moment Sam was a little confused. "Uncle?" he said sneeringly. "Him never show me no special treatment from him come back here."

It was not like the old man not to welcome an argument, heated or agreeable. It was well known to everyone, however, that life around the tree meant more to him than anything else. As he walked away they became aggressive to Sam and forcibly replaced him in his shop.

A few days after he had so alerted Castle, Sam's mother came to see her brother about the title. As the old man needed ownership of property to put himself forward as a candidate in the forthcoming elections he was more than anxious to win Sam and his mother over to his side. But as Sam also had the same ambition, the situation soon resolved itself into a straight fight for the lady's benevolence.

"When I get into the House," said the old man, "I will be able to do a lot of things for the two of you and this village."

But Sam was not impressed. "Who goin' to send you there? You think people fool? You goin' to promise dem heaven and promise dem earth and is only dust you can blow pon dem."

"Listen, my boy, the people of this village trust me. They know that I am champion of democracy and every one of them will vote for me. That will be enough to win me the seat."

Roy Henry

Whether it was the love of the mother for her son or the passionate persuasion of the younger man against the convictions of his elder one cannot say, but Sam had his way. In a week Castle would have to change his abode and as Sam gave notice of cutting down the fig-tree as soon as he came into possession of the property, it seemed that the old man had little else to live for.

That night he took a walk to the other end of his mile-long valley. In the distance, the lights of the American airbase could be seen. He sat down on a huge rock on the bankside. He picked up a small stone, clenched his fists and cursed. He cursed the Americans for coming so near to disturb the view with their neon lights. He wondered too what would have happened if Sam had not got his "break" in life from the good wages he had earned at the American base during the war. His nephew would certainly not have owned that shop; nor would he have been aggressive enough to force his uncle from his home. If it was a show of initiative he was happy he had not that virtue. The old man thought that earning those dollars had given Sam an ugly courage and even uglier manners. He shook his head and frowned. He could see no good coming from the association. Remembering the misery of his lean years in America during the depression, he felt he had a double reason for cursing.

He was cursing audibly now as he rose briskly from his stony throne. "Change! Change! Change! That's all you hear these days. And they all goin' to hell if you ask me." And he threw the stone away.

"Is that you, Uncle?"

As it was dark he did not realise that it was Sam. But he knew the voice was familiar. And as everyone in the village knew that he always visited that spot from late each afternoon till it was near midnight, he was not surprised that someone had recognised him in the dark. He was, however, surprised to know it was Sam.

"You know what, Uncle," Sam continued, "the people love you. You could really win the election." The old man knew when not to comment on suspect remarks. He knew Sam must have had other things on his mind. And he had. He had a proposition to put to him. His plan was to build a dance hall and a bar on the spot where the tree was situated. It was necessary to get the old man's co-operation to finance the venture. He took great care to show the financial returns possible.

But he had not bargained for the finer sensibility of his wiser and much travelled elder. "Let me tell you something, my boy. That tree has more history in one of its roots than all your shops and brains put together. My father knew it as a boy and my mother and grandparents before me. The emancipation was celebrated right here. You will cut it down over my dead body."

Sam made as if to leave without answering. It suddenly occurred to him that his proposal was not quite understood. "Who was talking bout history? I want some money, man. History can't clothe and feed me! No wonder you not better off. You and you history and big talk! You look as ragged as a dustbin."

The old man looked away and did not answer. Sam hissed his teeth in a fit of desperation and left him alone.

On returning to his shack, he could not sleep. He sat up and from his window he could see all that was going on under the tree. He saw market women unloading their mules and donkeys while waiting for trucks to take their goods away. He had an unusual urge. He wanted to go out and give a hand. But he was tired. Behind the tree, too, were the gamblers, intent and stooping. Opposite to them at the same time, he could hear a religious meeting going on. Nearby, there was a politician holding a meeting with its reception having all the hilarity of a comedy. A small boy was placed on the top of the tree with a pot of water that spurted on the honourable man's head whenever he made a point. The old man shared the crowd's laughter.

He felt a kinship with the tree. He wondered how many children in the village had been sired at its roots. He had heard a lot of rumours in his time but had not really given them any thought. The old man contemplated the virtue of the continued existence of a tree that took so much from the consecration of human life in its shadows. He pondered on and on until the sun rose early in the morning.

That morning Castle was unusually late in rising. The sun had arrived overhead yet the old man's door was still unopened. There was his audience, concerned, uneasy, fearfully expectant. Many had lingered, impatient for him to come and read the newspaper. They enquired about. He had not taken the morning bus that passed daily for someone would have seen him. In any case, they thought, he had never left the village for a single day for the past ten years. No one had dared to suggest the likelihood of his passing away.

It was Sam himself who must have become anxious enough to eliminate the fear and paralysis that was taking hold of everyone, for he came forward and went to the old man's cottage.

In his shack, behind the tree, Sam found him. There he was, asleep. Sam sat down beside the bed. Slowly, the old man awoke. From his window and the cracks in the roof, the sun came peeping through. On opening his eyes he could see the sky through the leaves of the fig-tree that overshadowed his shack.

He suddenly became aware of someone's presence and turned to see Sam sitting on the chair beside his bed. This time he was not alarmed. He recognised his visitor but did not speak save with his eyes. He turned away from Sam and looked at the sun.

Sam bent forward and tried to entreat the old man. "A have a better idea now, sir," he said. "Suppose we build a community hall wid a waiting-room for a doctor and a drugstore, we could call it an act of public spirit. That could help in the election, eh?"

The old man did not answer. He was still looking through the window at the sun between the leaves of the fig-tree.

Sam's eyes fell. He looked up again and the old man's calm detachment was apparent. As Sam rose to leave the room he knew he had been defeated and closed the door behind him. He had accepted the finality of the old man's decision after all.

My Fathers Before Me

KARL SEALEY

Dick, the yard man, took the big Rhode Island cock from the run and, tucking it under his arm, went back to the kitchen steps where he had been sitting.

He held the cock fast between his legs and, squeezing its mouth open with his left hand, took a pinch of ashes from the small heap beside him, between right thumb and forefinger. This he rubbed on to the bird's tongue, and began to peel the hard, horny growth from the tongue's end.

His grandmother, who had spent most of her usefulness with the family, came shambling from the house behind him, eating cassava farina soaked in water and sugar. She stood looking down at him for some time, her eyes, the colour of dry bracken, tender, before she took a spoonful of farina from the glass and, bending with the stiffness of years, put it from behind into his mouth. Through the farina in his mouth Dick said, like a man continuing his thought in speech:

"And your age, Granny? You've spent a lifetime here. How many summers have you seen?"

"More than you'll ever see if you go to England," she said, letting herself down on the step above him. "Eighty-four years come October, God spare life. Whole fourteen above-and-beyond what the good Lord says."

"Hmm," Dick said, and taking the cock to the run, returned with a hen as white as a swan.

The old woman said: "Just think of it, Dick, just think of it. Come this time tomorrow you'll be miles away, with oceans of

169

water separating you from everybody who loves you, and going to a land where you ent got a bird in the cotton tree, where nobody'll care a straw whether you sink or swim, and where black ent altogether liked." She scraped the last of the farina from the glass, and once more put the spoon to his mouth.

"You ent mind leaving us, Dick?" she said. "You ent mind leaving your poor old Granny and Ma? And Vere? What about Vere? You ent got no feelings in that belly of ye'n, Dick?"

Sucking farina from his teeth with his tongue, Dick said: "I'll send for Vere as soon as I can. Maybe Ma, too."

The old woman continued as though she had not heard: "No more Dick about the house to put your hands 'pon. Maybe some lazy wringneck governor in your place whose only interest'll be his week's pay."

"Time enough too, and welcome," Dick said.

From an upstairs window, whose curtains she had been pulling against the evening sun, Bessie saw her mother sitting on the concrete step above Dick. Going down to the servants' room she took a cushion from the sofa and went out to where they were sitting. She said:

"Up, Ma. Think you're young, sitting on this cold step?"

The old woman raised herself a few inches, and Bessie pushed the cushion under her.

"I's just been telling Dick, Bessie, how no good ent ever come to our family leaving our land and going into nobody else country."

"True enough," said Bessie. "Look at my Dick and Panama."

Then the old woman asked: "Ever teach you who the Boers was at school, Dick?"

"I ent ever learn for sure who the Boers were," said Dick, "save that they couldn't stand up to bayonets."

"That's right," Bessie said. " 'At the bayonet charge the Boers surrender.' "

"British bayonets," Dick remarked.

"Don't you let nobody fool you with that, Dick," said the old woman. "There wasn't all no British bayonets. Your gran'dad's bayonet was there, too."

"Oh, well, we're all British. At least that's the way I look at it."

"But British or no British," said the old woman, "your gran'-dad came back to me and his four children with a foot less, and as I often told him after, it served him in a way right. For what in the name of heaven had the Boers ever done him, whoever in God's name they was, that he should leave off peaceful shoeing horses, and go in their own country to fight them for it? What right he had, Dick, answer that question, nuh?"

Dick, having peeled the pip off the hen's tongue, handed the bird up to Bessie, who laid it in her lap and began to stroke its feathers.

"Didn't it serve him in a way right, don't you think, Dick?" the old woman insisted. "Going to kill those Boers who'd never done him a single thing? Speak from your conscience, Dick."

Dick said, turning the bit of callus from the hen's tongue round his fingertips: "Well, he went to fight for his kind. To defend the Empire."

"The Empire?"

"The Empire," Dick said.

"What Empire?"

"The British Empire!"

"Listen, Dick," said the old woman. "I can't ever get this straight though I must have tried dozens of times to get the old man to put it right in my brain before he died: Ent Britain England?"

"Sure. Britain is England," said Dick.

"And ent British come from Britain?"

Dick said, perhaps not too sure of himself: "Well . . . yes. British from Britain."

"And how come that your gran'dad lost his leg at a place called Mother River in Africa, as he was so fond of relating, and you says that he went to fight for the king of England? What right had the king of England in Africa?"

"Well, I don't think that the king of England was there in person," said Dick. "But he had, well . . . interests there."

"Interests?" said the old woman.

"Well, it's like this," said Dick. "Years ago, just as we from the West Indies are going to England now, English men and women, British if you like, went and made their homes in other lands, Canada——"

"That's where Vere's sister gone to a hotel to do waitressing," interrupted Bessie.

" . . . Australia, Africa, and so on," continued Dick. "And these places where the British made their homes became British and made up the British Empire. So the king of England had a right to interfere if any other nation tried to pinch the places where these English had made their homes, as the Boers wanted to do."

"Oh, I see," said the old woman, shaking her head up and down. "It's a little bit clearer now than I's ever understood it before. But how come you's all flocking to England like a parcel of sheep? Why don't some of you go to Australia or Canada? Sure, Vere says she gets sixty-seven cents on every dollar that her sister sends her. Why don't some of you try and work for Canadian dollars to send back home? Ent you just told me we's all British?"

Dick said: "Well, it's like this: A man had, say, twelve children. As the years passed by, the oldest grew up and left the old man and went and made their own homes. Mind you, you couldn't interfere with the old man and the younger kids they'd left at home for them to know, but at the same time the old man couldn't tell them who to let come in their houses and who not to. Well, it's like that with Canada and Australia and South Africa. They have grown up and are running their own homes, and they say they don't want us West Indians to come into them and that's the end of it."

"But we can still run about in the backyard of the old home," said the old woman. "Is that what you mean?"

"Exactly. If you put it that way."

"I see it all now. I see. Your gran'dad was never given to explaining. Still, I don't feel that your gran'dad had any right going to fight those Boers," she persisted. "Just as I don't feel you've got any right leaving bright, sunny Barbados and going to that bleak England, though I's often thought that with your reading and quickness maybe you could do better than you're doing."

"I've thought so too, for a long time."

The evening sun had struck through the leaves into his eyes, and letting himself down upon the lowest step he sprawled back, making a rest for his head with his interlocked fingers. The women looked down on his face, and when he spoke his eyes had a faraway look into the sky.

Bessie said: "Your dad thought the same thing, and it didn't do him no good."

Vere, the young cook, appeared round the corner in the yard, carrying a basket of groceries in her hand.

She rested her basket on the ground and sat beside Dick with a sigh, leaning her body heavily upon him.

"Your dad thought Barbados was too slow for him too," said Bessie. "He swaggered about singing the foolish songs of the money they'd made digging the Canal with the other fools just like, as Ma says, our dad used to sing about the 'pound and a crown for every Boer they down'. Only he hadn't the luck that your gran'dad had. He didn't ever come back."

The old woman said: "Died like rotten sheep in the Panama mud. No, no good ent ever come to our family leaving our land and forking ourselves in nobody else's. Not one bit of good."

"Three for luck," Dick laughed.

Bessie got stiffly to her feet, walked over to the fowl run, and put the white fowl in. Then she came back and stood looking down at Vere.

"You's a foolish girl, Vere," said Bessie, after a time. "Why don't you tell this Dick not to go to England?"

" 'Cause it wouldn't be any use," said Vere.

"No use, nuh?" said the old woman. "Hm."

Vere said, sitting up and half-turning so that her words might be taken in by both women:

"You two had husbands, *husbands* mind you, and nothing you could say or do could stop them from going away once their minds was made up. I ent see how I's been more foolish than either of you 'cause I ent been able to stop Dick here from going."

Dick executed a long stretch before he said: "My grandfather was sick of cleaning up the mess that Miss Barbara's dogs made in the morning, sick of watering the gardens under the big evergreen, sick of cleaning pips off these stupid fowls, sick of waiting for the few paltry shillings at the end of the week, just as heartily sick of the whole deuced show as I am myself now.

"And so when the chance of going to Panama came along nothing nobody could say could stop him from going, just as nothing nobody can say will stop me from going to England. My grandfather and dad didn't go because they were foolish, but because they were brave. They didn't go because they wanted to be rid of their wives and children. They didn't go because they wanted an easy life. They didn't go for a spree. They went because their souls cried out for better opportunities and better breaks. And just like them, I'm going for the same thing."

Bessie was still standing there her hands akimbo, looking down at Dick. When Dick finished speaking her eyes switched their measure to Vere, and with a fleeting lightening of her harsh face which none of the others saw she decided to play her last card.

"Still, Vere," said Bessie, "you're a foolish girl."

Vere pouted: "Say it again. A hundred times. Till you're tired."

"What're you straightening your hair so for?" Bessie asked.

" 'Cause other girls do," said Vere.

"And rouging your face, and plastering that red thing on to your mouth?"

" 'Cause other girls do." Vere hugged her knees, rocking herself back and forth on the step.

"You was always a rude brazen little girl. All the same, I hope you's got something else to make Dick stick by you. He going to England where he'll see hundreds of girls with real straight hair and really red cheeks and mouths natural like roses. Ten to one, one of them will get him."

Vere sprang to her feet, her eyes dilated.

"And I'd spend the last cent getting to England, and wherever they was I'd find them out and tear the last straight hair from her head. I'd tear the flesh from her red cheeks to the bone!

"I'd beat her rosy mouth to a bloody pulp! Oh Christ, I'd . . ."

She caught at her breath in a long racking sob, snatched the basket from the ground and ran into the house.

The other three were all standing now, and in the understanding of Vere's love, had drawn involuntarily closer to one another.

The old woman said, knocking a beetle from Dick's shirt with her spoon: "And will you still go to England, Dick?"

Their ears just barely caught the one word from his lips.

The women turned and, mounting the steps in the settling dusk, made their way together into the house.

The old woman said: "It's the same with him as it was with them, Bessie. Nothing will ever stop him."

"No. Nothing," said Bessie.

The Tallow Pole

BARNABAS J. RAMON FORTUNÉ

It was the day of the contest and everything was prepared. From the top of the pole dangled a ham, a bottle of whisky and a bottle of rum, fastened there by short ends of rope, and resting on the very top was a small cardboard box containing a hundred-dollar note.

I stood in the mixed crowd watching the pole that rose twenty to twenty-five clean, straight feet into the air like a ship's mast without rigging, greased from top to base with tallow after it had been planed and sand-papered to the smoothness of glass. The tallow stood on it in blotchy, white lumps like a strange, horrible fungoid disease; but it had begun to melt in the heat and the grease ran down sluggishly like ugly, shapeless drops of sweat from the hide of some pre-historic animal.

Standing at the foot of the pole, a couple of feet away, was the Mayor looking at his watch. He was dressed in a loose, linen suit that sagged about him. He seemed to be personally affected by the heat. He was a tall, massive, black man with a thick moustache that looked like a tangle of black shoelaces. His thick, kinky hair looked rigid and affrighted on his head.

It was Monday morning and you could feel the heat rising like waves below you from the bowels of the earth. It seemed as if the sun had changed its centre and that it no longer burned in the sky but somewhere close to the surface of the ground, waiting for the earth to crack, and leap out, a fearful, unformed foetus of fire. But when you shaded your eyes with your damp, clammy hands and looked up, you knew that *he* was still in his old place in the sky, sneering and relentless, grinning at you with his blazing teeth. The glare was all around you, enveloping you, penetrating the lids of your eyes, shining through your skin, so that as you held up your hand against the sun you could see its huge spider of bones.

At twelve noon the contest would begin. I saw it was two minutes to twelve.

The Mayor puckered his lips as he watched the face of his watch and then shouted:

"Start!"

The first contestant leapt at the pole and immediately slipped to the earth with great speed, striking it violently with his posterior. He wore a pair of old, khaki shorts and a merino. Tallow clung under his armpits, to his chin and all along one side of his face.

The mixed crowd of about four hundred let out a hollering burst of laughter as he picked himself up, an enormous, magnified fly that had just unstuck itself from flypaper.

The Mayor was mopping his brow and laughing while the sweat poured into his eyes.

The other contestant went up to the pole, turned to the crowd and bowed. Then he turned to the pole again. There was a feline quality about him, in his long, thin, nimble limbs, like a tree that had grown too high too quickly. His plan seemed not to attack the pole violently as the last man had done but to woo it like a lover. He made a short leap and held it. For a moment he was stuck there like a fly floundering on water, beating arms and legs furiously without making progress in any direction. Then he slipped gradually to the bottom, striking the ground with his knees and toes, while he embraced the base of the pole like a weeping mother fondling and trying to bring back a dead child to life.

The pole now, at least the lowest ten feet of it, was a clean and shining brown pillar of wood. All the grains of the wood could be clearly seen, like brushmarks in a painting. They flowed white and clean with artistic widenings and narrowings and now and then swelled into circular shapes that flow around a knot. The knots looked like onions embedded in the smooth, clean surface of the wood.

I observed now that the contestants were not slipping quite so easily down the pole. The same men, after cleaning themselves of the clinging grease with pieces of bagging, came back again and again to try their skill. Every now and then a contestant progressed about six inches, bringing down with him generous handfuls of tallow.

Many contestants brought sand and bags to assist them in their climb. Mounds of sand were stacked a few feet away from the pole and the coarse material of sugar and rice bags lay here and there in the small, human arena with the pole standing challengingly in the centre of it like Mount Everest.

Then gradually, but quickly gaining in intensity, there was a stir in the crowd and a rise in the sound of voices over and above the prevailing general hubbub. It echoed from one side of the crowd to the other.

"Greasy Pole! Greasy Pole!"

I had heard about him; everybody had heard about him.

But I had never before had the opportunity of seeing the great Greasy Pole.

The people fell back making a passage for the great man. Greasy Pole had won the contest continuously over the past five years.

The crowd flowed in again, closing ranks, like the return of the waters of the Red Sea after the passage of the Israelites, and Greasy Pole stood in the arena.

He was short, black; blacker than any Negro I had ever seen; true black—and shining; as if his sebaceous glands gave his skin a special glow. His kinky hair on his perfectly round head was cropped short and could only be distinguished from the round shape of his skull by its dusty dullness. He carried a heap of bags over his left shoulder. The span of his shoulders was broad and his arms looked like grappling tentacles where they emerged from his dusty white merino. He wore a pair of khaki shorts roughly patched in the seat, apparently by his own square, thick hands. But it was his feet and his toes that held my attention. They were long, unusually long for his height, with large middle joints that seemed endowed with extraordinary gripping powers. As he walked they gripped and clenched the earth, leaving a deep footprint where he had passed.

He stood before the pole and looked up and down as if measuring an adversary. Not a smile played on his face; his eyes were tense, ignoring the crowd as if he alone stood there. The long line between his thick, black lips was hard, straight and immobile. In the next instant, his broad face became as active as water stirred by the wind, and he smiled. He had discovered the weakness of his adversary. He turned to the crowd for the first time, and bowed.

"Greasy Pole! Greasy Pole!" the cheers went up.

He stood erect again but immediately stooped and gathered up some tallow from the ground. He rubbed it over the entire front of his body down to his legs in a thin film. Then he walked over to one of the heaps of sand and, taking up great handfuls, sprinkled himself liberally with it. The front of his body looked like a large sheet of sand-paper.

He walked back to the pole and taking a spring, leapt upon it. He did not slip down. His enormous, claw-like toes spread open to the smooth, circular surface of the pole and bit into it greedily.

The crowd screamed and swayed. Someone behind me thumped me on my back.

Greasy Pole remained there clenched upon the pole for a few seconds, gripping it like a wrestler in a stranglehold. His body jerked and he moved up several inches. Soon his hands reached the line of the tallow where the highest contestant before him had left his mark. I could see the tension in his legs. His toes were like talons. His body jerked again and his hands swept into the tallow.

He began to slip down, slowly but surely. Then he stopped. He seemed stuck to the pole—pinned upon the pole; gripping it with his thighs and looking like a hideous, misshapen, black butterfly.

He remained there, panting. His latissimus dorsi stood out like large wings. He took his hands one after the other from the pole and flung the tallow to the ground.

His body shook again. His great toes, completely spread apart, lifted him up and up again quickly to the high triumphant tallow mark.

He was hurrying now. His hands swept into the tallow greedily, quickly, rapidly, as he flung great lumps of it to the ground.

The crowd screamed again as he neared the top. There seemed no point in his pausing now; no point in his stopping and taking breath; he must get to the top now, or fail.

He passed the ham; he was going for the hundred dollars.

The heat and the excitement held us spellbound. A *cigale* was crying against the hot noon. Except for that, the world seemed to be cast in an eternal silence.

Suddenly, the crowd turned as if someone had fired a shot into the air. Greasy Pole stopped, too.

Someone was calling the name George Baker. It was a woman's voice.

"George Baker! George Baker!"

She was shouting from the back of the crowd but her voice cut over our heads like a scythe.

Greasy Pole turned and looked over the heads of the crowd to where the voice was coming from.

"George Baker! Don't forget you promise me dat money las' night! De money on top o' de pole is mine! George Baker, you got to mind you chile!"

Greasy Pole's body sagged. His muscles slunk back into the smooth, level surface of his skin.

There was a heavy sigh from four hundred throats as Greasy Pole slipped slowly down the pole and alighted to the ground. He looked at us with a sad, disappointed face as if he had failed us.

The Tallow Pole

In my mind's eye I saw the infant, not yet a year old, with large, black eyes, the paternity of which Greasy Pole was probably disputing. Was it boy or girl? I would never know. It did not matter.

Greasy Pole bowed his head in shame and defeat and walked through the crowd.

Later that evening I passed Greasy Pole. In fact, I stepped over him. He was lying drunk on the pavement.

Blackout

ROGER MAIS

The city was in partial blackout; the street lights had not been turned on, because of the wartime policy of conserving electricity; and the houses behind their discreet *aurelia* hedges were wrapped in an atmosphere of exclusive respectability.

The young woman waiting at the bus stop was not in the least nervous, in spite of the wave of panic that had been sweeping the city about bands of hooligans roaming the streets after dark and assaulting unprotected women. She was a sensible young woman to begin with, who realised that one good scream would be sufficient to bring a score of respectable suburban householders running to her assistance. On the other hand she was an American, and fully conscious of the tradition of American young women that they don't scare easily.

Even that slinking black shadow that seemed to be materialising out of the darkness at the other side of the street did not disconcert her. She was only slightly curious now that she observed that the shadow was approaching her, slowly.

It was a young man dressed in conventional shirt and pants, and wearing a pair of canvas shoes. That was what lent the suggestion of slinking to his movements, because he went along noiselessly—that, and the mere suggestion of a stoop. He was very tall. There was a curious look of hunger and unrest about his eyes. But the thing that struck her immediately was the fact that he was black; the other particulars scarcely made any impression at all in comparison. In her country not every night a white woman could be nonchalantly approached by a black man. There was enough novelty in all this to intrigue her. She seemed to remember that any sort of adventure might be experienced in one of these tropical islands of the West Indies.

"Could you give me a light, lady?" the man said.

It is true she was smoking, but she had only just lit this one from the stub of the cigarette she had thrown away. The fact was she had no matches. Would he believe her, she wondered? "I am sorry. I haven't got a match."

The young man looked into her face, seemed to hesitate an instant and said, his brow slightly wrinkled in perplexity: "But you are smoking."

There was no argument against that. Still, she was not particular about giving him a light from the cigarette she was smoking. It may be stupid, but there was a suggestion of intimacy about such an act, simple as it was, that, call it what you may, she could not accept just like that.

There was a moment's hesitation on her part now, during which time the man's steady gaze never left her face. There was pride and challenge in his look, curiously mingled with quiet amusement.

She held out her cigarette toward him between two fingers.

"Here," she said, "you can light from that."

In the act of bending his head to accept the proffered light, he came quite close to her. He did not seem to understand that she meant him to take the lighted cigarette from her hand. He just bent over her hand to light his.

Presently he straightened up, inhaled a deep lungful of soothing smoke and exhaled again with satisfaction. She saw then that he was smoking the half of a cigarette, which had been clinched and saved for future consumption.

"Thank you," said the man, politely; and was in the act of moving off when he noticed that instead of returning her cigarette to her lips she had casually, unthinkingly flicked it away. He observed this in the split part of a second that it took him to say those two words. It was almost a whole cigarette she had thrown away. She had been smoking it with evident enjoyment a moment before.

He stood there looking at her, with cold speculation.

In a way it unnerved her. Not that she was frightened. He seemed quite decent in his own way, and harmless; but he made her feel uncomfortable. If he had said something rude she would have preferred it. It would have been no more than she would have expected of him. But instead, this quiet contemptuous look. Yes, that was it. The thing began to take on definition in her mind. How dare he; the insolence!

"Well, what are you waiting for?" she said, because she felt she had to break the tension somehow.

"I am sorry I made you waste a whole cigarette," he said.

She laughed a little nervously. "It's nothing," she said, feeling a fool.

"There's plenty more where that came from, eh?" he asked.

"I suppose so."

This won't do, she thought, quickly. She had no intention of standing at a street corner jawing with—well, with a black man. There was something indecent about it. Why doesn't he move on? As though he had read her thoughts he said:

"This is the street, lady. It's public."

Well, anyway, she didn't have to answer him. She could snub him quietly, the way she should have properly done from the start.

"It's a good thing you're a woman," he said.

"And if I were a man?"

"As man to man maybe I'd give you something to think about," he said, still in that quiet, even voice.

In America they lynch them for less than this, she thought.

"This isn't America," he said. "I can see you are an American. In this country there are only men and women. You'll learn about it." She could only humour him. Find out what his ideas were about this question, anyway. It would be something to talk about back home. Suddenly she was intrigued.

"So in this country there are only men and women, eh?"

"That's right. So to speak there is only you an' me, only there are hundreds and thousands of us. We seem to get along somehow without lynchings and burnings and all that."

"Do you really think that all men are created equal?"

"It don't seem to me there is any sense in that. The facts show it ain't so. Look at you an' me, for instance. But that isn't to say you're not a woman, the same way as I am a man. You see what I mean?"

"I can't say I do."

"You will, though, if you stop here long enough."

She threw a quick glance in his direction.

The man laughed.

"I don't mean what you're thinking," he said. "You're not my type of woman. You don't have anything to fear under that heading."

"Oh!"

"You're waiting for the bus, I take it. Well, that's it coming now. Thanks for the light."

"Don't mention it," she said, with a nervous sort of giggle.

He made no attempt to move along as the bus came up. He stood there quietly aloof, as though in the consciousness of a male strength and pride that was justly his. There was something about him that was at once challenging and disturbing. He had shaken her supreme confidence in some important sense.

As the bus moved off she was conscious of his eyes' quiet scrutiny, without the interruption of artificial barriers, in the sense of dispassionate appraisement, as between man and woman, any man, any woman.

She fought resolutely against the very natural desire to turn her head and take a last look at him. Perhaps she was thinking about what the people on the bus might think. And perhaps it was just as well that she did not see him bend forward with that swift hungry movement, retrieving from the gutter the half-smoked cigarette she had thrown away.

Crossroads Nowhere

STUART HALL

I turned my back on the whirlpool of Marble Arch, the currents of cars that careened in and out of the Park, the crowd that shuffled and elbowed its way down Oxford Street, and began to walk up the Edgware Road. The evening had turned sharp, and the wind cut waist-high along the buildings. I turned up the collar of my coat, and stuffed my hands into the caves of my pockets. It was past supper-time, but the rooms where the young men and women sat perched on stools looked long and forbidding, the fragrance of fried chips and the towers of porkpies blunted the edge of my appetite. The vortex of Marble Arch drew a mixed crowd, but the permanent signs—the firmly shuttered cigarette kiosk and the pile of unsold *Evening Standards*—were desperately English. The tall Indian and the two girls speaking German who clutched his arm, the sprinkling of foreigners that salted and seasoned the pavement-crowds appeared as if drawn from the cones and threads of small streets that issue into the highway, as if thrust up from some vast, submerged international underworld that crouched behind the brassy frontage of the Odeon. In the surging throng I hardly remarked the coated form that passed me as I walked, and the voice that said, "A'right, sagga boy" was lost almost at once in the incessant hum of traffic. I stopped.

The lilt was unmistakable: West Indian—a greeting offered and over, like the flash of a trafficator or the sudden glare of a headlamp—a single sounded note of recognition that required no acknowledgement. For the form had passed on, that curious

West Indian roll carrying him around the corner and up towards the Corner House. I turned, and walked quickly after
him.

"Hey, boy," I said, "you know a good place to eat?" He was
tall, the face behind the thin edge of stubble that followed the
line of his chin burnt bronze beneath the neon. He wore a coat,
but no tie, and his shirt was collarless and open at the throat
with a kind of summer abandon.

I had surprised him. "Anywhere good round here to eat?"
He smiled at this and relaxed. "Well, lemme see now . . ." He
began to wave his hand, leisurely withdrawn from his pocket, in
an expansive arc that gestured me towards the farthest limits
of Oxford Street, and seemed to embrace the whole of north
London. "If you walk as far as de traffic-lite—not dese here, you
know, two or t'ree after . . ." I looked in the direction but the
traffic lights winked exasperatingly at me from every inter-
section . . . "an' turn lef', and lef' at the nex' street, you come
to a arcade on the rite han' side: tack thru' there, swing roun'
an' ease down the road a piece, an' is there, yu' boun' to see it."
His eyes searched my uncomprehending face, and he permitted
himself the luxury of an explanation.

"Tha's the Wes' Indian place you ask me for."

I grinned. "You work roun' here?"

"A doin' a job at Lyons, na? Til' a get a real work." He was
preparing to go.

I tried to think of something I could say to keep him. "You
like London?"

He smiled. "A livin'. After you dead a'ready. Whe' you goin'
do, boy?"

"I'm Jamaican too," I said. "Where you from, Kingston?"

He nodded. "Tha's a far place, boy." He looked down the
long stretch of Bayswater Road as if he expected to catch a
glimpse of the Atlantic.

What could I say? That I hadn't heard words slip off the
tongue like that, like a cascade of minted pennies, for months,
that we should go somewhere and talk, that we had something

to say? Out of a thousand mocking murmurs in a thousand foreign tongues, his had caught my ear, as the single call of a fisherman across the harbour brings the pasteboard canoes dancing and jigging together from the darkness. The when and the why of him, and that we were *not* strangers, might have filled a thousand fictions: exile gave a strange singularity to our meeting. The wind caught at these half-formed questions, and the shrug of his narrow shoulders helped me to silence. In spite of the huge trucks that burrow through Hammersmith to the Great West Road, or the vans that funnel their way to the river, in spite of the myriad taxis that weave and wind through the backstreets and knit the city together as with a network of veins—in spite of its restless, ceaseless activity, London is full of surprising silences. Livin'. After you dead a'ready. Whe' you goin' do, boy? For a moment our eyes crossed, the look framing his story better than his lips, the eyes dark without self-pity, the mouth smiling, unresigned: then the lights changed on us, orange, green and the traffic was gone.

"Right." I nodded. He nodded. Finished. Ships that pass. London opened its dark jaws, yawned once, and swallowed him like a snake.

Waterfront Bar

V. S. REID

They stood at the bar, belly-up to the rail, no light in their eyes at all.

The barmaid said, "Coming up!" When she said "Coming up!" her mouth was an inverted U, leaning on end. She whisked the three glasses into the sink and worked a limp half of a lime around the edges.

One of the three women laughed. Her laugh was a thin reed, stitching the scene. It went up to the octave and back again, was lost in the bottom of a hiccup.

Daylight slithered out of the bar on webbed feet, slithered over three empty baskets at their feet. The baskets were wash baskets. The women were washer-women.

The barmaid clicked on the lights. Three women and a barmaid stood under the lights. A limp half of lime went around the edges of three glasses.

The woman who had laughed brought her voice back from the bottom of a hiccup. She said: "Wash me in the blood of the Lamb."

Another woman said: "Who must wash you, Daph?"

Daph belched and said: "Give me a cigarette, Schooner."

Schooner said: "You hear what the woman call me, Peggy?"

Peggy pushed a cigarette to Daph and slid one in her own mouth. She spoke around the cigarette: "Don't you gone to wash for round-the-island boats?"

Daph searched her pocket for a match. The match was there but her fingers were fumbly. She leaned on the bar and belched.

Schooner said: "You drunk?"

Daph said: "You go to."

"Go yourself."

The barmaid used a gill measure. Seven-and-six white rum splashed over the edge of the measure. Peggy laughed.

"Treat we good, Miss Amy."

Miss Amy said: "Steel bottom?"

Schooner and Peggy said together: "Steel."

Daph passed her hand over her face and murmured: "Wash me in the blood."

Miss Amy steeled the rum with three gills of ginger wine. She wrinkled her nose and put the bottle hastily away. She pushed the bowl of cracked ice towards them. She said they should poison themselves.

Daph used a word.

A boy pushed the swing doors from Port Royal Street. His tray entered first. Light splashed on the burnish of a dozen pink combs tiered in the tray, on the curly hair tiered on his head.

The boy said: "Combs? Toothbrush? Hairpins? Shoelaces?"

Daph said: "Have a drink, Honeydripper."

Peggy said: "How much shillings for those sixpence combs?"

Schooner said: "Take a drink, Dripper."

The boy said: "Combs? Toothbrush? Hair . . ." His voice went with him into Port Royal Street.

Daph said: "Make the woman-boy gwan." She drank the white rum and ginger wine as somebody else would drink water.

Miss Amy said: "Jesus."

Miss Amy went to the radio-phone. She was searching for "The Donkey's Serenade". She liked "The Donkey's Serenade".

Four sailors came in through the Port Royal Street door. They wore oilstained dungarees and said: "Hi there, Amy!"

They said it heartily. They were oilboatmen in port for weeks, and drinking on tick. No ready cash. Tick.

A girl followed them in and leaned on the rail. Her slant eyes gathered gleams from the light.

Waterfront Bar

Daph said: "What a way things tight 'pon the water-front, Peggy?"

Peggy said: "Don't interfere with people, Daph."

The oilboatmen drank beer. Their voices were deep, like ships' bowels. American-accented.

"Hell, when we gonna get to sea?"

"A lousy town."

"You know Bill Doran on the *Alamein*?"

"Sure I know Bill. Sure, sure."

"Got a letter from his wife yesterday: Twins."

"Twins? Hell!"

"Tough."

"Yeah."

The tray came through the door before the man who carried it in. "Peanuts? Mint sticks? Guava cheese?"

"Have a drink, Honeydripper?"

"Daph, leave people alone."

"You guys heard what the A. F. of L. said about Panama registry?"

"Buy a mint stick, sailor?"

"Come again, Miss Amy. Steel."

"Jesus."

Miss Amy changed the record. Aluminium mutes on brass trumpets stitched a theme on the boogie pattern. The girl with the slanting eyes covered her eyes with her eyelids. She passed her palms down her thighs. She took her palms from her thighs and held them parallel with the ground. Her body quivered.

Daph said: "She feeling well."

"Leave people alone. Why you go wash for schooner?"

"Can't pick and choose these days."

"I hear 'Merican yacht coming in tomorrow."

"Lawd—them good to wash for!"

"Wash me in the blood."

"Daph, you drunk?"

191

V. S. Reid

The man with the tray held the door open with the tray so that the two men could come in. The two men came in and held the door open so that the man with the tray could go out.

Daph said: "See them two Russians here?"

The men were dockworkers. They didn't look like Russians: neither White nor Red. They were Negroes.

Peggy said: "Daph, you drunk? Leave people alone."

One of the men said to Miss Amy: "Comrade," and showed her a fist.

Miss Amy said: "Leave politics and order you liquor."

"Quarter-quart in two."

"Schooner, how you vote, me love?"

"Labour, Daph, me love."

The arm-rest of a crutch came through the swing door and the one-legged man hopped in like a big bird behind it. He steadied himself and his eyes searched the room. Daph tied a swift knot into her apron and said: "Cho! Bad luck. One-foot beggar-man!"

The one-legged man said a word. He went over to the oil-boatmen. The oilboatmen said naw. He went out again, saying a word as he went.

"Wash me in the blood of the Lamb."

"Daph, you must drink you rum and behave."

"So the guy said he wouldn't go to sea with no nigger on the valves."

"They are all wet, these Southerners."

"Personally, I wouldn't kiss a Sheenie or a nigger."

"Listen, punk, Christ was a Jew and Solomon a coloured-guy."

"Yeah? How does that make me kiss 'em?"

"Listen, punk. A guy named Hitler——"

"Pipe down, mugs. This is a foreign port, see?"

"Hell, sailormen nearly fight!"

"Daph, leave people alone."

"Steel, Miss Amy."

"Jesus!"

Drunkard of the River

MICHAEL ANTHONY

"Where you' father?"

The boy did not answer. He paddled his boat carefully between the shallows, and then he ran the boat alongside the bank, putting his paddle in front to stop it. Then he threw the rope round the picket and helped himself on to the bank. His mother stood in front the door still staring at him.

"Where you' father?"

The boy disguised his irritation. He looked at his mother and said calmly, "You know Pa. You know where he is."

"And ah did tell you not to come back without 'im?"

"I could bring Pa back?" The boy cried. His bitterness was getting the better of him. "When Pa want to drink I could bring him back?"

It was always the same. The boy's mother stood in front of the door staring up the river. Every Saturday night it was like this. Every Saturday night Mano went out to the village and drank himself helpless and lay on the floor of the shop, cursing and vomiting until the Chinaman was ready to close up. Then they rolled him outside and heaven knows, maybe they even spat on him.

The boy's mother stared up the river, her face twisted with anger and distress. She couldn't go up the river now. It would be hell and fire if she went. But Mano had to be brought home. She turned to see what the boy was doing. He had packed away the things from the shopping bag and he was now reclining on the settee.

"You have to go for you' father, you know," she said.

"Who?"

"You!"

"Not me!"

"Who de hell you tellin' not me," she shouted. She was furious now. "Dammit, you have to go for you' father!"

Sona had risen from the settee on the alert. His mother hardly ever hit him now but he could never tell. It had been a long time since she had looked so angry and had stamped her feet.

He rose slowly and reluctantly and as he glanced at her he couldn't understand what was wrong with her. He couldn't see why she bothered about his father at all. For his father was stupid and worthless and made their life miserable. If he could have had his way Mano would have been out of the house a long time now. His bed would have been the dirty meat-table in front of Assing's shop. That was what he deserved. The rascal! The boy spat through the window. The very thought of his father sickened him.

Yet with Sona's mother it was different. The man she had married and who had turned out badly was still the pillar of her life. Although he had piled up grief after grief, tear after tear, she felt lost and drifting without him. To her he was as mighty as the very Ortoire that flowed outside. She remembered that in his young days there was nothing any living man could do that he could not.

In her eyes he was still young. He did not grow old. It was she who had aged. He had only turned out badly. She hated him for the way he drank rum and squandered the little money he worked for. But she did not mind the money so much. It was seeing him drunk. She knew when he arrived back staggering how she would shake with rage and curse him, but even so, how inside she would shake with the joy of having him safe and home.

She wondered what was going on at the shop now. She wondered if he was already drunk and helpless and making a fool of himself.

With Sona, the drunkard's son, this was what stung more than

ever. The way Mano, his father, cursed everybody and made a
fool of himself. Sometimes he had listened to his father and he
had felt to kick him, so ashamed he was. Often in silence he had
shaken his fist and said, "One day, ah'll—ah'll . . ."

He had watched his mother put up with hell and sweat and
starvation. She was getting skinnier every day, and she looked
more like fifty-six than the thirty-six she was. Already her hair
was greying. Sometimes he had looked at her and, thinking of
his father, he had ground his teeth and had said, "Beast!" several
times to himself. He was in that frame of mind now. Bitter and
reluctant, he went to untie the boat.

"If I can't bring 'im, I'll leave 'im," he said angrily.

"Get somebody to help you!"

He turned to her. "Nobody wouldn't help me. He does insult
everybody. Last week Bolai kick him."

"Bolai kick 'im? An' what you do?"

His mother was stung with rage and shock. Her eyes were
large and red and watery.

The boy casually unwound the rope from the picket. "What
I do?" he said. "That is he and Bolai business."

His mother burst out crying.

"What ah must do?" the boy said. "All the time ah say, 'Pa,
come home, come home, Pa!' You know what he tell me? He
say, 'Go to hell, yuh little bitch!' "

His mother turned to him. Beads of tears were still streaming
down the sides of her face.

"Sona, go for you' father. Go now. You stand up dey and
watch Bolai kick you' father and you ent do nothing? He mind
you, you know," she sobbed. "He is you' father, you ungrate-
ful——" And choking with anger and grief she burst out crying
again.

When she raised her head, Sona was paddling towards mid-
stream, scowling, avoiding the shallows of the river.

True enough there was havoc in Assing's shop. Mano's routine
was well under way. He staggered about the bar dribbling

and cursing and yet again the Chinaman spoke to him about his words, not that he cared about Mano's behaviour. The rum Mano consumed made quite a difference to Assing's account. It safe-guarded Mano's free speech in the shop.

But the customers were disgusted. All sorts of things had happened on Saturday nights through Mano's drunkenness. There was no such thing as buying in peace once Mano was there.

So now with trouble looming, the coming of Sona was sweet relief. As Sona walked in, someone pointed out his father between the sugar bags.

"Pa!"

Mano looked up. "What you come for?" he drawled. "Who send you?"

"Ma say to come home," Sona said. He told himself that he mustn't lose control in front of strangers.

"Well!"

"Ma send me for you."

"You! You' mother send you for me! So you is me father now, eh—eh?" In his drunken rage the old man staggered towards his son.

Sona didn't walk back. He never did anything that would make him feel stupid in front of a crowd. But before he realised what was happening his father lunged forward and struck him on his left temple.

"So you is me father, eh? You is me father, now!" He kicked the boy.

Two or three people bore down on Mano and held him off the boy. Sona put his hands to his belly where his father had just kicked him. Tears came to his eyes. The drunkenness was gripping Mano more and more. He could hardly stand on his own now. He was struggling to set himself free. The men held on to him. Sona kept out of the way.

"It's a damn' shame!" somebody said.

"Shame?" Mano drawled. "An' he is me father now, 'e modder send him for me. Let me go," he cried, struggling more than ever, "I'll kill 'im. So help me God, I'll kill 'im!"

Drunkard of the River

They hadn't much to do to control Mano at this stage. His body was supple and weak now, as if his bones were turning to water. The person who had cried, "It's a damn' shame!" spoke again.

"Why you don't carry 'im home, boy? You can't see 'e only making botheration?"

"You'll help me put 'im in the boat?" Sona asked. He looked unruffled now. He seemed only concerned with getting his father out of the shop, and out of all this confusion. Nobody could tell what went on below the calmness of his face. Nobody could guess that hate was blazing in his mind.

Four men and Sona lifted Mano and carted him into the boat. The old man was snoring, in a state of drunkenness. It was the state of drunkenness when things were at rest.

The four men pushed the boat off. Sona looked at his father. After a while he looked back at the bridge. Everything behind was swallowed by the darkness. "Pa," the boy said. His father groaned. "Pa, yuh going home," Sona said.

The wilderness of mangroves and river spread out before the boat. They were alone. Sona was alone with Mano, and the river and the mangroves and the night, and the swarms of alligators below. He looked at his father again. "Pa, so you kick me up then, eh?" he said.

Far into the night Sona's mother waited. She slept a little on one side, then she turned on the other side, and at every sound she woke up, straining her ears. There was no sound of the paddle on water. Surely the shops must have closed by now, she thought. Everything must have closed by this time. She lay there anxious and listened until her eyes shut again in an uneasy sleep.

She was awakened by the creaking of the bedroom floor. Sona jumped back when she spoke.

"Who that—Mano?"

"Is me, Ma," Sona said.

His bones, too, seemed to be turning liquid. Not from drunkenness, but from fear. The lion in him had changed into a lamb. As he spoke his voice trembled.

His mother didn't notice. "All you now, come?" she said. "Where Mano?"

The boy didn't answer. In the darkness he took down his things from the nails.

"Where Mano?" his mother cried out.

"He out there sleeping. He drunk."

"The bitch!" his mother said, getting up and feeling for the matches.

Sona quickly slipped outside. Fear dazed him now and he felt dizzy. He looked at the river and he looked back at the house and there was only one word that kept hitting against his mind: Police!

"Mano!" he heard his mother call to the emptiness of the house. "Mano!"

Panic-stricken, Sona fled into the mangroves and into the night.

Minutes of Grace

E. R. BRAITHWAITE

I watched her come into the coffee bar: the skin-tight black jeans, thin shoes, soiled duffle-coat presented a picture of grubbiness, emphasised by the lank hair which hung unevenly about her shoulders. She paused just inside the door and looked around her, then walked towards where I sat apart from the lively, argumentative group of students who had apparently discovered the secret of stretching a cup of frothy liquid to last for two or more hours. There were several empty seats around the room and I hoped she would sit as far from me as possible, but she moved unhesitatingly towards my table, sat down opposite me and casually began unbuttoning her duffle-coat, her clear grey long-lashed eyes large in her pale narrow face.

"Will you buy me a coffee?" Her voice was low and clear: each word was spoken as if they had been well rehearsed in her mind. Somewhat surprised by that direct request I looked into her eyes, then signalled the waitress and asked for two coffees.

"May I have a cigarette?"

Without waiting for reply or gesture from me she picked up my cigarette-case from the table, opened it and carefully selected a cigarette; she placed it in her mouth and waited until I got the silent message and hurriedly struck a match for her.

"Do I make you nervous?" she asked.

"No, not nervous, but I am not quite accustomed to this sort of thing."

"Do you mind buying me a coffee?"

"No, you're very welcome." I looked around me, wondering whether we were attracting any attention. I prefer the women, in whose company I am, to be at least tidy looking.

"I suppose I'm embarrassing you." Suddenly she laughed, a sharp, brittle noise which somehow produced no change in her face or eyes. "It'll only be for a little while. I suppose you can stand being embarrassed for a little while?"

She had a trick of letting the smoke slip through her lips in a thick, slow curl, then inhaling it again through her nose lazily. Now and then she would tilt her chin upward and blow a thin spear of smoke over my head. Our coffee arrived and she put four spoonfuls of brown sugar into her cup. I noticed her hands, fingers long and finely tapered, the index and middle one of each hand deeply stained with nicotine.

"What's your name?" she asked.

I looked up. Her eyes were fixed on me; they were clear and clean to their very depths. Whatever it was that had produced the general untidiness had not yet reached to her eyes.

"Thwaite, Richard Thwaite."

She swung her eyes over me in comprehensive summary.

" 's funny, all the negroes I've met have had ordinary names, like Smith and Rogers. Guess what, my room-mate's name was Zutshi: she's white: English, funny."

"What's yours?" She paused before answering me.

"Nothing." Her gaze remained cool, level. "What do you do?"

"I write."

"What?" she asked bluntly.

"Books, articles, scripts, things like that."

"What are you?"

There was a slight pulling of the muscles around her mouth, the involuntary twitchings of a humour denied, rejected.

"I've just told you, I'm a writer," I said.

"I asked what you do and then I asked what you are." There was a mocking edge to her voice. "Can you see no difference in the questions?"

I caught on. I saw it all now, another of those beatnik smarties with their nothing philosophy. Anything for a laugh without laughter.

"O.K., I write and I'm a Negro." I was suddenly bored with her.

"Is that supposed to mean something?" Without taking her eyes off me, she killed the cigarette butt and reached into the case for another. I made a light for her.

"I'm sane and my sight is good." She went on, "No need to dodge behind your skin, its colour neither impresses nor bothers me."

She did the trick with smoke again.

"I don't suppose you understand. Let's try me. I was a singer and I modelled for artists. The modelling I did so I could live while I tried to be the other thing." She explained simply.

"What type of singing?" I didn't ask about the modelling. That was not hard to guess: posing for struggling young artists at a few shillings a time.

"What type of singing?" She repeated the question softly, as if to herself. "Blues."

She let the word hang between us for a while then continued: "Blues. That's the only kind of singing that matters. You should know, you and your dark skin; no, you and your black skin. They say it started with you, but who cares where it started. I always felt it, deep inside. Can you sing?"

"No," I replied, "but I like Blues."

She drew hungrily on the cigarette, squinting at me through the soft whorls. With her free hand she tilted her coffee cup on its side and made a face at the cold frothy dregs.

"More coffee?"

She nodded, and I ordered more coffee.

"How long have you been writing?"

"About two years," I answered. "Before then I taught in schools."

"They wanted me to do something useful, my parents, I mean. I started at art school but spent too much time listening to records and bands, then I quarrelled with my parents and left home."

She blew smoke into the silence between us, then I noticed the tears. She let them run freely down her face and onto the duffle-coat, but there was no sound from her. Then she rested her head on the table and put her hands over her ears as if to shut out the whole world.

"Can I help?"

"No." There was something remote about her voice, remote and final. In spite of the tears the voice lost none of its low-pitched clarity.

"Don't let this bother you." The hand with the cigarette made a circular gesture around her face. "I can't help them but they don't hurt any more. I can't stop them but they don't matter any more."

I took the handkerchief from the breast-pocket of my coat and handed it to her. As she casually wiped her face I looked around at the other people in the coffee bar and was startled to see that they were looking at us. I felt suddenly uncomfortable under the speculative stares and tried to avoid meeting their eyes.

"How did the singing go, any luck?" She shrugged her shoulders, her face half covered by her hair.

"No. It stayed inside, never came out the way it sounded inside. I started taking singing lessons and to pay for those I worked in coffee bars in the evening and modelling during the day. Then the men wanted me to do more than pose, so I went home." She blew her nose, wadded the handkerchief and put it into the pocket of her coat, then took another cigarette from the case, but instead of putting it to her lips, her fingers slowly shredded it, carefully separating the fragments of paper from the tobacco. Her shoulders had slumped somewhat inside the coat as if she were involuntarily retreating from some pain.

"They sent me away. Mother wouldn't have minded but she had to agree with Dad. Mother gave me twenty pounds, all she had, I suppose. Dad said he'd appreciate it if I did not return.

I took a room on my own. I needed money for my singing lessons, so I advertised, you know, as a model."

She looked up with those clear eyes, the tears had done nothing to impair their beauty.

"Are you shocked?"

"Not really." It was true. I wasn't shocked, or surprised, or anything. I had the feeling that she did not really see me, or care. I was an ear, a listening ear, needed for a moment. I felt that it helped her to talk; it just happened to be me.

"I used a different name and the men came, for all kinds of reasons. Some merely wanted to talk, others, well, you know. Most of them were mature men, and I often thought to myself, 'God, he's old enough to be my father.' They paid. None of it touched me, can you understand that? They paid for what they wanted, but it didn't touch me. At last I could afford to pay for my singing, and I knew that one day I'd walk out on it and be what I wanted to be."

She stopped talking and looked around her. There was a weariness about this simple gesture as if she were somehow trying to fix, to orientate herself. I tried to think of something bright and cheerful which would introduce a lighter note into our odd tête-à-tête, but she turned to me and continued:

"One day someone rang and made an appointment. His voice was vaguely familiar, but it meant nothing to me. He didn't say much, just asked if I'd be free at nine o'clock and when I said 'yes' he hung up. He arrived on time, exactly at nine. When the doorbell went I opened the door, and there he was . . . my father. . . ."

She put the cigarette end carefully in the ashtray and let her hands lie limply on the table. Her eyes were lowered and I could clearly see the faint network of tiny veins on her eyelids. The pattern of dark lashes against her face seemed to emphasise its pallor. "Needs a good, solid meal inside her," I thought.

" . . . We looked at each other, then he turned away. I heard him stumbling down the stairs." Her voice was now barely more than a whisper and I reached across the table and took her hands in mine, to comfort her; but she jerked them away with a little startled cry. There was something close to terror in her wide eyes.

"No, please don't touch me."

Her sudden action overturned one of the coffee cups and it clattered onto the table.

"I'm sorry, I didn't mean . . ." I began.

"I know, I know, it's just that I can't stand anyone to touch me. It's nothing to do with you, it's anybody."

As she righted the cup, the waitress hurried up with a damp rag, picked up the crockery and expertly ran the rag over the table. She looked questioningly at the girl, as if expecting her to make some comment, but my companion favoured her with a faint smile, and the waitress, with a short glance of hostility at me, moved off with her rattling burden. I supposed she thought we were having a fight about something and was in immediate sympathy with the member of her own sex. After she had got rid of the cups I saw her standing near to the students, whispering to them, then they all turned to look at us.

I turned again to my companion who had now stuffed her hands into the pockets of her duffle-coat; she was looking fixedly at me as if aware, as I was, that the thing with the coffee cups had broken our rapport.

"What happened after that?" I asked.

She smiled gratefully at me, and went on.

"I couldn't work after that. I couldn't do anything, just stayed in my room. I didn't answer the 'phone or the doorbell. Soon after then the nightmares began and he was always in them."

"God, it must have been awful for you," I sympathised.

"It was, but it's all right now."

She began buttoning up her duffle-coat, the movements of her fingers deft, unhurried.

"Thank you," she said softly. "You've been a tremendous help, really you have. It's been good of you, listening to me like this. I'm all right now. I wasn't quite ready, you see; I needed a few minutes' grace.''

She quickly stood up, carefully replaced her chair and walked away without another word. On her face was that look of resignation I had so often seen on the faces of aircrew just before take-off. I watched her walk through the door and past the glazed front of the coffee bar which overlooked the sidewalk.

I suddenly felt alone and exposed to the curious stares of the other patrons, some of whom were looking in my direction; I may have imagined the accusation I read in their faces, but avoided looking at them and started doodling on the back of the old envelope which I took from my pocket. I had come into their coffee shop to while away a quiet half-hour before keeping an appointment with a newspaper editor in the city. There was still about fifteen minutes before I needed to catch my train, so I decided to stay where I was a bit longer. I'd give the girl plenty of time to be far enough away so I wouldn't have to run into her in the street. The whole thing had been very unsettling, especially as I knew I'd been of no help to her. I wondered what she'd do. Go back to working in coffee bars, I suppose. I could have let her have a pound or two, but I don't suppose she would have taken it. Well, everyone has his own troubles. I hoped she'd pull through, somehow.

I signalled to the waitress. I wanted to order another coffee, but she came with the check. Still hostile. I wondered how she saw us, what kind of situation she has mentally placed us in. Probably thought the girl was in some kind of trouble and I was responsible. I took the check, paid at the counter and left.

There was no sign of my erstwhile companion along the short walk to the station; that suited me well, as I had no wish to see her again.

There were a number of persons milling around excitedly at the entrance to the station, across which a temporary barrier of short iron standards and chains had been placed. Against one of the standards was a blackboard with the notice advising travellers to make their journey by bus as the station was temporarily out of service.

I hurried to the nearest bus stop, rather sorry now that I had left myself so little time; there was a long queue of disappointed travellers, but just then I saw an empty taxi approaching and hailed it. As I climbed in I heard someone in the queue remark,

"They say it was a girl . . . jumped right in front of the train . . . poor thing . . . duffle-coat."

Ars Longa; Vita Brevis

JOHN FIGUEROA

In Kingston, when I was young the thing to have was a degree; now one does better to have an artist, or at least a friend who is the friend of an artist.

"My dear, you must just come and see the paintings of this man I discovered in Above Rocks. He used to be a cattle hand but you should have seen the chairs in his hut—painted, my dear, you know, I mean really *painted*, with love, I mean; every brush stroke, do you know. You could see him applying each jot and tittle of paint with, with, well—I think *genius* is the word."

"*She 'pon top, him underneath,*" the calypsonian announces to the stars. "*She 'pon top, him underneath deh move up and down.*"

"Have a drink, Henry," from the Jamaican host.

"Do you know I think I shall; rum, you know, rum—*Black Seal*, if you have it, old boy."

The host winces imperceptibly; he does his best to understand this expatriate European habit of drinking, of all things, *Black Seal*; he was brought up not even on the more expensive rums, but, of course, on Scotch.

"What was it you were saying about this man who paints chairs, Henry?"

"He *used* to paint chairs, my dear Thelma; he now paints pictures, do you know, just as you or I would, you know; real honest-to-goodness pictures; I mean, of course, with a difference. He's the nearest thing I have seen in the West Indies to Daumier

—a much underestimated painter Daumier, do you know, much under-rated."

"But, my dear Thelma, you seem to be dry. I say, Eustace, old boy, do get Thelma and me a drink. What will it be, Thelma; Scotch, oh yes, of course—I say, Eustace, Thelma will have a Scotch and Soda, and I, if you don't mind, another *Black Seal* and water will do me."

Eustace, the host, smiles his light-brown smile, just visible under the dim spot-light which gently illuminates the rather dried-up badminton court. He makes his way through the crush of guests to the table under the blazing Poinciana tree; many bottles are by this time "dead men", but there are many more under the table. Liquor flows as freely as the opinions and judgments of the various pundits, artists, critics, poetasters, and darling young things, with or without long ivory cigarette holders, all of whom are knotted about the lawn. On the one-time hard court the dancers are as earnest about their calypsos as are the others about their liquor or their painting and painters and discoveries—and of course culture, particularly *West Indian culture*.

When I was young it was good to have "culture"; but that meant to "speak well" and not "too flatly", to be interested in "classical" music, not to be too vulgar and to cultivate "old-world" manners; now, however, to be acceptable in progressive circles, where the liquor usually flows the fastest, one must have *West Indian culture*. One must for instance be ready to maintain (if needs be) that Roger Mais is the only "vital" novelist in the English-speaking world, and at least to assume tacitly, and now and again to state openly, that only plays in Jamaican dialect are moving, that Jamaican painters who do not use the most brilliant possible colours are basely imitating the culture of the foreign overlord.

Especially with regard to the foreigner this whole business of *West Indian culture* is not without its complications and ironies. A Jamaican for instance who has not heard of George Lamming and definitely not read him ("I believe that he has written a

Ars Longa; Vita Brevis

rather tedious book about growing-up in Barbados of all places," Thelma is whining on the lawn), such a Jamaican will now be dancing more and more like a Trinidadian. ("I wish they would play some *real* music," Marguerite is saying to Daisy and Dorothy as the new set of dances opens with a Victor Sylvester arrangement of an old-fashioned waltz. "Did you hear that Charlie Kunz stuff?" she asks in disgust and applies herself to the rum bottle—until such time as a dusky-voiced woman crooner should invite her to "*touch her pumpkin, potato but not to touch her tomato*".)

But "culture", in the abstract, is too complicated to be allowed to distract me from this gathering of artists (and their friends and patrons) drinking itself into still more flights of self-importance and honest jollity. Moreover, I am not "cultured" either in the older or newer meaning of that difficult word—notes towards the definition of which, in other circumstances, great men have written at length. First of all I went to college in the U.S.A., and was never old-world enough to wear a tweed jacket, waistcoat, a collar and tie in the Jamaican heat—so that my education and habits of dress ruled me out entirely in the old days; nowadays I have relegated myself to the outer darkness beyond the West Indian pale by various acts of indiscretion: I have thought our cricket umpires wrong on occasion; I have dipped my headlights; and I have, no doubt when alcohol had dissolved my entire super-ego, thought the History of the Romans more important to our young children than that of the Arawak and Caribs; I have had the temerity, also, to consider a really good Shakespearian production as satisfactory and commendable and as much to be supported as a production and play by Mr. Barry Reckord. ("I thought the language very powerful," Thelma is cooing; her right hand pats her brown upsweep, and her left pulls up slightly her deep-cut black taffeta blouse. "I think all these cults, Pocomania and the balm yard and obeah so interesting, and *so* much more vital than Christianity.")

"*Kitch, don't you advance; you late yu loss yu chance*"—the couples gather on the former hard court to dance—

John Figueroa

"Kitch, no more romance, yu too late, yu loss yu chance."

The dancers are being embarrassed by an argument taking place in the middle of the dance floor. There contend a loud-mouthed group consisting of men only—of course; women do not discuss, let alone argue at the usual Jamaican party; they might—and usually do—chit-chat among themselves while the men congregate together to drink and argue—usually about cricket. (There are exceptions, of course; but usually these exceptions are not true West Indians: they might be out-and-out foreigners or they might be people who are "playing big", that is who have studied and lived abroad and then have come back to our lovely shores to give themselves airs.)

But the argument which is embarrassing the dancers is apparently *not* about cricket. As we listen from our ubiquitous distance we are somewhat puzzled as to what the argument could be about, for the snatches that force their way to us across the waves of calypso rhythm—" . . . *not me. There's some that say that the men of today* . . ."—confuse our consciousness, roll our understanding back and forth, and with powerful undertow pull us out into the deeps of confusion.

"He has never seen a Rousseau, and yet it would take an expert to detect that what he has painted was not by Rousseau."

"If you will pardon me, I sink that you are mistaken—only Rousseau can—how you say—exist, no, be Rousseau."

"Precisely."

"I don't really know about this painting business, but it's just like cricket—take George Headley for instance—the world's greatest—you hear what I say—the world's greatest."

"I perplex myself with your game of cricket—what with ze bowling of a maiden over."

Hysterical laughter from all but the George Headley fan who continues: "You say this man paints like Rouss . . . whatever you call him. My friend here says 'impossible'. I know nothing about painting, except that I can't make head or tail of some of the stuff you see nowadays, BUT, and this is my point, BUT"—here he sticks his finger into the interrupter's face—"BUT if

210

this man can paint like the way George can bat then no other
person can paint like him. You listen to what I say, boy. When
George . . ."

"A fruitless occupation painting like Rousseau anyway."

"It's only by imitation that a man can learn anything."

"Why not imitate some of the old painters—at least you could
recognise what they were painting!"

"Why imitate at all—that's the trouble with all Jamaicans
—imitators. What we have here is not good enough for them."

"Paint what you feel."

"What you see."

"I say paint from ze guts—if zat's ze word—perhaps I should
say from ze intestines."

Hysterical laughter; heads thrown back; large black lips well
covered with lipstick, wide open, discovering rows and rows of
ivory teeth. One or two paler faces say their silent "peaches
and prunes", and call it laughter.

But we must leave this group for my partner has become
bored and wants to continue the dance which we have interrupted. "Oh Lord, men!" she spits out, as she loosens up her
hips to the tune of 'The men of today'.

"Men, they sure can talk; and with all this music too!"

I smile and think to myself how well *she* talks with those hips
of hers.

She, incidentally, has been rather hard on me; she seems to
think that I have wilfully organised all those men who are at
least eligible dancers, and in some cases eligible bachelors and
eligible husbands, into discussion groups on such promising sub-
jects as Picasso *v.* Renoir, Pound *v.* Dorothea Felicia Hemans,
Jamaican (I nearly said West Indian!) culture contra mundum,
Christianity *v.* Zen Buddhism, Weeks *v.* Worrell, American *v.*
English cars, and so on. But really, much as I like to hear the
choicer bits of wisdom which fall on this not too desert air, I just
could not have organised anything like this. Here is a man whom
the London Police were but two years ago dying to turn in for
living on the immoral earnings of various London ladies—here he

John Figueroa

is discussing with a drunk Zen Buddhist the "unnecessary trappings of Christianity". The Zen Buddhist, not unlike a porcelain Buddha himself, rests a steadying hand on the lovely little black piece he has just brought up with him from Hanover Street.

"It's in the East, my boy," he is mumbling, "that these difficulties have been solved. The body is not important, my boy. Action is nothing. What is action? Nothing!"

He is obviously about to treat us to something good, something as soothing as a smooth rum punch on a really hot summer afternoon. So I slip off; sermons, especially those rendered by lay people, have always bored me.

But as I stand under a flaming flamboyant, my glass refilled, the everlasting stars above me, the grass, the nature of which all men share, beneath me, I realise that I need not have run away from my Buddhist friend, for he has turned very silent, and is trying to follow a dancing couple round the floor in order to "cut in". Apparently while he was holding forth, a very cultured, artistic, and very Jamaican young man took the Hanover Street lady on to the floor. ("*It's nobody's business, business but my own; if a marry a coolie gal and change her for a Chinese gal, 'tis nobody's business but my own.*")

How *could* I have organised *anything* like this! The young Jamaican who is being pursued by the Zen Buddhist is brown, sharp and athletic; he puts his purloined partner through her paces. He is, of course, immaculately dressed in a dark tan suit, brown suede shoes and a wonderful maroon tie which has the following hand-painted scene on it: a tall, slightly curved coconut tree, with a grey trunk and intensely green leaves, stretches up to a shining silver moon: under this tree on some magic beach, close to fairy lands and forlorn seas, a pink body is seductively draped. The pink breasts are protuberant, and each is topped like a strawberry melba with a crowning cherry; the pink legs are shapely and the knees seem to point to the moon in an attitude of supplication. After some scrutiny one can discover, somewhere at the opposite end from the well-turned ankles, a blonde head with a red gash for a mouth.

Ars Longa; Vita Brevis

The young man swings out the Hanover Street lady. (*Ah what mek you deh wheel and tu'n me; ah wha' mek you deh tu'n and wheel me; gal you character gone.*) She "gives". Her black, dainty shoulders vibrate through the green nylon mesh of her bodice; her tiny pointed breasts describe circles against the invisible blackboard of the atmosphere, circles which are counter-pointed by the free activity of each of her buttocks. Her dancing is empirical and pragmatic, not controlled by any pre-existing form or idea laid up in heaven or elsewhere; her steps are rather adapted to the necessities of the music, and of her partner, with a scientific freedom, with an immediate suitability to the moment and situation, which would have pleased John Dewey. Moreover, although she does not strike one as being in any sense platonic, she justly illustrates Plato's description of music as being the palpable Erotics of the soul.

The young man flings her out; she wheels; she dips; she tosses her head. And all the while our English Buddha in corduroys, a violent purple and yellow check shirt resting on his uncarnal paunch, is stumbling around the floor after them, his eyes made out of finest glazed porcelain, his body now and again involuntarily taking on the rhythm of the "hot" music.

Were T. S. Eliot John Milton, I could imagine many of the highly cultured people here calling to mind, on observing this triad of dancers—black, brown, white—those suggestive lines:

> *The worlds revolve like ancient women*
> *Gathering fuel in vacant lots.*

How could I have organised anything like this? Am I a surrealist!

Enter now Freddy and his train. He has not been invited, but no matter. He does the odd water colour, and wherever women and artists (and liquor) are gathered together, there will you find this eagle. He is English; has been in Jamaica for two years; drinks *Black Seal* with the best of them; and is a staunch supporter and partisan of local art. He would hardly accept the free gift of a Turner but he pays ten guineas—which he can hardly afford—regularly for almost any ill-drawn local painting, provided that it is done in tropical colours and has one or two black figures lounging around in it. Freddy is a great sufferer; since coming to Jamaica he has been divorced twice—the second time from a light-skinned brown Jamaican girl whose innate intelligence and foreign training were not enough to overcome her family *mores*, were not enough to persuade her of the possibility let alone probability (nor God save the mark! per-impossible), even the desirability of marrying someone darker than herself.

They were together, once or twice, and he fell.

She soon divorced him, and now he suffers. Once a week in the evening he drives his car back and forth outside her house for about half an hour and then retires to a smart bar—with or without some local girl who is invariably well-built and of that local demimonde in which Freddy is considered definitely a good catch either as husband or escort.

I join in the loud greetings which Freddy and his train receive. He is a good type and very much to be welcomed at a party—especially when one is without a partner. As a matter of fact tonight his entourage is as usual predominantly female so that at the worst even if one did have a partner and Freddy should have decided, as he usually does, to be charming to her, one could quite easily return the compliment.

Freddy's party is not made up of artists, or even of would-be artists. Rather there gathers round him—and this is particularly true of his women—bored, tired, disappointed people; some, like himself, are sensitive; all are seeking some sort of respite, some sort of recompense or fulfilment; excitement they hope will be their Lethe water. So they crash parties at which the artists and the intelligentsia hold forth; the artists consider themselves "free" and so are in a position to provide thrills, excitement, forgetfulness, without, they tell us, reservations, scruples. In their art they *express* themselves; in their life they *are* themselves; and they devour whatever morsels they meet on life's way—whether this morsel be the rich man seeking status by buying the artists drinks, or whether the morsel be a pale, thin Englishwoman, physically starved, dehydrated, lonely, tired out with floor-walking in support of her two children, puzzled as to what happened to her ex-R.A.F. Jamaican husband who has without warning, and with an air of finality, set up house with an East Indian woman on the Spanish Town Road. All these morsels the artist devours and in this way he can have an interesting self to express!

The intelligentsia attract Freddy's puzzled women too; for now and again the intelligentsia sound as if they might have an answer or two to life's baffling problems. The members of the intelligentsia are reassuring when they speak—even when they are ill-informed. Their ability to place anything into a logical framework soothes Freddy's puzzled women, soothes them for a while until they have forgotten their rote-learnt lessons, and have to face the old problems once again alone.

Now, at a party like this, how does one distinguish those who are really having a good time from those who are pretending? It is not as easy as you might think. For instance, one of Freddy's women, dear Hilda, is already on the floor, her bare white shoulders swaying easily to the rhythm of a tango, her knees bending gracefully without putting more than a slightly perceivable strain on her rather tight pink gown, which, caught into a sort of bow on her left thigh, accentuates her easy hip movements. She moves easily, gracefully to the music, riding its waves, leaning steadily on her partner's shoulder. There is enormous control of movement in her tango; the slight hesitation, the dip, the "feather"—all are so quietly, charmingly, one would have said *happily* controlled, had one not known her.

The first time I saw her she danced in just this happy fashion; her control and grace were particularly arresting for the boat was rocking just enough to keep the inexperienced and uncertain off the floor. It was to this very tango, "Jalousie", that she gracefully moved as the ship swayed slightly from side to side, and dipped, every now and again, and with a certain regularity tilted all the dancers to one end of the floor.

When the rocking became so marked that the stewards would not allow us to continue dancing, she and I walked the deck. The enormous liner pitched right down till we seemed to be looking up at the waves. There on the semi-circular deck, bare-headed to the cold drizzle, but well wrapped up in our raincoats, we walked back and forth holding each other around the waist. We held on to each other tightly, partly because the boat rocked so violently and partly because it was warm and snug to feel so close together in defiance of the roaring ocean, and the cold salt spray, and the huddling leaden clouds. Up and down the deck we walked, and in that atmosphere of slight unreality and easy freedom which pervades an Atlantic liner, and in the warmth and conspiracy of the intimacy that was growing up between us, it all came out. All her unhappiness tumbled out, like soiled and clean linen from a suitcase that flies open as one is running to board a train. It was gracefully accepted unhappiness—but how could one have guessed it as she accepted one's invitation to dance, or as she followed one's rhythmic gyrations with such graceful intuition?

And who now, as he lifts his glass yet once more and pausing, takes note of Hilda, or who, breaking off from his interminable discussion of freedom and the spirit, and art and culture, and cricket, breaking off to notice the rounded solidity of her breasts pressing outward against her tight bodice, would imagine or guess what goes on beneath that smooth surface, would be able to interpret aright the slight look of soulfulness that sometimes shadows through the sparkling gaze?

"I was only eighteen," she had said. We sat on the deck, huddled against the so powerful and spray-laden puffs of wind. I was only eighteen when we got married; it was, of course, during the war; we had two days together. Then he went to the front. Haven't seen him since."

"Was he killed, then?" I asked tentatively. She had a daughter of about four with her on the voyage, and I guessed, from things she had said, that she had married again.

Ars Longa; Vita Brevis

"No, no," she said, "he lives in the States—he's American—and at the end of the war he sent for me."

"But you haven't seen him?"

"No; his mother gave me his telephone number. I 'phoned him; he said he was sorry but he did not want to see me. He was living with another woman."

"Had you known him for long before marrying?"

"Yes," she said, slightly moved by my sympathy and incredulity. "Yes. For two years. He came over with the Yanks and was stationed quite near us for training. He practically lived in our house. My mother and father simply loved him. Then he was posted to the front; I was still a virgin, and we got married before he left. At the end of the war he went directly back to the States. He wrote a few letters. Then he sent for me."

"Although he was living with another woman?"

"That's what I asked him. He said he thought I might like a trip to the States! Yet it hadn't been a hurried marriage, a nine days' romance. I had known him for two years. And he was so considerate and kind. He had never tried to take advantage of me, even after two years—and it would have been quite easy. I was so young and innocent—and foolish! I suppose it's the war. It just changed people. My poor parents, who were always so careful about me—they too had thought him wonderful, and loved him so much. The whole thing is like a dream, or something that happens to somebody else. I often feel as if I'm just looking on from the outside."

"And the little girl?" I asked. We huddled closer, and the boat seemed to pitch deeper and deeper into the ocean troughs.

"She is the child of my second marriage. I remained in the States when I discovered that Bob wouldn't have me back. His people even wanted to adopt me; and anyway how *could* I return to a small town in the North of England? So I stayed on. We were divorced. Then I met Roy. He seemed to be desperately in love with me and wanted to marry me, but I was *not* in a romantic mood. I explained my past, and remained frigid. Eventually loneliness and his desire got the better of me. And we had to get married. He has been a good husband; and he sent me to England to see my folks, but he is very cold; he is a Catholic and should not really have married a divorced woman. He couldn't wait before we were married, but now . . ."

She got up suddenly. And we walked the deck in silence for a long time.

On the way down to our cabins I offered Hilda a drink.

"Thank you," she said, "I'll need it."

Standing at the bar we had a brandy each.

When we got to her cabin as I said "Good night" she turned her face up to me as if expecting, as I thought, a fairly chaste goodnight kiss. I obliged. She threw her arms around me vehemently.

"Take me; take me," she said, almost biting her lips. "I *can't* stand it any longer. I have been alone in England for three months, and he ignored me for a month before I left home; he never seems to want me now. Be a good boy, George, and take me, take me."

Then she burst into choked sobs for a long time, and finally said, "I guess I'm just lonely, mad, tired, whatever you call it, but you can see why; can't you, George?"

"*Brown skin gal stay home and mind baby*" is the calypso starting as Hilda and Freddy are leaving the floor and going gaily towards the table under the poinciana tree. No doubt they're both thirsty.

I too drift towards the poinciana, not so much to speak to Hilda or to annoy Freddy by taking her away for a while, but just simply to refill my glass which has too long been dry—I think that for the rest of the night I should just take strenuously to drink and dance and forget

> *These matters that with myself*
> *I too much discuss*
> *Too much explain.*

Ars Longa; Vita Brevis

As I stroll over I hear on my left a heated argument about the bringing up of children—to flog or not to flog. The shiny-pated gentleman is repeating almost word for word what many of us heard at a lecture recently given in Kingston by a psychiatrist who was holidaying here but whose oral eroticism was such that he could not have wordless enjoyment of our tropical paradise. He had to lecture. And one of his themes, now being repeated by our shiny-pated friend, being repeated it must be admitted in a somewhat garbled and rum-developed version, was something like this: "Now today all ze world is Democratic. Now no more Authority. Now Democracy. Authoritarian father no more. Democracy in ze world. Democracy in ze family. We want self rule. You Jamaicans want self government. What about ze children? Ze children today demand Democracy. Self government. No more Authority. Now Democracy. And ze children will get zer demand. For we cannot stop ze forward progress of Democracy. It is going forward; we cannot stop it. Democracy for us; self government for ze children."

"*Six feet of earth, and we gone to eternity,*" is the calypsonian's wisdom at this point.

I do not know why I am so impressionable tonight, but as I approach the table and see Hilda and Freddy leaning on it and touching glasses to each other, I begin to relive a recent experience I had in Port Antonio two weeks ago. I think that my linking Hilda with the ship, and Port Antonio with *departure*, has something to do with my sudden translation.

Our farewells have been said; the departure of the boat has, of course, been delayed some hours. And now at sunset I am seated on a veranda on the hillside overlooking Port Antonio. It is now blue-green close of day; the hour in the North has been described as the "violet hour, that brings the sailor home from the sea"; the hour which long ago in Greece was so satisfactorily described as bringing home the sheep, and bringing home the goat, and bringing home the child to his mother. But now here in Port Antonio, Jamaica, the quiet and blue placidity of this

hour is the hour of departure. Departure is, of course, for many
—for my friends, for instance, who are now resting in their cabin
and wishing that the boat would leave—a moment of return. But
from this place *I* can only think of it as inevitable, final departure.

The white of the boat is mirrored in the violet of the sea
around the wharf. Beyond the channel, past Navy Island, blue-
green water and white pats of foam indicate the urgency of some
coral formation to leave the muddy depths and to stretch up-
wards for light and air. The sun is about to set.

The setting of the sun is inevitable and cannot be delayed.

The bunches of bananas, which were green on the brown wharf
and against the white boat, have all disappeared into the innards
of the ship, and its departure, which was delayed, is now im-
minent.

As I put my glass down, after a long pull of beer, I look out
to the ship, still quietly tied to the wharf. Suddenly but quietly,
I am convinced of the likeness between this ship's departure and
the final departure we must all, at some time, make.

I know beyond any doubt that the boat will leave, that my
friends will no longer be here. The pilot or the bananas or the
weather, or whatever you may think of, might *delay* its sailing
but will not put it off for good.

The journey which must be made is about to begin.

Health or doctors or whatever, might put it off, but in a year,
or two, or five or fifty, I must make my departure; the journey
to that land, from whose bourne no traveller returns, must begin.

My departure from this party of artists, intelligentsia, athletic
men, gay-time girls, of confused and lonesome people, all seeking
their Lethe water, I can now no longer delay: I must go home.
I suppose that I could hardly choose a better moment, for the
calypso to which my erstwhile partner and an intellectual are
now struggling, to which Hilda (with Freddy) is now gracefully
dipping, to which the Zen Buddhist and his professional partner
are now cavorting, to which our host and his lovely, even if
inhibited, partner are even now managing to maintain their

respectability, to which our athletic young man and his still more athletic girl-friend are jumping and jiving, to which Thelma and Henry are quick-stepping, to which the artists are forgetting their Art, intelligentsia their Reason, and the cricket enthusiasts their cricket, to which I am now making alone, through the white-washed gates, my irrevocable departure, goes like this:

> *Six feet of earth*
> *And we gone to eternity*
> *Death is so compulsory.*

Acknowledgements

Acknowledgements and thanks are due to the Authors for permission to publish their stories in this anthology. Grateful acknowledgement is also made to the following for permitting stories to be reprinted: the publishers of THE HOGARTH PRESS and the author for the excerpt from "A Morning at the Office" by Edgar Mittelholzer; the editors of *Bim* for "We Know Not Whom to Mourn" by Edgar Mittelholzer; the publishers of *Lilliput* for "A Wedding in Spring" by George Lamming; the editors of *Bim* for "Of Thorns and Thistles" by George Lamming; the publishers of *The Atlantic Monthly* (U.S.A.) for "At the Stelling" by John Hearne; the publishers of *The Atlantic Monthly* (U.S.A.) and *The Cornhill* for "The Wind in This Corner" by John Hearne; MESSRS. A. M. HEATH LTD. and the publishers of *Evergreen Review* for "Knock on Wood" by Samuel Selvon; MESSRS. A. M. HEATH LTD. and MESSRS. MACGIBBON & KEE LTD. for "My Girl and the City" by Samuel Selvon; MESSRS. A. M. HEATH LTD. and the B.B.C. for "Calypsonian" by Samuel Selvon; MESSRS. A. M. HEATH LTD., MESSRS. MACGIBBON & KEE LTD. and *The Evening Standard* for "Waiting for Aunty to Cough" by Samuel Selvon; the B.B.C. for "The Coming of Amalivaca" by Jan Carew; the B.B.C. for "Mr. Dombey, the Zombie" by Geoffrey Drayton; the editors of *Bim* and the editor of *Focus* for "Jamaican Fragment" by A. L. Hendricks; the B.B.C. for "Arise, My Love" by Jan Williams; the editors of *Bim* for "There's Always the Angels" by F. A. Collymore; the B.B.C. for "The Fig-Tree and the Villager" by Roy Henry; the B.B.C. and the editors of *Bim* for "My Fathers Before Me" by Karl Sealey; the B.B.C. for "The Tallow Pole"

Acknowledgements

by Barnabas J. Ramon Fortuné; MR. H. O. A. DAYES, literary executor, for "Blackout" by Roger Mais; the B.B.C. for "Crossroads Nowhere" by Stuart Hall; the editor of *Focus* for "Waterfront Bar" by V. S. Reid; the editors of *Bim* and the B.B.C. for "Drunkard of the River" by Michael Anthony; MESSRS. DAVID HIGHAM ASSOCIATES LTD. for "Minutes of Grace" by E. R. Braithwaite; the editors of *Bim* for "Ars Longa; Vita Brevis" by John Figueroa.